SEXUAL
AWAKENINGS

KATE STEWART

SEXUAL
AWAKENINGS

VOLUME ONE

THE WALTZ

FALL

I lit candles all over the house in only the scents he would tolerate. I covered our topiaries with soft, clear lights, and arranged fall flowers and large cornstalks into vases around the living room and porch. I loved fall, and by the way the house now smelled and had been transformed, it showed. Grabbing my pumpkin spice latte, I sat in my reading chair on the porch, watching the leaves sway in the cool breeze. I was already cold but refused to go inside, wanting to soak up the last of the sun as it made its way behind the trees, basking in the feeling in the air. Everything seemed clearer, crisper, and cold days were rare in the south this early in the season. Receiving an incoming message on my tablet, I tapped it, finding nothing new. He wouldn't be home for dinner. It was a good thing I hadn't bothered to cook. I knew better. A year straight of eating alone will do that to a woman. I opted for another night of wine and my vibrator.

Once inside, I chose my favorite bottle of red and poured a healthy glass. Surveying my beautifully decorated home, I rolled my eyes. What was the point? Maybe he was right. The last time I had decorated for the holidays, my husband had asked that same question.

"We don't have any children. We hardly have company. Why even bother?"

Prick. We didn't have children because he had a vasectomy three weeks after our wedding without telling me, only for me to find out in the first of many vicious arguments that ensued. We didn't have company because he was too occupied keeping his own, busy with his constant need to stick his dick in their throats. It wasn't enough for my husband to have one affair; he was in the midst of two.

I was not a woman scorned. Fuck that. I was a woman who had been freed, and too lazy to leave him, having no desire to start another relationship or leave my beautiful home. Alex was never here, ever. What was the point of giving up my life for a ghost I barely lived with? I took my wedding ring off months ago. He never noticed because, in all honesty, I couldn't recall the last conversation we had.

And then I remembered.

"You never loved me, did you?" I asked as he entered the house after another late meeting.

"Sure, I love you. Why are you acting so out of sorts?" He ran his hands through his hair, a signature move on his part that I used to find sexy. A stranger to me at that point when we had originally been so close, he stared at me as if I disgusted him, and I returned it. We had been best friends before we were lovers. We'd shared everything. I didn't even recognize the man who now took his place. There was not a damn thing wrong with me or the way I looked. All his fucked up issues about infidelity were his own.

"I'm not an idiot. Don't play innocent, Alex," I snapped.

"Drink your wine, honey," he said dryly, pushing past me.

That was our last conversation. When he was home, he called his mistresses from his office. I heard every word, because I listened. I listened to strengthen my resolve. I had already decided to ask for a divorce after Christmas. New year, new life, I guessed. He would let me keep the house and I would let him keep most of his money. He had plenty of it, due to old money passed down from his parents, and his newfound success at his advertising firm. I supposed he thought that since I wanted for nothing, I should just accept my circumstances as a good little wife, go shopping, get pampered. The truth was, I mourned my relationship with my husband, or at least the man I knew before things fell apart. The most frustrating aspect was he refused to admit anything was wrong; the man that had proposed to me knew something was wrong with me before I did at times. He was attentive and nurturing and…human. My tears saddened him; my smiles and laughter fueled him. He'd loved me.

I shook off the small amount of pain making its way into my chest. I had no more room for self-pity. I had done it all. I had worked out, tried new hair, new clothes. I had even gone so far as to get Botox. The only conclusion I came to after a few months of being refused in the skimpiest of lingerie was FUCK HIM. FUCK HIM. I had tried to make my marriage work. He was more interested in seeing it fail. Our relationship was too far gone from what it used to be. There was no trust, and definitely no lingering love. I had spent hours crying over him, now I just wanted my freedom. And freedom was becoming more important than comfort. I had to get out of this and soon.

I sipped my wine, thinking how completely unsatisfying it all was. I had waited until the age of twenty-nine to get married. It seemed the sensible thing to do after a few months of dating Alex. I couldn't even remember the last time we had made love or fucked. My last attempt to keep the home fires burning had failed miserably.

"We aren't a couple of fucking horny teenagers living out a fantasy, Vi. We aren't making a porno, and what the fuck are you wearing?"

I gave up that day, throwing every single negligee I owned away

3

and burying any remaining hope. Sex with Alex was never exactly hot. It had been enough because I had honestly loved him.

Drinking the last of my glass, I poured myself another. Sex, now there was something I was tired of living without. I had my trusty toy. God, how I loved that thing. Battery maintenance promised endless minutes of pleasure. The thought alone had me wanting to reach for it.

I was thirty-two years old, sitting in a big, beautifully decorated house, imagining the next session with my vibrator. I heard the shatter of the wine glass before I realized I was the one who had thrown it.

This was not my life! This was not who I was. This shit…this waiting, much like my marriage, was over!

Things were about to change and change today. First, I had to come up with a plan.

Sex, or lack thereof, was what set me off in the kitchen. I missed it. I wanted it. I needed it, but why? I'd never really had sex like most adults. Well, those adults who I envied, which included anyone who was having their needs met at this point. I abstained from having my own affair because, for a short time, I held out hope. Now that my mind was made up on divorce, I no longer had to justify my reasoning. Sex was a necessity for me. I had waited long enough. My body was starving for touch, my lips bankrupt from a lack of kisses. While a relationship didn't appeal to me, at least not immediately, the thought of a good hard fuck made me insane with want. Not that I'd ever been satisfied sexually.

My experience consisted mainly of missionary, with a few sporadic moments here and there in various positions. Alex was not well endowed and had by no means made up for it throughout our years together. I wondered what it was like to be with a man with a big cock. I moaned at the thought, never once having an orgasm from a man's dick. My girlfriend, Molly, told me that without a vibrator, I might never have one. She insisted girls who came with men inside them were either porn stars with amazing acting skills or had been divinely gifted in that department. It was a myth to me, an orgasm from a man's cock. I'd had fantasies for years about the possibilities of sex. All of it interested me, especially the kink. Alex would look at me as though I was insane when I suggested anything out of our norm. I would get hot and bothered reading my dark, erotic romances and begged him to try some scenarios with me. Looking back now, I could see why he thought it a little strange. It just wasn't realistic.

Do these people really exist, the people that explore the forbidden? Of course they do, but where were they? Certainly not on the outskirts of Savannah, GA. I laughed at the thought. I'd do good to find a decent looking, well hung, hardworking man in this area, period, let alone one that would explore my sexuality with me. Then again, what if? I mean, surely the insatiable and erotic sexual cravings of people are not limited to only large cities.

Where in the hell would I look for something like that here?

Of course there was the web, but some, or most, of those sites had a virus attached. I'd delved into porn a little when my imagination couldn't do it for me and I needed a little extra something. That got old as well. I was tired of watching. I wanted the experience. Pouring myself another glass of wine, I ignored the shattered glass on the floor. Who the hell would care about the mess anyway? After all, it was only me here.

⚮

Hours later, after watching Jimmy Fallon, my curiosity brought me back to the web. Fuck it; I'd been the well-behaved, jilted wife long enough. I wanted to know what was out there, especially those like me who shared the same curiosities. I would love to know if any other women in Savannah had a fascination with kink. After a few hours of searching, I stumbled upon a site advertising a local, adults only page. There was a large triple X on the screen and a flashing advertisement of what looked like a bar in or around Savannah, but my excitement was stifled when I realized there was no address. After a quick Google search for the bar, named The Rabbit Hole, I came up empty, and gave up. Yawning, I threw my tablet beside my pillow and laid my head down to watch *Nightline* when I heard a ping.

I looked at my tablet to see an incoming message asking for the password. After careful thought, I had nothing. I typed my plea.

Hint?

Rabbit Hole.

Not helpful at all. Shit. The possibilities were endless. I studied the XXX on the screen and saw an Alice in Wonderland cartoon encased in them. Inside the rabbit hole, in the middle X, was Alice kissing another Alice on the cheek as she held her pointer finger to her lips.

Making the best guess I could, I keyed it in.

Don't kiss and tell.

I was immediately redirected to the homepage, asked to create a username—Blue_Alice—and started navigating my way around.

It was a chat room, and from the subject matter floating in boxes around the screen, it was definitely a no holds barred kink fest. Perfect! At least the curious vixen inside me wouldn't have to show her face for now. I sat for hours in the various chat rooms reading the conversations. Most of them consisted of people hooking up and then agreeing to email in private. Great, hours on the site and I had only gotten a little hot reading what appeared to be an open and unashamed twosome having really kinky message sex. I could read a book and get hotter than this. I was just about to grab my trusty silver bullet and a new erotica book when I received an incoming message.

MadHatter: What are you doing here?

I froze, feeling completely busted. I shook my embarrassment off quickly. I had knocked on the damn door. Why not have a little fun?

Blue_Alice: Looking.

MadHatter: For what?

Blue_Alice: Anything but what I'm doing.

There, honesty. Honesty was good.

MadHatter: Why so blue, Alice? Bored housewife?

Blue_Alice: Fuck you.

MadHatter: So, I'm assuming I'm correct?

Blue_Alice: Maybe. What the hell does it matter?

MadHatter: We don't do married here.

Blue_Alice: I am getting a divorce.

MadHatter: That's not a new one.

Blue_Alice: Keep your boring ass chat room.

MadHatter: Temper, temper.

Blue_Alice: I could do a better job turning people on than this bullshit.

MadHatter: Wow, you really need a thick cock in that sassy mouth.

Blue_Alice: And I suppose you're the one who will be giving it to me?

MadHatter: Why not me?

I felt my cheeks grow hot and took a deep breath. Okay, now we are talking here.

Blue_Alice: Fine…talk to me.

MadHatter: Why are you here?

Blue_Alice: You already asked me that.

MadHatter: And you didn't give me a good enough answer.

I thought about it. Going into this with honesty would be the only way I would truly get what I wanted. But is this what I wanted? What if he was some nasty, fat perv with bad skin and greasy hair? Then again, he may have thought I was some nasty troll with a huge gut and overgrown forest in my pants. I shook my head, indignant at my own stereotyping. *Not cool, Vi.* This whole scenario meant taking a chance. I had been teetering on the edge of this for years, if I was honest with myself. I wanted to be fucked ruthlessly, worshipped and tortured, brought to levels of sexual awareness I'd only dreamed about. I was sure—no, positive—I had an undiscovered fetish or two. Honest, I'll be honest.

Blue_Alice: I want to explore a part of me I've kept hidden.

MadHatter: Why?

Blue_Alice: Because I don't have anything to lose.

MadHatter: That's dangerous.

Blue_Alice: That in itself is why I am interested. I want

to be fucked in ways I've only imagined, and I'm tired of only feeling half full. I have cravings and I'm ready.

A few minutes later, I was sure the conversation had ended, then a ping.

MadHatter: I'll be in touch.

Blue_Alice: Wait!

Okay that seemed a little desperate.

MadHatter: What?

Blue_Alice: Who are you?

MadHatter: I'm the guy with the thick cock you'll be wondering about tonight while you play with your toys.

Blue_Alice: Charming.

MadHatter: I can be.

And he was gone, if it had even been a he. For all I knew, it could have been a she. This too fascinated me. I thought of women and my sexual boundaries when it came to them and decided one leap at a time. Although women appealed to me from the waist up, I had no desire to explore the waist down. Then again, I'd really never had the opportunity.

⊛

The next day, I brought my iPad on every single errand with the chat room queued up. He could see me. He knew I was waiting. I looked desperate, but I needed this! I felt it in every part of me. I needed to be sexually free. I'd slept with six men in my thirty-two years. Two one-night stands, one when I was in college and the other right before I met my husband, Alex. The rest were boyfriends and not one of them was a freak, well not in the sense that I wanted

9

them to be. A few got me off with their mouth, but it wasn't earth shattering. It was more or less a struggle and an enormous amount of effort with constant murmurs of "Are you close?" during what seemed to be rigorous work. So, I rarely got off.

I had, as the mysterious messenger predicted, taken my toy to bed last night, imagining the man behind our brief chat. I was hot in a way I hadn't been in months at the possibilities alone. This had to be explored. I felt like I was a sexual creature on the verge of finally introducing myself. Once I was home, I unpacked my groceries, praying for the fucking iPad to ping. Just ping! When I got nothing, I decided to forgo cooking and treated myself to dinner at Tubby's, a nearby seafood restaurant on River Street. I sat on the balcony watching the boats glide down the river while the sun set. Couples passed by below me on the busy street holding hands and smiling while I dined alone. Minutes later I got my usual message from Alex letting me know he wouldn't be home tonight and I rolled my eyes. Why did he even bother at this point? God, how I hated him.

Later at home, I thought about looking up some listings to show. I had a real estate license I rarely used and knew it was getting close to time to put it back to use. I was good at it, and I enjoyed it, but when my marriage fell apart I dropped it completely. I had stayed at home for a month solid after hearing Alex's first conversation with one of his mistresses. I didn't need to see anything. The prick had no issue talking openly with her behind his office door. If you are going to cheat, at least have the smarts and decency to hide it. The devastating thought that he didn't care enough to hide is what really drove the knife into my heart. A few months after I had questioned him about his distance, I realized he had no intention of revealing his indiscretions to me. He was simply that fucking stupid. I heard every word he uttered to those women. It was eerily close to the way he used to speak to me. It hurt me horribly at first, now it just made my stomach turn. Why the fuck was I still here? What more reason did I need? He cheated; our marriage was over. I hated him. Why didn't I just ask for a divorce?

PING!

A wave of adrenaline shot through me as I looked at the screen. It was an address. It was obvious why. It was an invitation, and one that came too soon for my comfort.

Well that would be a hell no. I wanted to at least have a conversation longer than a few short sentences before I agreed to a rendezvous.

Blue_Alice: Hello?

No response came. I already knew the address would be my only message tonight. It was a challenge. He wanted to see what I was made of. If I was willing to step out of my comfort zone. All the reasonable reactions raced through me.

What kind of person barely introduces himself then gives an address to a total stranger?

Then again, what kind of person tells a complete stranger they want to be fucked six ways from Sunday?

I stared at the address for what seemed like an eternity. Okay, I could drive by. What was the harm? I would just look around, scope the place out. I could do this. Throwing my blanket off my legs and retiring my yoga pants, I took a scalding hot shower. I Googled the address with a towel wrapped around me, fear creeping into my thoughts. My search, of course, showed only results with possible directions. It had to be a home address. He gave me directions to his home? I shook off the towel, covered myself with scented lotion, and took in my body. I had long legs and curvy hips, a little extra weight made them even more pronounced. My breasts were pushing a C-cup, and though they weren't perfectly proportionate to my hips and ass, I was fine with them. I pulled out a thin black sheath dress that collared at the top, hugging my neck snugly, slipped on my spiked red heels and put on my best face. Thick eyelashes and perfectly lips later, I ran my hands through my dirty blonde hair that I'd ironed straight. I was ready.

After two small glasses of wine and a mini-breakdown later, I corked my bottle and made my way to my car. *You can do this, Vi. You can also back out at any time.*

My cell had no issues navigating the address. My GPS estimated my trip to thirty minutes, and in thirty minutes I could be in the midst of possibly the best or worst situation of my life. Then again, I couldn't imagine anything worse than the one I was already in.

I had enough heart left to give. I just didn't give a damn enough to use it. This wasn't about my heart; this was about a thirst I'd fought long enough. This would be good. This could be my something to look forward to.

Come on, Violet, divorce is not death and you've got a lot of living to do.

My something to look forward to ended up being The Rabbit Hole. The bar did exist, though the sign said private club. A wave of relief swept through me as I realized this was the perfect place to start. This club wasn't the private home of Mr. Thick Cock where I would be expected to do anything. The bar, though near the corner of nowhere and doesn't exist, looked to be newly built. The building was solid white and the entrance made up of two large oak doors. It seemed to be busy considering the number of cars in the parking lot. I stood in front of the doors, gathering my last bit of courage, and noticed they had been carved to showcase the characters of *Alice in Wonderland*.

So, I had a plan. I'd decided during my drive to give myself a year of no holds barred sexual exploration. No self-deprecating inner thoughts, no inner turmoil over the deeds after they took place, just raw indulgence. I would be safe, but I would seek out every avenue to find what pleasured me. I wanted it all. I wanted to fuck a professional escort, role-play, try my hand at BDSM, and maybe a ménage à trois. There would be no limits, only my preferences as I discovered them. I felt a tingle in my spine at the idea that tonight I might actually get to experience some small part of it. Down the rabbit hole it was. I exhaled, tightening my grip on my clutch. *Here goes nothing.*

I opened the door to be met by a huge man—more like a mountain—that reminded me of a lumberjack without the beard.

"Password?"

"Don't kiss and tell."

He looked at a list on a clipboard then nodded his head in confirmation. I thought it odd. I hadn't given anyone my name. He grabbed my purse and I stood back in shock as he went through the contents without apology. He handed it back to me, grunting as he took a step back, making way for me to enter. I was stunned at the absolute beauty of the club. There were oversized leather lounge chairs everywhere in black, white, and checkered patterns. Hundreds of intricate lights hung from the ceiling in different shapes and colors. There were glass dividers giving privacy in certain areas as well as hundreds of lit candles that had the entire bar smelling sweet and clean. Despite the amount of lights, the atmosphere was romantic. I'd expected ridiculous amounts of story time paraphernalia throughout; instead it was all done so tastefully. Unless you were looking for the fairytale details, you wouldn't really notice them. It was definitely a playground for grownups. A beautiful woman with ridiculously bright red hair greeted me as I took a seat at the bar then asked me for my order. I caught a few stares aimed in my direction and squared my shoulders.

"Martini, very, very dirty."

She winked at me as I studied the bar behind her. Mirrors lined the entire wall, and I could see myself clearly. I was shocked at my own appearance. I looked...confident. Taking a sip of my freshly delivered drink in an insanely large martini glass, I cautiously looked around. There were a few people scattered around the bar, but the ratio of people present to the number of cars didn't quite add up. At the end of the bar to my left sat a couple that seemed more than comfortable showing vast amounts of affection openly. I watched them for only a moment before the woman, whose naked breast was being inhaled by the man in front of her, winked at me. I winked back, feeling a small twitch of heat make its way below. A live show would be a first. Exhibitionists intrigued me. Maybe I would add this one to my list. He lifted her skirt, exposing her panties, and I almost gasped with her when he moved them to the side, sliding his fingers in. I felt heat flush through my body as I watched her head tilt back and a moan escape her lips. His fingers moved inside of her and I began to feel my sex clench with need. God, I wanted to be her right now.

"Having a good time?"

I nearly jumped off my stool when his breath hit my neck but maintained my seated position, refusing to look at the source of the voice. It was low and sexy, but I was so in tune with the couple, I couldn't tear my eyes way. Her panties were off now and she was on her knees, his cock in her mouth. I gripped the side of the bar, trying to keep my voice level.

"It could be better," I replied to the man seated to my right. A million silent prayers went up in that moment as I tore my eyes away from the couple, hoping at least one would be answered, and turned to the man talking to me. I parted my lips slightly as I took him in. Gray eyes, strong jaw, full lips, a strong brow. Fucking hot!

"Mad Hatter, I presume?" I hoped I sounded coy, but the level of heat coursing through my veins led me to believe otherwise.

"Blue Alice?"

This could very well be the best answer to any prayer I'd ever gotten. He had broad shoulders and was dressed professionally in a three-piece suit. His tie had been loosened, and his wavy, jet-black hair was slightly disheveled. This man wasn't just good looking, he was a slap in the face to good looking. I took my gaze away to study my martini, trying not to give too much away. I felt his intense gaze as it covered every inch of me, and it unnerved me and heated me at the same time. I wouldn't worry if I was pretty enough for him, if I was the right body type, had the right color hair. Now was not the time for insecurity. Now was the time for me to be comfortable in my own skin and flaunt it as much as possible.

I boldly turned to him again, taking my turn to peruse him from his wing tipped shoes to his perfectly fitted suit pants. I lingered on the promising bulge resting between his thighs and then trailed up further to his chest, appreciating the crimson color of his tie before stopping at his face. He smirked and I found it incredibly sexy the way his lips twisted, his eyes never straying from mine.

"Vi, short for Violet, and I told you I'm getting a divorce."

"Rhys," he said, grabbing my hand and turning it over to kiss my wrist. I gulped down the moan that threatened as he lowered my hand back to my lap, caressing the top of my hand as he left it. Smooth. "Can I offer you another martini?" His voice was deep and unnerved me further. I jumped at the chance to numb myself a little.

"Grey Goose, dirty."

"Very, very dirty," the bartender said, grabbing my empty glass and winking at me.

I heard a gasp to my left and saw the man had fully immersed himself into the woman who was no longer able to wink, or even breathe for that matter. Her eyes were shut and her mouth parted as she wrapped her legs around him as he pounded into her. My body flushed, my breathing changed, and I didn't have a chance in hell of hiding it. He gripped her throat roughly as she came and he picked up his pace as she screamed out. By this time, my limbs were weak with want. I felt my entire body come to attention and turned to look at Rhys who was watching my reaction intently.

15

"Beautiful," he whispered as the bartender set my drink in front of me.

I was consumed by the scene that had just unfolded and intoxicated by the man whispering to me. I turned my attention back to him quickly. He didn't seem interested in the couple at all.

"I've never seen anything like that," I noted. "That didn't turn you on?" I questioned, no longer able to keep my voice steady.

"I'm concentrating on you at the moment. Tell me, Violet, what do you want to happen tonight?"

"I want to be fucked exactly like that," I said without hesitation. He chuckled as he finally looked over at the couple, watching them closely. I followed his gaze to see the man pumping the last of his orgasm inside her, holding her tightly to him.

"This is the extent of your imagination? This is you exploring your darkest desires?" His brows pressed together, as if he was confused with my admission.

"Not exactly, but I've never done anything publicly, either," I admitted, sipping more of the martini than I should have. I was nervous, and it was obvious. So be it.

"So," he said, sliding his finger around the rim of his tumbler, "let's talk about that."

I took another sip of my martini. He caught a small drip of vodka off my lower lip with his thumb and brought it to my mouth. I immediately responded, sucking the tart liquid off. FUCK ME. He smiled in response, and as soon as I was able, I kept talking.

"The thing is...I'm not exactly sure what I'm looking for. I just know. I want...something. I've been reading a lot and studying the different types of scenarios, fetishes, and I think—"

His laughter brought heat to my cheeks, which prompted a bite from my tongue. "This isn't fucking easy for me, you know," I huffed, embarrassed.

"Sorry, it's just you really are so green." He slid a hand down my arm, causing my entire body to lean into his touch.

I recovered slightly. "What's wrong with that? Being green...Isn't that what you people love? Aren't I what you look for?" I gripped my glass stem, twirling the drink slowly around and he stilled my hand, commanding my attention.

"You people?"

"Yeah, you know..." I widened my eyes as the couple who had just been power fucking now walked past us, fully clothed with sated smiles.

"No, I don't know," he said, amused.

"If you are going to make me feel inferior and childish for being here, I'll just cut my losses right now." I grabbed my clutch and opened it, searching it for my card to pay for the drinks.

He stilled my hand again. "I apologize. It was brave of you to come here. I won't make jokes at your expense again. Tell me what you want, Violet." My name rolled of his tongue so smoothly; my body gravitated toward him a little more. We were a whisper away from a kiss.

I took a deep breath and got lost in the blue hue surrounding his gray depths. He seemed to be searching for something when he looked at me. His lips looked soft. I leaned in and pressed my lips to his. He seemed only faintly surprised and retuned my soft kiss, reaching up to cradle my face with his hand. God, I loved that simple gesture. But a kiss wasn't exactly what I was there for. I pulled away from him as electricity lingered and quickly explained.

"What do I want? I want to do things like that, indulge on my sexual whims. I want to experience everything I feel I've been missing. I want to try it all and tonight I think I want you." Honest, bold and barely able to keep my shaking hands from showing, I kept his intense gaze. "But mostly I want to find out *what* I want."

He seemed slightly stunned and even more amused. I'd made a fool of myself. I quickly grabbed my bag and stood. "I can see I'm wasting your time."

"Come with me." It wasn't a request. It was an order. My core clenched and I felt the dampness from my now soaked panties as I followed him down a long hall behind the bar. I watched his confident walk, he was much taller than my 5'9" and I loved it. I felt the anticipation building, overjoyed at the thoughts racing through me. He led me into an office, shut the door behind us, and walked to sit behind a desk, gesturing for me to do the same.

"What is this?" I asked, looking around the spacious room.

"My office," he answered without further explanation. Ah, so he owned the bar. Nice, this wasn't an inexperienced man. This excited me.

He sat behind his desk, watching me carefully. My sex clenched again at the weight of his stare. What the hell was going on here? We sat in silence as he watched me sit, legs crossed and muscles clenching nervously as I fidgeted with my bag.

"I'll make you an offer," he said, placing his hands on his desk. "I'll help you explore your boundaries and figure out just what it is you want, and in return, you follow a few simple rules."

I shifted in my seat, my growing need outweighing my ability to reason, even though his offer didn't seem unreasonable. The sweat between my legs mixing with the unhappy ache was enough to make me agree to anything. Still, I had to ask, "And the rules are?"

"Everything you have at home, throw it out. No books, no toys, no other partners. I become everything you need sexually. No exceptions."

"That's a lot to ask of someone you've only just met, not to mention it throws a wrench in my plans," I said nonchalantly.

"Which were?"

"Delve into all areas BDSM, fuck a professional, maybe a ménage. I kind of want to try it all." To this I got another smirk, but had no shame in my admission.

"And you can do all of those things with me. But you won't know the when or the who, and you'll find out quickly you'll be fucking a professional." His tone was dead serious. I believed him.

This was definitely safer than allowing random, willing strangers to violate me. One partner, one person to show me the ropes, suddenly seemed more appealing than going in blind.

"And you are so sure you can fill my every need?"

He raised a brow as if to say "Are you kidding?" but humored me. "Violet, I am far from the adventurous man I once was, but even being half that man, I can get the job done."

"Wow, that's quite a bold statement. And will you be monogamous as well?"

A sharp nod was his answer. He gave me a heartbeat to absorb his response then said, "Take off your dress." When I hesitated, he started in, "Don't fear me, Violet. I never do a thing to hurt a woman. This is about pleasure. I don't want you to feel anything but safe with me."

I was up in seconds, bared to him. I stood naked before a man I had met only minutes earlier. I had to admit, it was fucking hot, and the part of me that protested what was left of my innocence was being beaten down by my determination. He appraised me carefully, studying my every curve, taking in my chest, letting his eyes drift to the swollen wet mess between my thighs.

"You're wet now."

"Yes," I breathed, barely able to control the tingle escaping my every pore.

"Come here," he said, turning in his chair to point to the empty space beside him. I walked over slowly, standing inches from him between his parted legs as my body begged for his touch.

"Spread your legs." I parted my legs as he studied my sex. He took a single finger and skimmed the surface, covering the tip of my clit as I cried out. My nipples peaked as I watched his eyes wander back up to mine.

"You are absolutely beautiful. Go get dressed," he said, dismissing me, turning back to face the door in his chair.

My heart sank, my sex screamed, and my mouth let out an immediate protest. "But I thought—"

"Trust me," he said, his jaw clenching tightly. What the fuck was going on here? I had barely stepped into my dress, frustrated, and furious when his next question came. "Are you on birth control?"

"Yes," I clipped tightly.

"Make an appointment with your OB, get a full screen and come back in a week."

"And just why the hell would I do that?" I snapped, zipping up my dress and catching his eyes watching it happen.

"Because I only fuck bare." His voice was dangerously low. My pulse picked up as I watched him closely. His face gave nothing away, but his eyes told me that I wasn't alone in my frustration. "I'll have the same results when you come back. Also, I've had a vasectomy, but I prefer you keep your method as well."

"This is all very clinical right now," I said, crossing my arms. "But I can totally appreciate what you are saying. I…was worried…you know, about this kind of thing. Do you do this often, you know…" How did I ask if this was the norm? When he didn't answer, and continued to watch me, I tried a different approach.

"What's in this for you?" I asked as he stood and came toward me quickly and with purpose. I was flat against his office door in seconds, his eyes burning into mine, my palms flat at my sides. He gently grazed his erection along my stomach and I gasped at the bulge. I felt even more warmth spread in my panties. I would be sliding in my leather car seat on the drive home. He stood, his arms braced on either side of my head, and said nothing. I became uncomfortable and couldn't control my panting.

"I think we both know what's in it for me," he whispered, now an inch away from my lips. "One week, Violet."

He leaned in, brushing his lips on my neck, and I arched my back, begging for more. I stood in front of him, about to burst with need, my chest rising and falling, my eyes pleading. He turned the knob behind me and I followed his cue, walking out completely deflated as I looked back at the closed door. One week, just one week and that man's mouth would be on me, his hands touching me, not to mention what that hard bulge silently promised. I shivered with anticipation; every step back to my car was agony. I needed release. I let my head fall on the seat rest and recalled the stormy eyes, chiseled cheekbones, and soft lips of the man I'd just handed myself over to.

God, I got lucky. I was willing to settle for several semi-attractive men with experience, instead I got an arrestingly handsome Mr. Thick Cock who seemed to have a wealth of knowledge. I clapped my hands together with glee.

Here we go…

Against my better judgment, I did as Rhys asked and threw out my bullet. I didn't have toys. I had a toy. Now, I mourned the loss of it but saw a brighter future ahead, so I kept it short and sweet. There was no point deleting my erotic romances, but I would refrain from reading them. I made an appointment the next morning for a full STD panel, blood work, and to make sure I was doing well with keeping my birth control on track. Although I didn't need birth control—that had been handled for me by my husband—it kept my periods regular and less painful. I spent six days thinking of the man whose gray eyes haunted me. Hours were spent picking out the perfect lingerie to wear to my kink debut. I cleaned my house frantically, to pass the time, and had even shown a listing or two. Being a part of the work force again felt good. I had pampered myself and even gone to lunch with a few girlfriends who had sworn me off after my endless months of hermit behavior. I'd begun to make peace with my circumstances, my failed marriage and my new arrangement—an arrangement that excited me to no end.

By the time the day came, I was so worked up, I had to drink a glass of wine to calm myself before I hit the shower. I scrubbed myself viciously and exited the shower, slathering on a new body tonic that smelled amazing. I had myself waxed the day before and was smooth as silk, already wet with thoughts of what the night might bring. I clasped my brand new silver see-through bra and put on the matching panties. I shadowed my hazel eyes with a dark bronze and tinted my lips a glossy nude. I pulled on my favorite black silk slink dress and matching fuck me heels and gave myself a "go get 'em" smile in the mirror.

Arriving at The Rabbit Hole thirty minutes later, I smiled at the same bartender who took my order after she complimented my appearance. She was absolutely beautiful with a heart-shaped face, overly pouty lips, and a small nose. She looked like a living doll. Her bright red hair and colorful tattoos only made her more appealing. If I had a female type, she would be it. I asked her name.

"Tara," she said, delivering my martini with a smile.

"Tara, nice to meet you. Call me Vi." She nodded and shot down to the end of the bar to help others who were patiently waiting for their drink orders.

"Red or green?" A man sat next to me on the stool and I took in his appearance. He was only marginally attractive and had a slightly large nose and thin lips.

"Pardon?" I asked, completely clueless to his question.

"Red or green," he asked again, confused at my lack of knowledge until realization hit him. "Ahh, I get it. You're new."

"That I am..." I lingered, waiting for his name.

"Paul," he answered, making himself more comfortable on his stool, a little too comfortable as he invaded my personal space, making no attempt to mask the fact he was checking out my tits.

"Paul, Vi, nice to meet you. So, tell me. What does it mean?"

"They are the levels of kink you are interested in for the evening. Red being the most extreme and anything goes type of night and green, well, it's not quite as intense."

I nodded, taking in his words, wanting further explanation, but was interrupted from asking when Tara addressed me.

"You can go back," she said, turning to Paul, shaking her head no. I caught that I was off limits to Paul by order of Rhys and it made me feel wanted for the first time in months. I smiled and nodded to Paul who regarded me with the eyes of a man who had just lost his favorite toy.

I walked the hall, adrenaline spiking to levels I hadn't felt in years. I turned the knob to find Rhys in the corner of his office, his hands on his hip, staring at the security screen until I entered the room.

"You look beautiful." His comment caught me off guard, and I smiled as I closed the door behind me. "Hope you aren't too offended by what I do about it."

My reaction was instantaneous, my pulse sounding in my ears as I struggled to breathe as his words lingered between us. His eyes were fierce and a menacing smile graced his lips.

I quickly asked the question weighing on my mind. "Will tonight be red or green?"

"You're nowhere near ready for red. Papers, Vi." He held out his hand and I opened my purse as I walked over and handed them to him. He looked at the bottom line with satisfaction then rounded his desk, handing me his own. I looked it over, noticing the date was recent and his last name was Volz. When I was content with what I'd seen, I handed them back.

I licked my lips as we both stood taking inventory. Jesus, he was hot. Tall, broad, slim at the waist. Tonight, he wore slacks and a simple collared shirt. He walked around his desk and bent over, catching the hem of my dress before lifting it slowly over my head.

He pulled me close to him, our stomachs touching and chests apart. He kissed me sweetly but pulled away quickly as his eyes glittered over my breasts with appreciation.

"I think it's time for an introduction," he said, pushing me slightly away as he pulled his cock out from his pants. "Hit your knees."

My sex twitched and I fell straight to them, mouth watering. I kept my hands away, studying the fucking gorgeous, thick cock in front of me. The head was huge and I couldn't wait to wrap my lips around it. Another prayer answered. Mr. Thick Cock, indeed. I looked up to him as he gripped the edge of his desk with both hands, waiting expectantly. He had every right to be confident about what he had to offer. He was already slightly hard, and I couldn't wait to see him at full potential.

I gave him a small smile in appreciation before shoving the entire length in my mouth, hollowing my cheeks as I pushed through a gag, feeling his body flinch. Looking up, I found his eyes closed tightly and gave myself a mental pat on the back. Giving head was my favorite sexual act and I made damn sure I was good at it. I sucked him so hard, the noises were unmistakable. I opened my eyes to see him grip the desk with white knuckles and heard his breathing, but quickly realized I was the only one moaning. Sucking harder, I played with his sack, swirling my tongue on the huge tip, fisting his huge dick and still I had no moans. His expression was filled with lust as he stared down at me, but I couldn't hear him and it bothered me.

"Do you want me to stop? I asked, gripping him roughly.

"Did I tell you to stop?" he said through clenched teeth. I shoved his pants down to his ankles, grasping his ass with both hands and shoving as much of him in as I could. Minutes later, he withdrew from my mouth and pulled me to my feet. His breaths were heavy, his eyes hooded. I knew he was turned on. I hoped I had delivered and all the evidence below certainly pointed to the fact that I had.

Huge, thick cock, amen.

He reached behind me, unclasping my bra and sliding the material off with his fingertips, letting it fall to the floor. My nipples peaked with his stare alone and his eye shut briefly before he covered a nipple with his tongue. I gasped out his name and his gaze shot up to me. His eyes dilated, telling me he liked the sound of his name on my lips.

He released a perfectly peaked nipple from his mouth and led me to the chair on the opposite side of his desk. He carefully removed my panties and sat me down, slowly hooking each of my legs over the armrests, spreading me wide before him. Wrapping his arms around my middle, he pulled my ass to the edge. I had never been so exposed and had never been so wet in my life.

"Did you like sucking my dick?" he asked, kneeling down while sliding the tip of his finger up and down my ridge. I shuddered and barely got out the words.

"I loved it, " I murmured.

"Good to know," he said as he slid that torturous finger inside me. Another gasp and I was having a hard time keeping still. He slid that single finger over me again and again, tracing my pussy while exploring it with his eyes. I closed mine, gasping as he added another finger, sliding them easily in and out.

"Eyes on mine, Violet." I did as he said as he leaned over and sank his tongue into me, causing me to jump. He stopped his movement, and when I whimpered, he scolded me.

"Don't move again, or tonight my tongue will be the only thing you get." It was a threat I knew he would make good on. I willed my legs still and kept my hands planted on the rests, gripping the handles.

He licked me from my ass to the top of my folds and I couldn't stop my limbs from shaking. It felt amazing, but I knew I had to warn him.

"I…I can't come like this. I mean, it's hard for me to." His gaze hot on mine, he lifted his head slightly, his lips glistening with my juices.

"I've had my tongue on your pussy for ten seconds, Violet, but I could eat it all night. Stop talking."

He licked his lips clean and it took everything I had not to grab his head and take his lips because I loved what they were saying. Yes, sir. I held my breath as his tongue flicked at my clit again and again. His fingers circled me sweetly, the stroke of his tongue gentle and coaxing. I kept my body still while inside I was screaming. I felt the pull coming faster than it ever had. His tongue, now more aggressive, swirled and licked and sucked, and by the time I had figured out he had twisted his fingers and was fucking me relentlessly with them, I was screaming his name in praise. Oh…my…God.

I came hard, shuddering and pulsating in places that hadn't existed until this minute. Fuck, fuck, fuck. "Fuck yes."

Rhys was still on his knees, plunging his sinful fingers in and out of me, rubbing my wetness all over my pussy. "Glad you approve."

He didn't seem surprised at all. I, however, was floored. He leaned in again, sucking my lips clean, taking every single drop of the pleasure he just gave me back. When he had his fill, he looked up at me with a lust I'd only ever dreamed about. I burned it into memory and leaned in, cradling his head, taking his soaked lips, tasting and sucking them mercilessly. He grabbed the back of my head quickly with both his hands and our tongues mingled perfectly. Our kiss was almost as intoxicating as the cloud that lingered from my orgasm. The fog was amazing. We got lost in tongues and lips and sucking. I slid from the chair into his lap and wrapped my legs around him, squeezing his hips.

"Violet," he protested. We both inhaled sharply as my soaked sex hit his hard dick. "Violet," he mumbled, his lips still covered in mine.

"Enough!" he said, pushing me off his lap gently. I was instantly humiliated and quickly apologized.

"I'm sorry. I got carried away," I said, biting my lip in apology.

"Don't be. It's just that isn't what you are looking for, right? I have other plans for us tonight."

"That would have been pretty vanilla, huh?" I smiled deviously.

"Exactly," he said, putting his cock back into his pants as my pussy twitched in protest.

"What, um, about you?" I asked, nodding toward the obvious and painful looking erection in his pants.

"He's a big boy. He'll be okay for now." He gave me a full smile and I damn near lost it. This man had just feasted on me, had my juices on his lips, and was absolutely stunning.

"So how are we going to do this?"

"Didn't I just give you a screaming orgasm?" he asked, locking up his computer before turning to me with that now familiar amused look.

"Yes, but now I thought we…" I replied sheepishly, knowing I was acting like a needy nymph.

"Now we eat." He nodded toward my dress on the floor. I quickly realized I had been standing naked in front him without an ounce of bashfulness.

I could eat, but that was the last thing on my mind. And why wasn't it the last thing on his? Wasn't he tempted by me at all? I pushed the thought away as I grabbed my dress.

Then another disturbing thought occurred to me.

"Wait, are we going on a date?" I asked, sliding my dress over my head and adjusting it until it laid correctly.

"Not exactly," he said, locking his office. He grabbed my hand, leading me out to the parking lot, which confused me even further. Handholding was not exactly the act of a casual sex partner. I said nothing as he led me to the passenger seat of a sleek black sedan. Once my door was closed, I shivered slightly as the air swooshed against my legs. My face, still burning with heat from being blasted in his office chair, welcomed the cold. What he had just accomplished in mere minutes took most men months. I was soaking wet and couldn't wait to feel that huge cock fill me up. I was suddenly irritated I had to wait longer. Then again, I loved the idea of his plans.

He sat next to me and started the car. I stayed quiet, not wanting to break the hum of my limbs. I was suddenly ravenous and now a little happier about dining. He stayed silent as well as he drove, adjusting the temperature for comfort, and turning on some music to fill the silent cabin. I looked out of my window, remembering the feel of his tongue and fingers. If the workings of his mouth were any indication of what this man could do, I was all for the game we were playing. We pulled into a Mexican restaurant. I waited in my seat as he opened the door for me. When we were seated, he must have noticed my frown.

"What is it, Violet?" he asked, taking a tortilla chip from the bowl that had just been set down before us.

"Nothing," I said, looking around the restaurant, none too pleased with the fact we weren't dining in a classier place.

"Ah," he said smirking. "You were expecting to be dined at a five-star restaurant and fed buttered lobster from my fingers, is that it?"

"Well, not exactly," I said, completely busted.

He opened his menu, trying to hide his deep smile, but I saw it.

"Okay, fine. Maybe I was hoping for something like that," I said, picking up my menu.

"Uh huh," he said, his chest moving with his chuckle.

"You're doing it again, Rhys," I said, a warning in my voice. "Laughing at my expense."

"You make it too easy." He closed his menu and leaned over. "Sorry, but you have obviously read one too many erotica books."

I crossed my arms and sat back, defiant. "So what? That's what we women crave, to be worshipped and showered with gifts and adored while getting our brains fucked out."

He leaned over, closed my menu, and looked directly at me, his stare hot, making me shift suddenly. "I intend to make you crave me after I worship, shower, adore your pussy and fuck your brains out. But tonight, I'm in the mood for Mexican, okay, princess?"

I nodded quickly as I opened my menu. "You're right. I'm sorry. I have no right to expect anything like that. And please don't call me a princess or the next time I have your dick in my mouth I'll bite hard and not in a pleasurable way."

To that, he chuckled. "Noted."

When the waiter came, we ordered fajitas and margaritas, keeping our conversation light. I finished my plate and looked at him with a question.

"Do you take all your tourists to dinner?"

"Tourists?" His lips curled at the edges. "I guess that would be an appropriate word for you at the moment. And yes, all the ladies that I have a sexual relationship with get fed at some point."

"Why? That's more of a dating type of thing to do." He looked at me incredulously and shook his head.

"Well, this is not a scenario where you are fucking a man with no heart. Again with the books. I have feelings, emotions. I'm not made of steel, I bleed and I like to get to know the women I fuck. It's a matter of feeling them out, seeing what they prefer, their wants and needs. Sex is just as psychological as it is physical, Violet. I date. I have relationships. Not all people into kink have some sort of demon to battle. It's a sexual preference."

"That club is like something out of one of my books."

He exhaled. "Violet, that club was handed to me. None of it was my idea."

"So what you're saying is you're normal?" I asked, the disappointment in my voice unmistakable.

"Sorry to disappoint you again. Would you prefer I acted like a pompous ass with mental issues and ordered you around like a bitch in heat?"

"I don't know," I said, sipping my margarita.

"That's the point, you don't. We are going to find out. For now, why don't you just go with it? Why are you getting a divorce?"

That question threw me for a loop and I downed my margarita and gave him an honest answer.

"I started listening to his home office conversations months ago and realized he was cheating on me with two women. When he comes home, which is rare at this point, at precisely eleven p.m. he calls who I refer to as *the girlfriend* and talks to her. She seems to have him on a short leash. It's like a meticulous ritual with her and doesn't make sense to me, but it's every night he's home at the exact same time. Other days, and at all times of the day, I'll catch him calling the other. He's either never realized his conversations aren't muffled or doesn't care. He cheated. It's over. I'm fine and I never ever want to talk about him again." I glared at him for bringing up such a personal topic so soon.

He motioned for the waiter to get the check, paid quickly, and grabbed my hand and led me out to the patio. A mariachi band was walking from table to table playing upbeat songs. I felt numb as I took in the small stone waterfall and strategically placed lights hanging above us. To the right of the patio around the corner of the building there was a tiny gazebo close to a small pond hidden under the cover of a tree and he led me there without a word. He took a seat at the tiny bench inside of it and gestured for me to sit on his lap. He turned my body sideways so that my legs were spread over his.

I stared at the pond, still uneasy from my admission to Rhys, and breathed the cold air in deep, trying to gain back some small sense of peace. This really wasn't what I had in mind at all when I set out to explore my sexuality. I thought I had been perfectly clear about what I wanted, and so far, we'd only had some mind-blowing oral. We sat in silence for a few moments before his breath was on my neck. I turned to see his eyes full of the same lust he'd shown at his office. I was instantly back there with him, lips parted as he slid his hand underneath my dress and began to massage my pussy over my panties in mesmerizing circles. I instantly left the dark place from our conversation and felt my body start to hum. He moved my panties to the side, entering me suddenly with his digits, and I lost all sense of reality. I bucked under his hand, my body begging for more. He pulled his fingers from me, sucking them sweetly before putting them back into my warm center, in, out, in and out, in and out. He leaned over and took my neck with his mouth, trailing his tongue to my ear.

"I love the way you taste."

My clit pulsed as he brushed it with his thumb. Wrapping my arms around his neck, I opened wider for him as we held each other's gaze. I licked his lips and he squeezed his eyes shut, his hard dick bulging beneath me. He stood suddenly, forcing me to my feet, and turning me away from him as he placed my hands on either side of the arch of the small gazebo. He wrapped his arm around my waist, pulling my ass toward him, bending me over slightly. Looking around frantically to see if anyone was coming our way, I started to protest when he lifted my skirt so it hung on my back then pulled down my panties. I was in a panic. Anyone could come by at any moment. Oh God, this was...hot! My arms buckled slightly when I felt the tip of his huge cock at my entrance, sliding up and down. He ran one hand up and down my ass and smoothed it over, caressing my thighs as the other finger fucked me roughly. On edge and full of adrenaline, I kept my mouth clamped as his raw touch pushed me into a frenzy.

"You're going to stand there and take this dick, Violet," he ordered, his voice making my sex clench. There were people just a few feet away. My skirt was hanging over my ass and my front was covered, but there was no mistaking what we were about to do. His huge tip entered me again and I bit my bottom lip so hard tears sprang to my eyes.

And then I felt him. His width slid into me one painful and achingly delicious inch at a time. I thanked God out loud as the mariachi band started another song very close to where I was being impaled.

Rhys pinched my nipple, finding it easily over my dress as he thrust the rest of his hard length deep inside of me. The band muffled my scream while I held on tight as his cock stretched my drenched pussy. He gripped both hips, showing no mercy as he fucked me viciously. I called out to him, my pleas lost in the air. He bent me over further and my entire body twitched when he hit me deep, fucking me harder than I'd ever been fucked in my life. I braced myself, taking all he would give me, savoring every amazing amount of beautiful friction. He squeezed my ass painfully, driving in deeper, and all I could do was hold on as I prayed for him to never stop. The more he fucked me, the wetter I got.

He wrapped his arms around my waist, his dick still pulsing inside of me as he again sat on the bench. I writhed in pleasure, feeling the depth of him even more. Now sitting on his lap, his cock buried deep as I faced away from him, unable to see, only to feel, I moved my body, grinding my hips into him.

"Violet," he grunted, pumping into me as I braced my hands on his knees and bounced up and down with his thrusts, my legs hanging limp on either side of him. I was out of my fucking mind moaning as he pumped into me, his balls slapping my ass and finger pressing on my clit. I felt the pull and second-guessed it until minutes later Rhys had his hand over my mouth, muffling my now easily heard moans. I shattered, completely coming apart as he pressed hard on my clit and buried his cock deep. My legs shook uncontrollably and I went limp as he pounded into me and spilled himself inside.

I opened my eyes to find us unseen, or at least I hoped so, but deep down I really didn't give a shit. Rhys pulled out of me and I felt the evidence of his orgasm seep down my leg as I used my panties to wipe the mess away, stuffing them in my purse. Rhys buckled his pants and turned me to him to straighten my dress. I looked at him with wide eyes as he rubbed his thumb along my jaw then placed a soft kiss on my lips.

"I love Mexican," he said, his eyes twinkling with mischief. I could only nod as he led me to the car, staying quiet until we arrived at The Rabbit Hole.

He kept his car idling, to keep the heat in, and asked for my cell. I watched his profile as he programmed his number into my phone. The glow of the dash lit the shadows and highlighted the perfect, strong lines of his face.

"Why are you single?" I asked before I had a chance to weigh my words.

He handed my phone back. "I haven't always been."

"That's an answer?" I asked, thrown off by the open book my life had been so far to him and the vague answer he had just given me.

"It's one you will have to accept tonight." He got out of the car and cornered my side as I smoothed down my dress. I accepted his hand, and he kissed my wrist in a way that made my now sore sex ache to be filled again.

"Thank you?" I said, grinning widely as he nodded his head to accept, and returning my grin.

"I'll be in touch, Violet." He watched me walk to my car, and when I was safely inside, he returned to his. I drove away with a smile plastered to my face and an ache that I reveled in. Thank you, indeed.

At home, soaking in the tub full of Epsom salt for the second day in a row, two things were apparent. I was ridiculously out of shape, and I had been well fucked by a man with a dick the size of a tall Red Bull. I had winced throughout the last two days, wondering if I could even handle another hit of him. I checked my cellphone constantly, but had received nothing, not a word from him.

Alex walked into the bathroom, straightening his tie. "What's on your agenda today?"

I sat stunned. There would be words between us today?

"I'm sorry, are you talking to me?" I looked behind me at the shower tiles to emphasize my sarcasm.

He looked down at the floor, studying his shoes. It was the first time I had really looked at him in months. With chestnut brown hair, deep blue eyes, and a boyishly handsome face, it was no big mystery to me why I fell for him. Smart, good-looking, funny, a persuasive way with words, now all I wanted was his silence.

"Vi, I know I've been distant," he offered. I immediately waved my hand.

"Absent, not distant. Absent. And I really don't even fucking care to talk about it today, Alex. I've tried too hard for too long." I stood up from the tub and saw him take in my naked form. He gave me a good once over and grabbed a towel, handing it to me, and averting his eyes as if it bothered him. I made a small hmpf sound and walked past him.

"Can we have dinner tonight?" he asked, following me from the bathroom to our bedroom where I held my towel tightly around me.

"Absolutely fucking not." I heard my phone ping. I thought it ironic. I looked at the message and smiled. "I have plans."

"May I ask with whom?" he said, putting his hands on his hips.

"Are you for real right now, Alex?" I asked, mocking his gesture, my hands gripping my hips.

"Bye, Vi," he said, giving up so easily I had to add fuel to the fire.

"I'm sure she'll forgive you. Just buy her something!" He paused in the doorway and then kept walking.

Looking at the message again, I quickly let it go as a flutter of excitement raced through me.

RHYS: I want a kiss. Meet me at the club at 8. Green.

Hmmmm, green had been good to me so far. As a matter of fact, I was terrified of the pain tonight's escapades might induce, no matter how mild. I couldn't wait to see him. Wait.

I sat on the edge of the bed. *I couldn't wait to see him?* My phone rang in my hand and I jumped at the intrusion.

"Hi, Mom." I blushed as if she knew what I had been up to.

"How's my baby?" I grinned. I loved the sound of her voice. It took me back to a better place and time.

"I miss you, Mom." My voice trembled, surprising me, and I shook my head to dismiss my sudden emotion. This had to be PMS.

"What's wrong, baby?" she asked. I heard her walking and a door close behind her. Though my father and I were close, she never revealed anything said in confidence between us. I had an amazing friendship with her my whole life. My best friend in the world was my mother. I had a few close friends growing up, yet there were times we were at odds, even years we couldn't connect. Now that I was older, that wasn't even a possibility. I was an only child who had been both spoiled and disciplined.

"Mom, I'm divorcing Alex. You know I've been unhappy—"

"I know," she said quietly.

"You know?"

"Honey, I was prepared for this statement the day of your wedding."

I sat stunned at her admission. "What? You are telling me now you knew it wouldn't work out?"

"Yes. I knew he couldn't make you happy. I'm sorry, baby. I thought about it a hundred times then realized it was better not to tell you. I guess I was hoping I was wrong."

I knew my mother loved me with everything she had. She

would never intentionally keep something from me to hurt me. I probably wouldn't have heeded her warning anyway.

"He's been unfaithful," I said, then bluntly added, "and now so have I."

"Not surprised about him, but, baby, you too?"

"It's recent. He's been unfaithful for over a year, I think."

"Well, baby, I know I'm not supposed to say this, but honestly, what's good for the goose. When is this happening?"

"Soon. I haven't asked him for one yet, is that weird?"

"You will when you're ready. What's the hurry? The damage is done and paperwork is just that, paperwork. Don't you let him have that house. I know how much you love it! Why don't we get together this week? Or better yet, pack a bag and come and stay with me. We can have one of our weekends."

"I'll be over Friday. You have a date."

"I love you, baby. Just remember who you are and take her with you. The worst thing you can do is lose a piece of yourself to this because of him."

"I think I'm in the middle of doing just that, Mom. Kiss Daddy for me. I'll see you soon."

Who knew? I thought my mother loved Alex. I would go home this weekend and be my mother's daughter. It may be just what I needed.

But tonight, I would be Rhys's student, and I couldn't wait.

I took a ridiculous amount of time getting ready. I wore a long red skirt and white blouse, finishing the look with my new black and white checkered heels with a red sole, courtesy of Alex's new American Express. I thought it was a nice touch. Tara greeted me and told me Rhys was running late and would be along shortly. She rounded the bar, which was slow, and kept me company, pouring us an insane amount of drinks in a short amount of time. We laughed until we cried and the more drinks that went down, the closer Tara got. Instead of beating around the bush, I asked her directly.

"Are you trying to seduce me, Tara?"

She batted her false lashes, which made her clear blue eyes pop, and gave me a sweet, "Maybe."

"You do know I'm fucking your boss?" I hiccuped, pushing the drink she set in front of me away.

"He shares with me once in a while," she said, raising her brows and leaning in closer.

"I've never been with a woman," I said, my eyes sweeping over the curve of her breasts. "I think you are beautiful."

"Well, it wouldn't hurt to play around a little," she said, unbuttoning the first three buttons of my blouse. I looked around to see we had an audience of one. Rhys was in the corner next to the entrance watching us intently. I gave him a smile as Tara slipped a hand underneath my shirt, sweeping a hand over my breast. I saw Rhys's eyes light up and moaned as Tara's soft lips took my nipple into her mouth. I was wet instantly, watching Rhys get hot over our exchange. I watched him carefully, waiting on him to object when Tara kissed my chest and glided her lips and tongue up my neck. Her hand reached between my legs and I parted my lips as she stroked my clit with expert skill. I couldn't tear my eyes away from Rhys and could feel his tension and growing need as Tara stroked me, sucking my tits and my neck, drawing my eyes closed when she slid her fingers inside of me. FUCK THIS WAS HOT.

I felt lips brush mine and opened them, grinning at Rhys, who was now standing between Tara and me.

"That's enough, Tara," he said, lifting me off my barstool, encouraging me to wrap my legs around him. Tara protested as I smiled at Rhys, who carried me away as I gave her a thumbs up.

"Thanks for my first outstanding lesbian experience."

Rhys burst out laughing as he led me down a different hall than the one that led to his office. I saw a few numbered doors and we entered door number three. The room was painted red and had a huge black ottoman in the center of it. I hadn't bothered to explore the club any more than Rhys's office, but it had been in the back of my mind that there was much more to it than just the bar.

I looked up to Rhys with rose-colored glasses, due to the amount of drinks, and kissed his neck. "You smell so good. Mmmm, did you miss me?"

"I missed your pretty pink pussy." He grinned, tossing me on the ottoman. "And maybe a little of that mouth."

I turned on my stomach and pointed the tips of my heels in the air. "I've been sore for two days, you know. I don't think I'm going to be able to service you tonight, sir." Another hiccup escaped me and I giggled.

"I could just take it," he said, throwing his jacket on the ottoman and loosening his tie.

"I'm a little buzzed, Rhys. Don't you think you should wait until I'm of sound mind and not take advantage of the situation?"

He laughed as he unbuttoned the side of my skirt before sliding it off me. When I was in nothing but my panties, he'd given me my answer.

"What were the rules?" he asked, spreading me out on the ottoman on my stomach, pulling down my panties to just underneath my ass. He massaged my shoulders, placing small kisses on my back, trailing down to my ass before he took a mouthful of it. I was already soaked from Tara's skillful fingers, now I was drenched from Rhys's tongue.

"What rules?" I couldn't think with him stroking my skin, it felt so good. "Oh, the rules. No toys, no books, no other partners."

I felt the heat on my ass before the sound registered. He had just spanked me and it fucking *hurt*.

"What in the fuck!" The sober me would have realized this part of the evening was designed to test my ability to withstand a good spanking. The buzzed me wanted to punch the fuck out of him.

I rose from the ottoman and was brought back down by his hand flattening my back and pinning me down.

"Shouldn't we have a safe word or something?" I reasoned, with every intention of using it as soon as possible.

"How about stop?" Another hit on the same exact spot he'd just branded me on had me screaming out.

"Motherfucker!" Another round of slaps had tears coming out of my eyes, but I refused to ask him to stop. I was getting what I asked for. This was all part of it.

"So, you broke a rule tonight. I can't fuck you and I'm the one who's the motherfucker?" He was amused. I could hear it in his voice. I had no skin on my ass and this was amusing to him. I glared at him over my shoulder.

"I'm awake now," I said, sobered from the pain of my seared ass.

He sat at my feet, leaning over to soothe his handprints with his tongue, and I instantly forgave him, sighing his name. "Rhys?"

"Yes, Violet?"

I turned over on my back, sitting up at the same time to pull myself to him as my legs cradled his body. "I thought you wanted a kiss."

"All in good time. Should I feed you?"

I waved off his concern. "No, I'm good. I swear," I said as my vision cleared and his beautiful face fanned the flames of my burning insides. I leaned in, wetting my lips. He refused my kiss, turning his head away with a tsk.

"You have to earn it," he said, unbuttoning his shirt with one hand, tracing the other down my chest before pinching my nipple hard. I cried out to him in pain and he looked at me, unaffected. After I got my wits back from seeing his bared chest for the first time, I returned the favor, pinching his nipple as hard as I could. He didn't flinch. Instead, I felt his erection grow on my leg. Holy shit.

He pushed me back on the ottoman as he revealed his full chest, letting his shirt fall to the floor. He was cut and had a bare chest, which I loved. What turned me on most were the sharp indents of either side of his stomach. They were well defined and I gestured with my head, demanding to see more. He obliged, his pants falling to the floor, his boxer briefs the only thing keeping me from the rest. His thighs were thick and muscular. Who knew he was hiding that body underneath those clothes? I felt my sex twitch.

"And the rest?" I asked, resting on my elbows, legs crossed, my heels still on.

"You have to earn that, too," he said as his eyes glittered, no longer playful, the feeling in the air growing insanely intense. He came toward me and I flinched slightly as he reached me, tossing me easily on my stomach.

"You ready for your punishment?" He didn't hesitate. He took my panties down my legs and lifted me on all fours. His fingers dipped into me suddenly and he thrust them in front of my face.

"Who did this to you? Wasn't me! What are the rules, Violet? No one but me." His voice was full of contempt, and I was instantly on guard. He gripped my head roughly and stuck his fingers in my mouth. I moaned out in surprise before sucking myself off him.

"I wanted to taste that pussy of yours tonight, but you let someone else play with it. Now it's all ruined."

His hand came down again, softer now as he took another handful of ass before sliding his digits in again. I screamed out in a mix of pleasure and pain, no time to register when he spanked me a second time.

"I don't want to hear it. Matter of fact," he barked as he made his way in front of me and pulled his stiff cock out. I had to fight the smile as he pushed it past my lips into my waiting mouth, slowly sliding it back and forth, coating my tongue with his tender muscled flesh. He twisted my body so he could access my entrance while I sucked him off. He licked his fingers clean and slid them in again.

"Tastes so good and you ruined it!" Another spanking had me clamping my mouth down around him, and I heard him hiss through his teeth. "I hope you know that just encourages me to keep going."

I sucked harder, thrusting him as far as I could fit him, swirling my tongue, anything to keep the fucking hand from swinging down again. He got lost in my mouth, holding onto my head with one hand, feeding his thick length to me with the other. I loved every second of it. I glided my tongue up and down his shaft, taking his length with enthusiasm, making a popping sound when I pulled it out, opting to work on his sack as I sucked it gently. I felt his whole body stiffen and I moaned with pleasure, knowing how I was affecting him. I looked up to see his eyes hot on me. He began stroking my back, smoothing my ass with his hands and then massaging my clit slowly.

I took his cock back into my mouth, never letting my eyes leave his. He stroked me as I fucked him with my tongue and lips. His fingers started to make noise with the moisture that had built inside me and his dick became harder, letting me know he was close.

"Stop," he said, suddenly pulling his dick from my mouth. "So fucking wet," he said, working me over with his touch.

I mourned the loss of his cock, eagerly waiting for his next move. He sat on the ottoman, pulling me onto his lap so that I straddled him. I gasped at his cock prodding my entrance.

"We're going to take it slow. I have to have a taste of that perfect, wet pussy tonight. If it hurts, let me know."

I nodded as he picked me up easily by my underarms, sliding me slowly down the length of his cock. We fit together perfectly, our eyes locked and both our mouths parted.

"Rhys, oh God. Rhys, oh God." I already felt like I was going to come. "Please kiss me. Oh God, this feels so good."

He let go of my arms, thrusting his hands into my hair, his mouth crashing down onto mine. Our tongues thrashed wildly as

I felt his cock throbbing inside me. I'd never felt so good in my life. We licked and sucked as our tongues tangled and still we didn't move. We stopped only when we had to take a breath. As soon as my eyes opened to meet his, he started grinding into me gently.

I felt the stir immediately, the pull of my release close.

"Wait," he said, reading my body. "Just hold on a little longer," he urged, catching my bottom lip and sucking it slowly. I tossed my head back and felt his lips cover my chest as everything inside of me became unglued. I was quaking already and felt the pull getting stronger and stronger.

"I need you to fuck me, right now," I ordered to Rhys who replied by turning us around and pinning me to the ottoman. He spread my legs as far as they would go and buried his dick deep, hitting me exactly where I needed him. He drilled into me as I screamed out, praising him and cursing him at the same time.

"Fucking pussy is so tight, God yes," he said, tearing me apart with his perfect cock. I reached between us, circling my fingers and squeezing on his slick width made available as he pulled away before pounding into me again. He hissed and grunted as he watched us connect, watching my pussy contract and surround his cock. I felt the pull even stronger now and gripped his shoulders, digging my nails into him. Sensing it coming, he nailed into me, pulling my ass off the ottoman. With one more deep thrust, I came apart, clawing and scratching as my body spasmed out of control. He pressed on my clit hard and began massaging it. Seconds later, another tidal wave hit me and I saw white as I writhed and moaned beneath him. He slowed his thrusts until I caught my breath, opening my eyes to see his dilated, his chest glistening and stained with my nail marks. He slowed to a stop, pulling his cock out of me, stroking a few times as his eyes took me in.

"Fucking beautiful," he mouthed, his voice barely audible. He seemed to be taken with my reaction to him. "I don't want to hurt you. I got carried away."

"Please, Rhys, I want to see you come, and I want you inside of me when you do it." Those words were all it took and he was gliding inside me, touching me deep. I got to appreciate him then as my hands roved his biceps and chest. I wrapped my legs around him and squeezed, feeling him harden further as he hovered over me, thrusting deep. Minutes later, he threw his head back and grunted as my pussy milked him for everything he had.

It was the best fucking kiss of my life.

⬥

At home that night, I cursed my stupidity in the tub as I smiled with the memory of his face so close to mine, his beautiful body glistening as he fucked me so hard I came twice. Multiples, my God, multiples!

I had to text him.

VIOLET: Hey, just wanted to thank you for the kiss.

A few minutes later, I got my response.

RHYS: My pleasure.

VIOLET: I want to thank your thick cock too.

RHYS: Soon.

VIOLET: Goodnight.

RHYS: Goodnight.

⬥

As I prepared to spend the weekend with my mother, I texted Rhys, letting him know I was taking a short trip and he was on his own. His return text was vague.

RHYS: OK.

I had no obligation to let him know my whereabouts but didn't want an incoming text like the one I'd received a few days ago flashing across my smartphone.

RHYS: Pretty pussy, here now! Green.

I had no complaints with green so far and enjoyed the large candlelit table that could easily seat twelve he had set up in one of the club rooms. When I asked what we were having, his reply was his tongue inside me for hours on top of that very table. He sent me home with a sated smile, promising me more of where that came from.

The man was a fucking miracle.

I put one last piece of clothing in my bag, only to meet Alex at the door. His arms were crossed. He must have caught me smiling and thinking of Rhys. I didn't feel any guilt as I pushed past him.

"Where are you going?"

"Away, Alex. Have a good weekend." He stopped me with his hand on my shoulder.

"Whatever I've done to hurt you," he said, staring at the floor between us, "I really didn't mean to."

I sighed heavily, fighting my emotions. Why the hell did I still care? Why the hell did this man still get to me?

"Why are you suddenly so concerned with my affections, Alex, and with the state of our marriage? It's too late, even to keep up appearances. Despite what you think, I'm not an idiot. This, the way you're acting right now—" I gestured to him "—isn't genuine, and whatever your reasons are at this point, I don't give a damn. Don't play concerned husband now. There is nothing left for you here," I said, holding my chest, my voice shaking.

"I know you still love me. You are my wife." He pulled the bag from my hand, setting it down in an attempt to pull me to him. I brushed him off easily.

"It's too late. Way too late. I'll be back."

I walked out on him then, a small amount of satisfaction and a little sadness accompanying me as I went.

I spent the weekend doubled over with cramps and eating my mother's homemade fudge. It was the perfect set up: my mother, the movie *Fried Green Tomatoes*, and endless amounts of chocolate. We laughed and cried, made huge breakfasts, and spent a large amount of time snoozing on the couch. Sometimes a girl just needs her momma, and this Southern belle was no exception.

I came home refreshed on Sunday and texted Rhys right away.

VIOLET: Home safe. Hope you are well.

I waited hours for my reply.

RHYS: Ok.

Wow, he was on a roll. I felt I owed him some sort of explanation. We were exclusive, but only sexually. It appeared he didn't give a damn, so I left it alone. I wanted to see him. I wanted to talk to him, but I was still bleeding and casual talk wasn't exactly our arrangement. I would just have to see what he did next.

Son of a bitch! I moaned as I stomped around my house. It had been a week since I'd gotten back from my mother's. It was Sunday afternoon and I had listings to show in the morning. I had put myself back to work full time, no longer having an excuse to be a lazy, moping wino. Giving myself a kick in the ass, I got back on the treadmill, even if it was only twice for twenty minutes. I felt better about myself and this was progress, but my tour guide seemed to have quit without resignation and I was beyond frustrated. I heard the ping and leaped for my phone. Man, he had me. It was another address followed by a 'green.'

I was still furious with him for making me wait but couldn't keep my feet from taking the steps to my shower for a quick scrub.

Putting on a pair of jeans and a dressy top, I slipped into a more comfortable pair of heels. Running my hands through my long, blonde hair, I noted that I needed a cut and got into my car.

Play it cool, Vi. If he's kept up his end, he should be fit to be tied as well. You can do this. Be cool.

I pulled up to a house that sat on a square on in downtown Savannah across from Forsyth Park and studied it. It was a huge family home, and I was utterly confused. It looked like something out of a *Southern Home* magazine. Minutes later, he was at the front door, waving me in. I walked up the three hundred steps to the door—okay, that's a slight exaggeration—and greeted him with a false smile.

"Out of breath, huh?" He was bare chested and looked incredible in nothing but a pair of jogging pants. His torso was ripped and his sweats clung to his toned waist. His black hair, normally styled to perfection, was disheveled and hung loose on his forehead. Full lips turned up at the corners in a familiar smirk as his eyes met mine. It took everything I had in me not to lunge at him.

"Screw you, buddy," I said, walking past him.

"I've got something for that mouth of yours," he said, swatting my ass hard as he closed the door behind me.

"This place is beautiful," I said, taking a look around. The hardwood floors were, of course, antique, and the house looked to be restored. There were modern furnishings and it had an amazing homey feel to it. "Whose is it?"

He furrowed his brows together and tilted his head. "Mine."

"Oh," I said, feeling my cheeks heat, "it's just…I didn't picture you in a place like this."

"Uh huh, let me guess, a high rise with stainless steel appliances and fur covered floors?" He was laughing at me again.

"I really don't like you right now," I said honestly, walking past him to take a tour. A walk around downstairs revealed two large living areas, a study, and a huge kitchen. I took the first step of the staircase and was stopped short.

"Let's keep it down here for now." He gave me a stern look and I crossed my arms.

"You hiding a wife up there?"

He crossed his in reply, his biceps bulging as my mouth went dry. "Depends, are you hiding a husband?"

"I told you about my husband," I said, cowering under his glare.

"I want to believe you, I do, but a weekend trip, Violet?"

Was this why I hadn't heard from him in a week?

"I went to my mother's. I didn't think you'd care," I said, shrugging.

"Do you live with him still?"

My lie came quickly. I couldn't lose Rhys, and Alex would be gone soon, anyway. "No."

"All right," he said, eyeing me appreciatively. He closed the gap between us and yanked my shirt over my head.

"Why are you half-dressed and what are we doing today?" I said, half laughing as he tugged my jeans down.

"We are working out," he said enthusiastically.

"Uh, Rhys, it's Sunday, which is technically a day of rest. It's God's law."

"Lady, you might have to pray for forgiveness for the kind of workout you are about to get."

I shut up, because I wanted him, because the urge to reach out and kiss him was killing me. We didn't share like that and I couldn't show him how much I'd missed him, though my treacherous body gave me away.

When he had me naked, he pointed to a large solid oak coffee table. "On all fours," he barked, picking up my clothes and laying them neatly on the stairs.

Walking over to the table, I did what he asked, a little embarrassed at the setting. His blinds were closed, but I felt completely vulnerable, ass in the air. It was getting chilly and being in an old drafty house had me covered in goose bumps. Rhys came back a few minutes later with a small yellow box and set it beside me on the table. I was intrigued.

He sat on his couch as I waited on all fours, giving him a strange look when he turned his TV to a college football game. He stretched an arm behind him, holding his head with his hand. Minutes passed as he watched the game, looking completely relaxed.

"Hell of a workout plan you got here, Rhys," I joked as I waited for him to make a move. He didn't acknowledge or look at me as I waited patiently. Surely this had to be a joke. Any minute he would burst out laughing. He pulled his phone from his pocket to send a text and I gave him wide eyes and a "Hello!"

He continued to ignore me and I went from horny and expectant to furious in nanoseconds. I moved to get up and he snapped to attention.

"Get back on all fours, now!" I went back down quickly, trembling. His bite was fierce and I was pretty sure the conversation we had next to his stairs wasn't over. Rhys wasn't happy. I shouldn't have lied to him. God, maybe he knew I still lived with Alex. I should come clean.

"Rhys, I—"

"Did I say you could fucking talk?" he bit out viciously. WHOA. And then I was wet. I had to remind myself that I asked for this, that I wanted to experience being dominated. I needed to let go.

"Can you at least tell me what the exercise is?"

"Woman, you have no idea when to shut your mouth." He snatched the yellow box and came behind me. I looked back at him and gave him a smirk. Bad idea. His return smirk was scary.

I heard the box open and close as Rhys circled the table, rotating two small silver balls in one hand. His eyes were on fire as he circled me, taunting me.

"We are exercising the art of stamina and discipline today, Mrs.

Harvell." My eyes widened as my pulse quickened, sure I had just begun sweating in the cold room. He knew. He had just caught me in a lie.

"Rhys, I—"

"Not another word, Violet, or you won't get my dick today," he snapped. I clamped my mouth shut, my arms growing weak as he continued to circle me, rotating the balls, the sound breaking through the cheers of the football game; it was all I could concentrate on. He leaned over and rubbed my backside, gently moving over my folds and dipping a finger in.

"So wet for me already and I haven't even touched you." I parted my lips and pushed back on his hand in reply, moaning for him. Seconds later, I felt the rub of a single cool ball at my entrance and gasped at the feel of it. I moaned again as he slipped it inside of me.

"We gotta keep this pussy tight if you want to play with the big boys, don't we, Mrs. Harvell? Don't you dare let it go or we'll start all over again." I clamped down as hard as I could, the task not seeming to be much of a challenge until the weight of it hit me. FUCK.

I kept my thighs tight, clenching as much as I could. It was agonizing. I looked up to meet his eyes filled with that familiar burn. He circled me, watching me struggle. I felt the ball slip as I gave just an inch of leeway to relax. I sucked in a breath, clenching as tight as I could when he surprised me by adding the second. The fear set in as I gripped my muscles tight. He tortured me, stroking my thighs in a relaxing manner as I held onto the balls for dear life. I found no pleasure in this and was about to start begging when he joined me, kneeling on the table, placing a hand on each of my thighs. He licked my center sweetly as I tightened with all my might, trying desperately not to lose his game.

"Very good. I'll reward you." He dipped his finger inside, pushing the balls slightly further. This was my reward? I moaned in agony as my knees began to hurt, my thighs aching for relief, and my arms starting to shake.

49

"Look at that sweet ass," he murmured, massaging my puckered hole. I sucked in a breath and squeezed as hard as I could as he rubbed me sweetly. The feeling was so foreign but felt so fucking good. I knew I couldn't hold on much longer.

"Oh God!" I cried as he dipped a finger into the unchartered territory, a ball crashing to the table.

"You get one, Violet, no more." I shook now, the ball barely inside me, and the wetness only growing as he fingered my ass and blew on my sex. I moaned for him, begging for relief, but he kept me there. I was drawn so tight; my nipples were aching and I felt the tears hot on my cheeks. It was pure frustration pouring out of me at this point.

He took his finger and his mouth away and I screamed out in frustration. The pull was there, but I needed his help and he knew it.

"What do you want, Violet?"

All I could feel was the heavy weight of the ball and the need for his cock. I didn't answer as he slapped my ass hard, the second ball falling out only to be replaced swiftly by his length. He slammed into me and I came so hard my front half collapsed on the table as I called his name. He never slowed his pace, his strokes punishing and exquisite. I recovered only slightly as he again massaged my ass while punishing my clit with his finger. I came again minutes later and he grunted, pulling my hair as he shot his orgasm onto my back in hot spurts.

We lay on his couch, tangled up and panting an hour later after another round. This one didn't involve balls or discipline. This one, though just as devastating as the first, consisted of me being bent over every surface of the bottom floor of his house.

"About my husband…" I said, catching his gray eyes, the small grin fading from his face.

"Jesus, lady, no man, no matter who they are, wants to hear those words after sex."

"It's just that, I want you to know...I don't know why, but there's nothing going on there. I mean, we have to be honest, right?"

He was lying flat on the couch and I had my leg over his torso, enveloping him with my hand on his chest. This was way different than our rendezvous at the club. I wondered why he had brought me here to his home. This screamed personal, yet he never really pried, never really asked me questions about myself. Maybe this was just the way he treated his partners, and I respected him for it. He gave way more than he took, and it seemed to satisfy him. And yet, the more I studied his profile as his breathing evened out, the more I felt my chest tighten. He said he was a relationship kind of guy, or that it wasn't so out of the question. I wondered if he'd consider that with me. And then I sort of panicked...I shot up off the couch, racing to the stairs for my clothes, and heard him laugh at my lightning streak across the house.

"Where's the fire?" He had just tied the string on his sweatpants and rounded the corner to the stairs when I clasped my bra.

"I'm sorry. I have to go. I forgot..." I couldn't think of one damn good excuse to give him and sat down on the bottom step of his stairs, sliding my shoes on.

"Wow, that's the worst excuse I have ever heard. I wanted to cook you dinner, but hey, you forgot..." He shook his head slowly, his usual grin at my expense covering his face.

"I'm sorry," I said, standing up, throwing my shirt over my head. He helped me pull it down and lifted my hair out of the collar as my heart did a summersault.

"It's okay, Violet. If you have to go, you have to go," he whispered to me as he kissed my cheek. I nodded and walked toward the door, mumbling about errands and that it was pointless to thank him for fucking me and I would talk to him soon. He stopped me as I placed my hand on the doorknob.

"Don't leave. You don't want to, so don't." His breath tickled my ear. The smell of him mingled with the sex we'd had was intoxicating.

"If I stay, then everything changes, right?" He moved my hair away from my neck and placed a soft kiss on the back of it.

"Don't you want to find out?"

My chest squeezed at the thought and I turned to him, kissing him sweetly before I left him at his door. I fumbled with my keys, not looking to see if he was watching me, and got into my car. I braved a look at his entrance, but he wasn't there. I laid my forehead against my steering wheel, not wanting to leave, but knowing if I stayed it meant we would start something I wasn't sure I was ready for. I was barely a few weeks into my year of being sexually free. On the other hand, the man was beautiful, smart, intuitive, well endowed, and seemed successful. Oh, and he was a fucking stallion in bed who had blown my mind with his impressive skills with his hands, dick, and tongue for the last two weeks. What the hell was I thinking?

I dashed for his door, taking the four million steps quickly and twisted the handle. Locked. Okay, so it wouldn't be the grand entrance I pictured in my head. I knocked on the door and got no answer. I knocked again and waited. Nothing. What the hell? I had been in the car less than five minutes. I didn't see a car leave. I knocked again, this time more of a bang, and got nothing. Completely confused, I ran down his steps to the driveway and saw his sedan parked next to the house. I ran back up to his door and knocked again. When he didn't answer, I became furious and kicked a potted plant down his steps. He picked that exact moment to open the door and stood watching me curse as my toe pulsed with my heartbeat. He crossed his arms, soaking wet with a towel wrapped around him.

Ah, he was in the shower. You should probably find a rock to go crawl under, Violet.

He stood there dripping on his beautiful antique floor, torturing me, his half-baked smile on the verge of hysterical laughter. I quickly started talking.

"I'm definitely not as subtle as I used to be." I nudged over my shoulder at the plant that I had just massacred. "I have a bit of a temper. I've horrible allergies and I look disgusting when I have an attack, like disgusting." I circled an opened hand over my face for emphasis. "I have good things going for me too. I hate raisins, but I love wine. As a matter of fact, I can pair wine and food like no one's business, I give a mean massage, I know the location of all the prime and potentially lucrative real estate in Savannah, and I can hold a ben wa ball in my vagina for at least ten minutes."

"Five," he replied with a chuckle.

"THAT WAS FIVE MINUTES!" I said, disgusted. "Fine, I'll make it ten by Christmas. I love a challenge." I stood there with my pride hanging in the air as he watched me carefully. "God, why couldn't you have just left the door unlocked?" I threw up my hands. "Now you've seen my crazy."

He looked gorgeous freshly wet and still dripping. I wanted back in that house bad. "Yes. I want to see where this can go, Rhys."

He dropped his towel and tugged me inside by both hands, shutting the door and placing my back on it. And then he kissed me, really kissed me. I melted into his arms as his tongue gently stroked mine, my moan this time sounded like a sigh. I opened myself to him, letting him strip me bare. He clasped our hands as he led me upstairs. I took a quick look around his spacious bedroom as he led me to his adjoining master bath. He turned the faucet on the tub and plugged it, adding some bath salt. I raised my brow.

"What? It's cucumber, and I like the smell."

I burst out laughing and he swatted my ass playfully. He tested the water, letting it run as he pulled a towel from the cabinet, placing it on his sink. The bath was a beautiful, old-fashioned, claw foot tub and I couldn't wait to get in it. He pulled me to him and kissed me again like he meant it, leaving me breathless and aching for him.

53

"Take a bath and I'll start dinner. Chicken fettuccine okay? I'm pretty sure there are no raisins in it." He winked and I nodded, my cheeks heating slightly. He kissed me again sweetly and let me go. I stuck both feet in, wincing as my sore toe hit the water. Rhys turned to me as an afterthought as he was walking out the door. "I'm glad you said yes."

I smiled at him and replied, "Me too."

God, how naïve was I to have thought all people into kink were subhuman? Rhys seemed to be a really good man. I looked around his subtle but tastefully decorated bathroom and thought now this is a man who might appreciate decorations on the holidays. His house was a home, even if he was the only one who occupied it. It seemed warm and inviting and I felt right at home in his claw foot tub, sudsing my body and enjoying his hospitality...and his cucumber bath salt. I giggled again, taking a look at the brand he liked, burning it into my brain. I was sure it would come in handy later, either as ammo or a present. God, was I already planning to prank him in the future? The truth was, I hoped so.

Downstairs, dressed and freshly cucumbered, I found a drop dead gorgeous man tooling around in his kitchen with ease. He wore a fresh pair of sweats and had pots going heavy on the stove. I was saddened at the loss of his bare chest now covered by a white -shirt.

"Anything I can do to help?" I piped behind him.

"No, just sit there at the bar. I poured you a glass of wine." I took a seat at his bar and sipped the wine. It was amazing.

"Okay, straight up," I said, snapping my fingers, "if you can't be this amazing in a year, don't you dare do it now." I saw his cheeks puff, his back still turned to me as he stirred the pot of noodles. He set the spoon down and walked over to the bar.

"Well, I can be a real prick too, but I figured I'd start you out easy." He snatched my wine glass out of my hand as I protested with a quick, "Heeeeyyyy." He drank a big gulp, leaving me with a sip left and I crossed my arms. "I'll shut up now."

He pulled the bottle out of a cabinet, poured me more, and then turned to his task at hand.

"So, I love your house. When did you get it?"

"Thanks," he answered, draining the pasta. "I moved in about three years ago."

"And you decorated this place yourself?" *Okay, what the hell with the loaded question, Vi? Easy.*

"No, I had help," he said, shooting a careful glance my way.

"And that's my prying quota for the day," I said, taking a nice gulp of wine.

"I highly doubt that, Violet," he said with a grin, mixing the pasta and gesturing for me to sit at his kitchen table.

He joined me a few minutes later with two full plates of steaming goodness paired with fresh garlic bread. I dug in, absolutely starving from the smells that had tortured me while he was cooking. I took heaping forkfuls into my mouth in clear appreciation of his amazing cooking skills. I moaned, closing my eyes after a few bites. Catching his eyes on me, I turned my head and gave him my best smile, twisting my fork in the air with flair.

"I'm not sure I like that moan, woman."

"And why the hell not?" I asked, offended. "It's a compliment to your cooking"

"And it's an insult to my cock. I'm not so sure you moan as well when you compliment it."

"Well, anytime you want to make me moan in your kitchen with your cock, let me know. I'm game. And this food is delicious. Thank you."

"I love that you eat like you mean it," he stated, taking a mouthful of noodles.

"Not that I need to." *Shit, self-depreciating slip, Vi. Not attrac-*

tive. Then again, give yourself a break. It's been a while since you've dated. You are dating! I went in for a smooth recovery, "But I do love my food and I mean that."

"I love the way your body looks. I wouldn't change a fucking thing."

I snapped to and saw that he meant it, and I fell a little for him right then. I stifled the emotion I was sure was showing in my face. It had been so long since I felt this type of affection, since I was this full, this appreciated, this...happy. I wanted it to last.

When we finished our dinner, I insisted on cleaning the dishes and he made his way to the couch to watch football. When he saw me enter the living room, he pulled a small pillow from the side of the couch and placed it between his chest and his arm. If he could see my insides, he would see them falling to my feet.

Who the fuck are you, Rhys?

I had every intention of finding out.

⟠

Twenty extremely boring minutes of football later, I spoke up, perfectly relaxed with my feet snuggled with his on the coffee table he had violated me on hours earlier. It was hard to believe this was the same man.

"How old are you, Rhys?"

"Thirty-four."

"Where are you from?"

"Here, born and raised." He lifted a piece of hair covering my eyes so he could glance down and catch mine. "You?"

"Thirty-two. Thirty-three on Halloween and born and raised here, too." I snuggled further into him; he seemed to like the affection or faked it well.

"So, before you owned the bar, what did you do?"

"What I still do. I work a boring ass nine to five installing computer updates for the company I work for."

"You have a nine to five?" I sat up, completely thrown.

"The bar is great income. I could live off of that, but being there day in day out isn't very appealing."

"I get it." I lay back down in his arms, resting my chin on his chest. "But you still love it, right?"

He leaned down and whispered, "If you're asking if I'll ever get tired of fucking your pretty pink pussy in a variety of light and dark ways, I'm almost positive the answer is no."

I smiled and buried my head in his chest. He cupped my chin, bringing my eyes to his. "Never ever be afraid to tell me what you want."

I was so close to bursting, I simply nodded and put my head back on his chest, making sure he didn't see the lone happy tear that fell down my cheek. I woke some time later to the weightless feeling of being carried and looked up to see Rhys cradling my body as he moved us easily up the stairs. He looked down at me with an intensity that had my already rapid heartbeat kicking into overdrive. Standing at the edge of his bed, words failed us both as our eyes locked.

He kissed me and my clothes seemed to fall away naturally, as if they didn't belong between us. Naked and laid out for him, he took his time stretching his lips and tongue over every single inch of my skin. I felt worshipped and beautiful, and when he brought his mouth back to mine, I kissed him with my whole being.

"Violet," he said as he held my face in his hands, tracing my jaw with his kiss. I basked in his tender touch, wrapping my limbs around him, unable to get close enough. He slid inside me gently; the friction of his cock mixed with the emotion in my chest led me to orgasm in minutes. His strokes took me to a blissful state, murmuring as I kissed his chest and arms. He made love to me for hours as we took turns swallowing each other's moans, exploring each other's bodies until we were too weak to move. He held me to his chest tightly as we drifted off into a deep sleep.

The next morning, I woke up to his kiss, smiling as he trailed it to my nipple. I covered my mouth, pushing his head away and sprang up from the bed.

"Violet, what the hell? I had a perfectly good erection."

"Toothbrush?" I questioned, scared to say more.

"I think there's an extra one in my medicine cabinet."

He shook his head and smiled, falling into bed, his black hair a total disheveled mess and his morning stubble sexy as hell. I knew what I looked like and was terrified. I scurried into the bathroom and checked my appearance. Past the age of thirty, I had never looked well in the morning. I always had pillow face and Tina Turner hair. Today was so...different. My hair, by the grace of God, while a little tousled, still looked good. My skin was glowing, face slightly puffy, but not too shabby. I grabbed the spare toothbrush and went to work, remedying my morning breath. After using the restroom, I opened the door in a "ta-da" fashion, naked as a jaybird.

He chuckled and patted the bed next to him. I looked at the clock.

"It's eight a.m. on Monday morning, don't you have a job to go to?" I asked.

"Get over here," he growled. I walked excruciatingly slow and giggled when he snatched me by the waist, throwing me onto the bed.

"Woman, service me!" He kneeled in front of me, turned his head to the side as he placed his hands on his hips, proudly displaying his glorious morning wood.

"Okay, I'll earn my keep, but you better be thinking about this at work today." I swallowed him whole and minutes later he pounded me into thinking of him for the rest of my life.

Pulling into my drive, I noticed Alex's car there. I walked in, expecting him to be dressing for work, but he was in our bed and sick as hell. I rolled my eyes at his pleas to talk to me. Showering and dressing quickly to prepare myself for a few listings to show, I granted him a small amount of mercy by leaving some cough tablets and hot soup by the bed. The only thing worse than being sick was being treated like shit when you were sick. Besides, I was feeling generous today. I'd just started something amazing with a man who treated me well and worshipped my body.

Deciding today probably wasn't the best day to ask Alex for a divorce, I set out to sell houses. I was on top of the world and had nothing but huge smiles for complete strangers. I looked like a lunatic, but a happy one. When I got home later that night, I found Alex face down on the floor, burning with fever. I rushed him to the ER and stayed with him as they got his fever under control. I looked at my phone hours later and saw I had two missed texts from Rhys.

> **RHYS: It's 5 o'clock and all I can think about is your Jedi jaw movements this morning. Please come now for a repeat performance. My cock will thank you.**

> **RHYS: Maybe it wasn't as good for you as it was for me?**

I looked at the clock. It was one a.m. Shit. Somehow Alex had found a way to taint the only good thing that had happened to me. I texted him back.

> **VIOLET: So sorry. Crazy shit. I'll explain later. And yes, it was incredible. I will take your cock up on that offer.**

I got no response and tucked my phone back into my purse.

"I love you, Violet." I looked to see Alex studying me from the hospital bed. He looked pitiful and I almost felt sorry for him.

"Yeah, love you, too, honey." I rolled my eyes away from him and sat up in my chair.

"Where is your wedding ring?" he asked, studying my empty finger.

"Wow, a sick and desperate man," I said, shaking my head.

The doctor came in and discharged Alex with a long list of prescriptions. Alex had the plague, as far as he was concerned, and begged me to stay with him. I spent the next day at home nursing his health. The sooner he got better, the sooner I could ask for a divorce.

Rhys had extended his invitation again and I had turned him down again. I hated when I had to text my reply. On day three, his text came and my heart sank.

> **RHYS: You aren't running away, are you? You can talk to me.**

> **VIOLET: No, God, please don't think that, Rhys. I promise I will explain. I wish I were with you.**

I got no response. It took Alex five days to get up and moving, and I could feel Rhys slipping away. I shouldn't have lied to him. And I sure as hell shouldn't be ruining my fucking chances with him to nurse Alex back to health. I went to check on Alex after waking on the couch and found him missing. I looked at the bedside clock, 10:59 p.m.

I stood against the side of his office door, the way I always did when I eavesdropped. Listening to his conversation, I assumed it was Sandra he was speaking to. I had met her twice at office parties and other occasions for the firm. Alex was the head of commercial accounts at his advertising firm and had recently received an award for his work on a shoe campaign. He hadn't bothered inviting me, stating it was an afternoon ceremony and he didn't want me to have to miss work. I found out later through our credit card statement the fucking bastard had booked a suite that day. I listened to him speak to her the way he used to talk to me.

"You are so fucking perfect. I don't want to hide it anymore. I love you, Kris."

I choked on a sob. I didn't care how much I hated him, how much I was ready for my marriage to be over. It fucking hurt to hear him profess his love to another woman. Especially when I had been the woman who had been nursing him back to health. Clutching my chest, I turned my body, my forehead to the wall as my tears of rage fell silently. I wouldn't wait for Christmas. I wouldn't wait for tomorrow. As soon as he finished his conversation, we would have ours.

"I want to fuck you so bad. I need you right now." Alex's voice sounded desperate, needy.

I felt a hand clamp over my mouth and started to scream out when I heard his voice.

"It's me. Don't scream."

I tried to turn to face him, tears still damp on my face. Rhys was here, in my house, and my husband was on the other side of the door. What the hell was he doing here? He held my back to his chest as I stood still, facing the wall, completely wide-eyed and terrified we would be discovered at any moment. He stroked the wetness of my face, his voice coming out in a whisper.

"You cry tears for a man begging for someone else's pussy."

I shook my head no, wanting to tell him it wasn't true, to tell him it stung a little. I hated Alex. Alex, who was just on the other side of the door! I tried to break free, but he kept his grip on my hips.

"He doesn't want you anymore, Violet. He doesn't want this."

He slid his hand up my thigh, only partially covered by my baby doll nightie, straight up to my sex. Fear set in as I listened to my husband's voice as he proclaimed his love to another woman. The slip of his hand beneath my underwear and the flick of his finger hard on my clit woke up the woman who didn't give a fuck about

Alex, didn't give a fuck about inhibitions, and didn't give a damn if Alex came out and saw her impaled on another man's dick. Though he wouldn't let me turn to face him, I gave him permission by sliding my panties down as far as I could before it hit the hand resting on my hip, the other stroking me with his fingers. Alex's voice was a blur as a wealth of wet came pouring out of me. His lips brushed my neck and his voice took me into a whole new world with his next words.

"He may not want you anymore, but I wanted you. I wanted this," he said, pressing hard against my clit. I had to stifle a moan as he slid to the floor, taking my panties down. He pulled my ass out and spread my legs.

"He doesn't want it anymore because you were never wet for him the way you are for me. You were never his. You never wanted him the way you want me."

He swiped his tongue from the bottom of my folds to the top, completely knocking the breath out of me. Two fingers slipped into my slick center as his tongue circled my clit hard. He did this with no mercy as my body twitched with anticipation. I wanted to see his face, take in his beautiful gray depths. All I could do was give him a low moan as his fingers glided in and out. A third entered my ass and I almost collapsed to the floor. He was doing this slowly, but the tension was building and my core began to hum. His tongue joined his fingers and I could barely stand when he'd had his fill, dragging the flat part of his tongue back to my clit. I stood there getting my pussy eaten in a dark hall, not hearing anything but the gasps caught in my throat. I was close to coming and I could hear Alex's call coming to a close. Rhys paused behind me.

"You want me to stop? I could leave right now, or he could walk out and see me devouring your sweet, pretty pussy." He worked his fingers, stroking the nerves that set me off, my body convulsing slightly. "Violet, what do you want to happen?"

"Don't stop," I said on a whisper, still on the edge as his digits slowly fucked me. Seconds later, I felt his tongue resume the circles it was making on my clit. With a few more strokes of his tongue, he shoved his finger fully in my ass and I came, trembling from head to toe, scratching at the wall, rubbing my forehead back and forth over the textured surface as I fell apart, hot liquid sliding out of me as he continued his strokes, pulling my wetness with him. When the last shudder left me, he stood and whispered in my ear.

"I wanted you. I wanted you so much. You fucking lied to me. You made a fool out of me. I'll never let you make a fool of me again."

Heavy tears fell down my face as he turned my head to the side to claim my mouth in a long, slow, sensual kiss. His rock-hard chest behind me rose with his breath, his cock heavy, stiff and pulsing against my back. I tasted the tanginess of my sex and inhaled the soothing scent of him, a mix of soap and spice. And then he was gone, just a shadow moving down the hall and out the door. I shook my head no violently, still completely floored by what had just happened. I wanted to run after him, to tell him how sorry I was, but he was right. My white lie had reared its ugly head. I had waited too long and it looked like I was fucking mourning Alex outside his office door. There was no way he would believe me. *I* wouldn't believe me. I had just lost Rhys.

I heard Alex end his call with another "I love you" and the rest of the woman who had any feeling for him died in that moment. I slid my panties back up and walked to the kitchen to get a glass of wine. I was dripping wet from my orgasm and felt my panties soaking as I stood uncorking a new bottle. The evidence that Rhys had just been here fucking me with his mouth wasn't something I wanted to rid myself of...not right away, anyway. I sighed as I sipped my wine. How in the hell did he know where I lived? How insane was he to just stroll into my house and claim me while my husband was here? I shook my head at the thought of Alex actually walking out and seeing Rhys stroking me with his tongue. I would have been furious to miss that orgasm. I laughed out loud at the thought, at the insanity of it all, my heart crumbling in my chest.

How could Rhys not see me as anything but pathetic, standing outside a door crying as my husband confessed his love to another woman? This whole situation went from clean lines to fucked up in minutes.

Alex walked in moments later and gave me a smile as he eyed my wine with nothing but assumption behind his stare. Back from the dead and just as dreadful as ever.

"I'm not an alcoholic, asshole. You would know that if you lived here."

"Vi, what the hell did I do to deserve that?" he challenged, his arms crossed.

"I've been fucked." I said, both figuratively and literally I almost added, though I decided to keep this civil.

"Pardon?" Alex asked, slightly shocked at my vulgarity. I was hardly ever this candid with him. I took a sip of wine, looking forward to this. I thought before, in my denial, that I was being strong. I thought I was just too uninterested to fight for my freedom when the truth was, I wasn't strong enough...until now.

"You fucked me out of a life you promised me. Companionship, a home, not just a house and kids. I won't even go there. The truth is that I don't love you anymore at all...either."

He spoke up to protest, but his words died on his lips as my distant stare became a glare.

"Don't fucking do it. Not tonight, Alex. I don't love you, you don't love me. Let's get a divorce. I want the house and I want you out of it tonight. I could get you on adultery but I'm afraid now I'm guilty, too."

He stood, mouth gaping as I gave him a little more. "Yeah, Alex, what did you expect? I'm not an emotionless robot. Let's make this civil for the long run, but for now I just want to say you're a total fucking disappointment. You shouldn't have asked me to be your wife if you had no intention of being a husband. I wasted years of my life on you and I can't get them back. That leaves me a little pissed off."

"You don't mean any of this. You're just drunk." I poured my wine out and set the glass next to the counter.

"Alex, I don't know why you want to keep me captive. It's fucking cruel, honestly, and I have no more patience for it. Get out, tonight, and don't come back. Go to Kris, except I thought it was Sandra. Either way, leave now." His eyebrows raised in surprise.

"Oh, please...Do you really think I'm that stupid? I wanted this relationship and I cared, so I know all about you. Now I just want you fucking gone, a memory."

He turned to walk away and I watched him go, kicking him as he left with my next words. "I will get everything I am entitled to and I won't take any more than that. Don't make this dirty. I can bury you."

He paused at my words, and when I was done, he walked away. I wrapped a blanket around myself and went to the porch. An hour later, he was gone, my marriage was over, and for the first time in years, I was free.

I quickly texted Rhys.

VIOLET: Please come back. He's gone. Please, Rhys, don't leave things like this. Please talk to me.

No reply brought a pain to my chest that blinded me with tears. I had definitely lost him.

✦

Two weeks and not a fucking word, I was past the point of crazy. I stood frozen outside the bar that now had a closed sign in front of it. I really had to get a grip. I had signed up for an exhibition, not a love affair. That's what I got, a taste of everything and the love affair. I was desperate to stare into those gray eyes, strung out on a man who obviously didn't mean what he said. I had texted him for days with no reply. I didn't show up to his house. It seemed too desperate, and if he wouldn't respond to my texts, then he damn sure wouldn't answer the door. Maybe I wasn't cut out to be a mistress. Maybe I was a one-man woman.

No, fuck that. I was made for Rhys and him alone. He knew it and I did, too. I know he felt what I felt and I know I would be just as finished with him as he was with me had the circumstances been switched. *This is what happens when you fucking lie. This is why you're getting a divorce.*

Lies, deception, no matter how harmless you think they are or whom it would protect, someone always gets hurt.

Okay, back to square one. I had everything I truly wanted, and had lost it. I was in between love and lust and couldn't discern it because I was too busy mourning it to dissect it further. I wanted him. I couldn't have him, and that's what bothered me most.

He didn't even give you a chance to explain.

Just as the thought popped into my head, the message came.

RHYS: The Barracks. One hour. RED.

I couldn't help the smile that tugged the corners of my lips.

VOLUME TWO

THE TANGO

THE BARRACKS

One hour later...

My elation from his sudden invitation was short lived by the three-letter word that followed it.

RED.

I knew he was angry. I knew I was about to pay for my lie. I knew I had hurt him and I had no idea what I was about to walk into. What I was sure of was that he wouldn't physically hurt me.

RED.

I had so many things I wanted to say, an apology to make first and foremost. I also wanted to ask him why the club was closed. Surely, I had nothing to do with it. No, he might have been a little hurt by my actions, but something told me this was much bigger than me. And who the hell was I to think it could have anything to do with me? We'd had one day to explore our relationship further. Even then it was filled with light conversation and nothing heavy. Well, except for the sex. I still didn't know much about him, but in the time that I had known him, I *knew* he was a man I could fall for. And I had ruined it.

I'd been too slow in leaving my worthless husband, who was now completely out of my life, divorce pending. I had filed the day after I kicked him out. All I had to do was tell Rhys the truth. I just didn't want to lose him. I beat myself mentally until I arrived at The Barracks. Putting my car in park, I surveyed the building, instantly on edge.

What a shit hole.

If the meeting place was any indication of the feelings he now harbored for me, I was in deep shit.

RED.

The beat down shack, known as The Barracks, was located on the outskirts of Savannah. It looked to be in shambles, resembling a hideout for crack heads, on the verge of being condemned.

I can't go in there!

I took deep breaths, on the brink of a panic attack. What the hell was Rhys doing here? This was not his style. I was tempted to text him and call it off. Walking quickly from my car, I scanned the lot to make sure I got in safely.

Stepping into the dark bar, I saw him immediately. He was standing at the far end, and as soon as the door closed behind me, his eyes were on mine. They were as cold as ice. Sweat covered me instantly, and I could feel heads turning my direction but couldn't tear my eyes away from Rhys. There was an electrical shift in the air then a crackle, and it didn't have the kind of pull that had me gravitating toward him. This was the kind that made my steps careful. I was just a few feet away from him when he turned and walked around the corner then down a flight of stairs. Swallowing the lump in my throat, I followed quietly. At the foot of the stairs, he continued walking down a dark hall with a set of rooms to the right and left. I stood behind him, silent, as he reached into his pocket. When he turned the key and walked through the door, I hesitated.

He inspected the room as I quickly surveyed it. There was a large iron chandelier with cheap yellow bulbs hanging from the ceiling. Large black silk ribbons were draped from the center of it. I hadn't noticed before that Rhys had been carrying a small black bag, which he dropped to the floor with a thud, making me jump, his back to me. He was waiting.

It was then that I understood exactly what RED meant. My Rhys was gone, and I was about to meet the version of the man that took his place.

I took a tentative step into the room and closed the door.

"Rhys, I just wanted to say I—"

He turned suddenly, taking long strides toward me, and gripped my neck with one hand, nailing me to the door. I gasped in surprise; his grip was tight.

"Don't ever call me by my name again. You will address me as sir, and I don't want to hear a fucking word come out of your mouth. Sir or stop, that's all you get, Mrs. Harvell."

OH FUCK. OH FUCK. OH FUCK.

My limbs were shaking at the power in his voice and the weight of his words. His grip was tight, but he wasn't cutting off circulation. He didn't want to hurt me, and I knew that. I trusted him, though the look in his eyes was deadly. He loosened his tie, still holding my neck, keeping me pinned to the door.

He watched my chest rise and fall with interest. Using his spare hand, he pulled my sweater up and pulled down my tank top along with my bra underneath so that the material supported my breasts, leaving them exposed and clustered. Trailing his hand down my stomach, he unbuttoned my jeans and shoved it inside my pants as his grip tightened on my throat. I heard the sound of my arousal as he plunged his fingers inside. I was dripping. He stroked me roughly as he squeezed my neck. I screamed out when he drew two fingers up to my clit and pinched it. To my whine, he smirked. I had to keep cool; apparently, my pain fueled him. I wondered if my moans would do the same.

Rhys was one beautifully pissed off man.

"Tonight, I will exhaust you, sate you, and make you hungrier at the same time. You will think of nothing but my cock until you come, begging me to do it all over again." He grabbed my chin roughly, forcing me to meet his eyes. "Eyes on mine at all times, Mrs. Harvell, or I will it make it more painful than it has to be."

He soothed my now aching clit with my wetness as he stared at my nipples. Taking one with his mouth, he pulled and sucked hard as I writhed beneath him and arched my back, begging for more. He bit down on my nipple and I jumped in his hold as it grew tighter. I thrashed my head back and forth, caught somewhere between heaven and hell. And just as suddenly as he started, I found myself alone at the door, gasping and holding my neck.

He undressed slowly, his back to me.

"Take off your clothes," he barked, making me jump out of my skin. I felt the pinch in my clit, the soreness in my neck, and more than anything else, the need in me. I stripped down quickly as I admired his beautiful broad shoulders and the curve of his perfect ass sitting on top of his thighs. I was dying to ogle the front of him, but he refused to turn around. He stood underneath the chandelier filled with hanging ribbons and gestured for me to come to him. As soon as I was within reach, he gripped my wrist, yanking me closer, and tied the ribbon into a smooth knot, pulling the other side down so it dangled my hand over my head. Once both hands were suspended, he moved to my legs, tying a longer piece of silk to each of them. I was hanging like a rag doll. He tested the hold by pulling on one of the ribbons and my arm stretched painfully.

"Perfect," he said as he watched my reaction. I had no idea why his anger spiked my arousal, but it turned me on more than anything. I gave him a wicked grin and saw surprise in his eyes.

Bring it, baby.

He shifted behind me, smoothing my skin with his hands. He ran his hand up and down my sex then shoved his fingers into my mouth without warning. I sucked hard, taking my arousal off him. I felt his cock bump me from behind as he circled me. Stopping in front of me with a sneer, he leaned in, his breath hot on my skin.

"I'm going to let you ride my cock tonight, but you won't be in control. Nice and slow, Mrs. Harvell, or I'll make it hurt."

I stood on my toes, practically hanging from my arms, the burn becoming more intense by the second. I whimpered and was scolded by the slap of his hand hard on my ass. I kept my yelp to myself as his eyes challenged me. I wanted to drink him in, to admire his beautifully muscled chest and mouthwatering cock. Instead, I was forced to face his cold eyes and unforgiving expression.

As soon as the burn in my arms became intolerable, he lifted me up quickly to straddle him, filling my pussy with his thick shaft. I swallowed air and clawed his back, holding myself to his chest as I adjusted to him. Hearing a rush of air escape him, I moaned and he pulled back, glaring at me. I wanted to move but knew better. My arms were now hanging limply above me, due to the slack of being held up. Although I felt a small amount of relief, they were becoming numb. The sensation of being filled by his thick dick and the numbing of my arms was overwhelming. The need to move became unbearable.

His lips were so close, only a whisper away. I needed to touch him so badly, to kiss his lips, to feel his tongue.

"Remember what I said," he said as he twisted a nipple painfully, "and don't test me."

I began to move excruciatingly slow. Staring into his angry eyes was agony. It was the worst kind of torture, knowing what I could have, seeing it in front of me, and not being able to touch it. I felt the pull to move faster and tightened my legs around him as he kept his grip on my waist. I moaned and he loosened his grip so I was forced to cling to him to keep the burn out of my arms. I widened my eyes, suddenly afraid he would let me fall.

"Watch it," he said, enjoying every minute of my discomfort as the burning between my thighs brewed.

I died a little with each slow movement of my hips as I pumped slowly, squeezing his thick length. He felt amazing, but I wanted more. Deciding to get constructive, I moved myself away from him, pulling myself up on the ribbons so I slid down his cock fully with each thrust. His mouth parted as I held my own weight, taking every inch of him. He fit me perfectly, and with each push of my hips, I saw his eyes blaze and his desire grow more intense. My arms were on fire, but it felt so damn good that soon I got lost and quickened the thrust of my hips.

His victory grin was not the one I'd grown to crave.

"Thank you."

He let go of me immediately. My arms were wrenched painfully tight above my head and I was once again on my toes. I grinned back out of spite, surprising him again. He knew it hurt. He watched me twist and turn my body, trying to help ease the suffering, and then slapped my ass a few times for good measure. I struggled with my restraints as he pumped his cock, ogling me strung up before him. I could tell he liked what he saw. My body pulsated as my center screamed for relief at the sight of him stroking himself. I'd never been so damn uncomfortable and yet so turned on. My arms were useless now, almost comfortably numb. I whined as I saw his pace pick up and almost spoke up to protest his climax. Challenging eyes told me that was exactly what he wanted, so I remained silent. Licking my lips, I watched him rub my wetness all over his shaft. Filled with desire for him and longing to be the reason for his release, I whimpered as I saw the drop of arousal fall from his tip. He had brought himself to the edge and I was helpless to stop him. Despite his constant threats to keep my eyes on his, I bowed my head and closed my eyes in defeat. Seconds later, I looked to find he had dropped his hand, and when our eyes connected, a slow smiled spread across his face.

I glared at him as he untied one wrist, pulled the ribbon down, freeing them both before massaging my arms as the blood pumped back in and the tingling subsided. Rhys chuckled and trailed a single finger around my nipple, dragging it down as he traced it around my stomach as he walked behind me. His touch continued as it trailed under my arm and to my back. He rubbed my back with his open hands and I lifted my head and closed my eyes, enjoying his caress. His thick head bobbed at my entrance, his breath hot in my ear.

"Bend over and grab your ankles."

I did as I was told, and seconds later, he was under me, tying the ribbons so that my wrists were attached to my ankles. His fingers entered me, moving around and dragging up and down my sex. My breath hitched as he put just enough pressure on my clit to start the pull and then pulled it away as I began to fall. There was no mistaking the begging in my moan. I felt a swish of air and then he was buried inside of me. I screamed out at the intrusion and moaned at the intensity.

My orgasm was building quickly as every solid inch of him filled me deeper than I had ever been filled. I tilted my hips, backing myself into his thrusts, taking all of him deep. His fingers dug into my hips without mercy as he pounded into me roughly. My thighs and calves burned out of control as I began to whimper.

"What's wrong, Mrs. Harvell?" He grinded into me again and again, fucking me so hard tears sprang to my eyes. I couldn't breathe. I couldn't do anything but feel the huge cock that tore me apart, and I fucking loved it. His strokes were violent and rapidly pulling me to orgasm.

I really wished I had stopped the next words coming out of my mouth.

"Harder, sir."

He pulled out of me abruptly and I cried at the loss of him. He was under me in seconds, cutting the ties. I moved to rise to my full height when he grabbed my hair, pulling my face to his roughly.

"WHAT THE FUCK DID I SAY?" His eyes were pure steel, cold and devastating. "Get on your knees."

He let go of my hair and I sank to my knees on the cold floor. I didn't have time to prepare myself as he pushed his dick in my mouth and I immediately started choking on him. It lit a fire in me, making me work harder. He let me use my hands and I lightly massaged his thighs before moving them around to grip his ass, taking him deeper. I moaned at the way he was looking down at me. I could see a hint of surprise in his eyes as I took him as hard as he gave it. I loved every second of him fucking my mouth.

"You like that, Mrs. Harvell?" He gripped my head, holding it with both hands, and I felt his cock pulse. "Open wide."

He came then, shooting his hot load straight down my throat, gripping the sides of my head and jacking into me without mercy. I swallowed every drop, licking him clean then moved to his sack and sucked hard as I continued to pump his cock. His legs trembled, and I got another moan from him. I couldn't hide the curl of my lips.

"Enough!" He pulled away and turned his back to me. "Get out."

I stood, stunned. He hadn't given me what I needed. I walked away slowly, sure he wasn't done. When I was dressed, I waited at the door, hoping for something, anything.

"Get. Out."

I moved to the door and turned around one last time to see him pull on his jacket. His face twisted as he looked up and saw me standing there. I also saw hurt. I hoped he saw mine.

"I'm sorry." I didn't wait to see his face as I turned and walked out, shutting the door behind me.

It was the first time Rhys had ever left me unsatisfied, and I knew I deserved it. I walked to my car, legs shaking, unsure of what to do. I sat in the parking lot, and less than a minute later, I saw Rhys leaving, his bag in his hand. He didn't even look my way. I pulled out before he had a chance to.

⚭

Days later, I stood at the glass double doors of the house I was showing, thinking of him. If he wanted me to crave him, he had done his damn job.

How the hell had I made it out of that situation without a mark on me? My arms had burned like hell afterward, and I had to once again soak in Epsom salt.

God, that whole experience was incredible. And if loving it made me a freak, so be it; I had walked into the land of misfits and fit right in. I loved the power that man exuded. His influence over me, with only a gesture or one word command, was mind blowing. Without hesitation, I would do anything he asked. I trusted him, even though I had never seen him so angry.

And I really needed to learn when to shut the hell up.

The ache in my body told me I was the worst submissive ever, yet I loved it. The look in his eyes, his parted lips as I rode his cock, made me squirm and tighten my thighs. I wanted him so badly. My new revelation was that I loved being fucked viciously. I still remembered the slight amount of surprise in his eyes when he had taken me so roughly and realized I loved it. Not letting me orgasm was definitely a good way to get back at me for my lie. Although, I was sure if I hadn't fought him so hard, he would have given me what I wanted.

Thoughts of him consumed me and I couldn't stop thinking about the way he filled me and gripped my throat. It was just so raw...so damn...HOT. My body was screaming for relief, but I refused to do anything about it. And then I would remember how beautiful he looked the morning after we'd made love. It was always in the forefront of my mind. The way he kissed me, the way he smiled at me while he faced me on the pillow, his dark hair a mess and adoration in his eyes, for me. Rhys made me feel beautiful, cared about, wanted. I craved that side of him. I'd ruined a good thing with Rhys. I'd had a chance to be with him and blown it. I'd spent the last three weeks mourning the thought of *what if* with Rhys, but I'd spent the last year doing the same for another man. Maybe I'd lost the chance of a relationship with Rhys, but I still had the chance to explore my dark side with him. The problem was, I wanted both. My only hope was that he wouldn't punish me the same way twice.

"Mrs. Harvell?" I quickly realized there were tears running down my face, which was humiliating. The couple I was showing the house to had stopped their discussion as they walked around the empty house while I'd been lost in thoughts of Rhys.

"Sorry," I said, catching my tears on my sleeve. They looked slightly concerned, but had grace enough to let me recover. "So, what do you think?"

"We love it! We'll have an offer to you soon." They stood so close to each other, it was easy to tell they were recently married. How did I get from where they were to where I was?

Easy answer, Vi. Alex. Fucking Alex.

"That's wonderful. I'm so happy you love it. I knew it would suit you two. I hope you'll be happy here."

As I walked them out, I noticed they had to be in their early twenties. Ending my inner musing, I locked the door and turned to leave, watching as he opened the door for her and sighing as I remembered the last man who had done that for me.

I had to get over this. This was supposed to be an adventure, not the focal point of my new life. But Rhys knew it was more; I knew it was more. And now it was just sex...again.

How could he just emotionally shut me out so quickly?

I either had to accept my fate as his new RED playmate or move on. This was a dangerous game. My heart was involved. I was already hurt by the way he treated me, but then again, it had turned me on. I'd been right about my desires all along.

I'd had my warning. RED was RED. It meant extreme, and from what I'd been shown, I knew it could only get darker.

I hated that he wouldn't speak to me. I wanted to be his play-mate. I also wanted to be the girl who fell asleep in his arms. I could have had both. Now I couldn't and he gave me no choice. The next time he wanted to play, I would have to be ready. I had to take my heart out of the ring, but with Rhys, it seemed impossible.

I walked into the building feeling like a foreigner in a strange land. It was amazing what a year of being out of someone's life could do, how you see things differently, more clearly. I was a stranger here. Some of the office personnel took a double take as they noticed me. I guess it really had been that long.

"Violet," Alex's assistant greeted me sweetly, "so good to see you. You look amazing!"

"Thanks, Serena. Is he in?"

"Yes, and he's expecting you." She smiled and twisted the knob, ushering me in.

I walked into Alex's office and noticed his attorney present. When he had called and begged me to come, I should have known better.

Alex spoke first. "Have a seat, Violet."

"What the hell is this?" My blood was boiling. Did this bastard have no shame?

"It's a divorce you want, isn't it?" Alex said smartly, taking a seat behind his desk.

"I'm outta here. If you want to talk with attorneys present, you need to prepare me." I glared at both of them, ready to stand my ground.

"Sit down, Violet. I'm prepared to make an offer," Alex said carefully. He looked at his attorney then back to me as if to ask 'Am I doing okay?'

The red flag went up. Instead of fleeing, I was suddenly curious to hear his offer, so I sat. Alex was a man with connections, which came from being a part of an influential Savannah family. They were traditional to the core. The type that held several charitable functions every year. His family deemed me acceptable, due to my own upbringing at the careful hand of my parents who knew and were social with the Harvells. Although it hadn't been, our courting could have easily been arranged. I knew I'd be in for it if he decided to fight. I just didn't know if he had the decency to play nice or would choose to play dirty after he'd abandoned me. From the looks of it, it was the latter.

"Mrs. Harvell," his lawyer—who happened to be a mutual friend of us both until that very minute—spoke up, "Alex is prepared to offer you the house, a lump sum, and pay your car note."

"Don't address me like you don't know me, Joseph," I snapped. "How much?" I never let my eyes leave Alex, who now looked away. I couldn't help but smile at the amount of power I had at that moment. Over a year of feeling powerless could do that to a woman.

I turned to Joseph, who had been his best man at our wedding, and saw his resolve to be the lawyer I was sure Alex had paid handsomely for, though he was worthless. Joseph, who had made a pass at me a year after we'd been married, looked at me now as if I was weak, pathetic, and gave me a laughable sum. "Sixty thousand dollars."

I stood up and nodded. "Sweet offer coming from a man who has a trust fund worth over three million dollars. I'm not looking to get rich here, fellas, but you can both kiss my ass with that offer."

Watching the two of them squirm, I knew the amount in his trust was now inaccurate. Alex was worth much more. He was probably worth millions more, but I had no intention of breaking him. I just wanted it to sting a little. I didn't need his money and could support myself, but I wanted him to feel the small slap of our divorce so that he wouldn't make the same mistake twice. The women of Savannah didn't deserve a prick like him on the loose. I felt guilty for giving him back.

"Joseph, let me have a word with Violet," Alex said as he excused him with a wave of his hand. Joseph immediately protested, but Alex stood firm.

"We tried it your way, Joseph. Let me speak to my wife." Alex opened the door, ushering him out.

When he closed the door, he stood in front of it, cowering under my glare.

"That was low, Alex. You know I'm entitled to more. And you know why, or do I need to remind you?"

"I'll take care of you," he said, defeated. "I don't even know who I am anymore." He took the chair next to mine.

"Wow, a Scooby mystery for us both, but in lieu of Daphne and Wilma, let's finally talk about Kris and Sandra."

He paled. I would never understand how I ever loved such a coward, or how I turned into one. I should have walked into his office a year ago demanding an explanation.

"Please, don't, Vi. Let's keep this clean. It's what you wanted."

"Well, seeing as how I was just ambushed by you and that jackass, I could very well get my hands dirty."

"It's over now and I knew you would never fall for it," he said, rubbing his temples. "Vi, while I was in the hospital, I watched you. I saw you get a text from someone and truly smile. I told you I loved you right after, but what I didn't tell you is that I am sorry for the way I've treated you and I want you to be happy. What I did was wrong, but I didn't know how to explain it to you. If you had your shot at being with someone that made you truly happy, I wouldn't want to stand in your way. I did love you, just not in the way you deserved, and you will always be a dear friend—"

"What is this?" I said, truly confused. "I wasn't your friend. I was your wife! You want me to say it's *okay* that you abandoned me because you decided to have an affair and it made you happier than you were when you were with me? Not one affair but two!"

"It's not that simple," he said, rubbing his palms on his pants. He was clearly terrified and I couldn't for the life of me figure out why.

"Don't worry, sweetie, just make me an offer I can't refuse. Your reputation will be safe. I mean, it's not that big of a scandal." He buried his head in his hands.

"Vi, you know it is. You know my parents would flip. I would lose my trust. I'll have Joseph draw it up. I shouldn't have listened to him." He looked at me, and for the first time, I could see the red around his eyes.

"What do you want, Alex? I want this over." I crossed my arms as I glared at him.

"I'll give you a divorce settlement and you will give me confidentiality. I don't want a scandal. Irreconcilable differences stated as the reason."

"Fine, I don't care. Let's get this over with." I stood, watching the perspiration roll down his forehead. Incredulous at his reaction to me, I continued, "Is it really that hard to admit you were a shit husband, that you abandoned me and had an affair?"

"You know my parents," he snapped.

"Yeah, I know them, but I don't know a damn thing when it comes to you anymore," I said, watching him squirm. "Make a better offer and do it soon. I want this done just as much as you."

"Vi—" He grabbed my arm and I pulled it away quickly, disgusted at his attempt to touch me.

"Don't touch me. Don't look at me. Stay far the hell away from me. Have your offer sent to me. I really don't ever want to see you again."

"Vi, I'm sorry I hurt you, but it's better for the both of us." He stood then and met my eyes.

"I have to agree with you on that. You weren't the man for me." My confidence was undeniable when I left his office with my head held high. I was finally about to be free of the hell of being Alex Harvell's wife.

I strode through his floor with no intention of staying a minute longer. I stood waiting for the elevator when I noticed a meeting going on through the glass in the adjacent room.

It was her.

Sandra stood at the head of the table, a commanding presence. She truly was beautiful. She had a lean body and curvy hips. With long dark brown hair, blue eyes, and perfect, high cheekbones, it was easy to understand an attraction to a woman like her. I couldn't hear her talking, but I could see she exuded confidence. I couldn't tear my eyes away. The few times I had met her, she had been formidable but stiff. This was the woman who ruined my marriage. I watched her walk around the room, gesturing with her hands here and there. She smiled at her audience before her eyes drifted over to me. She'd seen me watching her. I stood my ground, hoping my confidence showed in my stance. I wondered if she knew she wasn't the only one Alex was seeing, and then resigned myself quickly to the fact that it didn't matter; I no longer cared. I was done playing detective. I was done with him.

He's all yours, honey. Good luck.

Her smirk was unmistakable in its meaning, and I almost didn't catch it. She thought she had won, and in a way, she had. I felt sorry for the fool she was; the way you feel sorry for a mouse at play before the snake strikes to swallow it whole.

The elevator dinged, and as the doors closed behind me, I realized I was smiling.

I'd made it a new routine to work out in the mornings with both cardio and lightweights. If I had a chance in hell of keeping up with Rhys, I needed strength and stamina. I made it a point to start hanging out with a few friends. I'd been out with my old school girl-friend, Molly, a few times for drinks. She was fun and had a mouth like a sailor. I enjoyed my time with her, but still kept my relation-ship with Rhys a secret. I hadn't heard from Rhys and knew the text was either coming soon, or wasn't coming at all. I had dealt with enough shit in the last week between being the man of my house after a busted water pipe, to failing to make a sale, and my confron-tation with Alex. I was about to explode. Not to mention the insa-tiable need in me that made its presence known more often than not. I was on edge. I needed him. I hated him for it. As if he sensed my distress, his text came.

RHYS: The Barracks. One hour. RED.

I sat in my car, debating my next move, because I was sched-uled to show a house shortly. His texts had never come at a time I couldn't get to him before. Then again, it was beginning to irritate me that I was at his beck and call. He was in complete control of the when and where. My sex was throbbing already at the thought of him filling me, but I had an obligation, and I had to see it through.

VIOLET: I have an appointment in thirty minutes.

I got no response. I called the potential buyers who assured me they were on their way. Thankfully, they were not impressed with the home I showcased, and fifteen minutes after I opened the door, they were gone. I flew down the highway, furious with the situation. My heart pounded at the thought of what was to come. Why couldn't we go to his club? I hated The Barracks. I parked and noticed I was ten minutes late. I was irritated and strung out, and really needed to get off. When I walked into the bar and saw he wasn't there, I made my way down the stairs to the same room we had used and twisted the knob. His hand grabbed mine and I was brought in quickly and pushed against the wall.

"You're late!" he yelled, smacking his palm against the wall next to my head.

"I have a job!" I said, facing him head on.

His eyes glittered. This is what he wanted. We both stood, chests heaving, glaring at each other. I could feel the tension in him, as he could mine. We were both desperate for relief.

He ripped my blouse open, exposing my breasts, and grabbed one roughly.

"When I tell you to get your pussy here, I don't give a fuck what you are doing, you get it here!"

"Says the man with the nine to five that texts me after six!" I screamed a little louder than I should have. He pinched my nipple hard and I cried out and arched my back as he captured it with his mouth. He sucked greedily and I moaned at the contact. I felt his hard dick brush my leg. He released my nipple and began circling it with his tongue as I watched him. He grabbed the other breast and I felt the warmth spread quickly between my thighs as he licked and sucked my nipple. Damning the consequences, I threaded my fingers through his hair and pulled hard.

"Cranky little pussy, aren't we? What's the matter, Mrs. Harvell, you need to come?" His smile was full of menace and I looked away, disgusted.

"EYES ON MINE! You don't get to look away from me. You get to *see* me and what I do to you."

My blouse ruined, he removed it from my shoulders.

His lips curved into a wicked grin. "Get naked."

"Sir," I hissed in response. I quickly got to the task and pulled down my slacks and kicked off my shoes.

I was furious and out of my mind with need. Nearing a month since my last orgasm, I was about to lose my mind. The room went completely dark and I panicked. I couldn't see anything. I reached out in front of me and felt nothing. As I waited, my breathing escalated with my fear. This was Rhys, damn it; I had nothing to be afraid of. But I was. I was also intrigued. I listened closely but heard nothing, so I called out to him, feeling ridiculous for saying the word.

"Sir?" I could swear I heard a chuckle, but the second I thought that, I felt a brush across my breast. Gasping, I reached out, but he was gone.

"Please, I don't like the dark. I need to know where you are," I begged, the desperation in my voice apparent. Reaching behind me, I put my hand on the knob for a quick retreat. Naked or not, I was ready to flee. My body now facing the direction of my escape, I froze when I felt his breath on my neck. I immediately relaxed.

I felt the bite on my shoulder and melted into his mouth as he soothed it with his tongue. He spread my legs then swiped his finger down my sex and felt me wet with need. I whimpered as I continued to feel his breath on my skin, not an ounce of light in the room.

"What can I do for you, Mrs. Harvell?" His tone was vicious. I jumped at the sound of it.

"Fuck me, please," I said in a plea.

"Please, what?"

"Please, sir."

"Why should I give *you* my cock?" I heard the bite in his question.

"Rhys, please forgive me—"

"I told you not to call me by my name." His voice was calm, even. It scared me more than his angry words. I stood there, shaking and unsure of what to do next. Seconds later, his hand was circling my sex. I cried out, so close to coming, and my forehead fell to the door. He jerked me away from the door and turned me around. I reached out for him and felt his chest rising and falling. I slid my hand down his chest, desperate to touch him, to feel more.

"Don't you dare. You don't get to touch me." I whimpered again.

84

As soon as I took my hands away, he brought my leg up, nudging my entrance with his thick head, and then slammed his cock into me. I screamed, clawing at his shoulders. He held my leg underneath my knee and when he pushed up, my back hit the door with each thrust. His cock was unbelievably hard and I could feel his desire for me more than ever. This was how he truly liked it. I knew it then.

I thrashed my body against his, giving him what he loved, and heard a moan escape him. There was a light and dark side to Rhys, and it seemed my villainous lie had released the dark. I was both devastated and elated by it. He filled me with his fucking, hard and hungry. His lips brushed my neck and I couldn't stop the word from escaping my lips.

"Rhys," I breathed.

He went still. His lips were close, his breathing matching my own. I could feel his need to connect, because it mirrored mine. I licked my lips in anticipation. One breath away from his kiss was enough to make my eyes water. I leaned in and he moved away, lowering my leg to the ground before pulling out of me.

Curling my fingers in frustration, I dug my nails into my hands. I was losing my pleasure because I couldn't do one simple thing: shut the hell up. I wanted to be intimate with him, but right now, I wanted release more.

I stood, my thighs shaking, now alone in the dark again, until I heard the strike of a match. The flare from the phosphorus lit his face and I saw nothing but lust as he eyed me briefly. I began to shake as he ignited a large red candle and set it down on the floor next to a red leather chair beside him. He pumped his cock a few times, showing me what I craved most and patted the chair, ordering me to sit.

I walked over slowly and was about to sit when he turned me around quickly, lifting my knees onto the seat of the chair. I gripped the head of the chair, my body tilted down and out, leaving me exposed.

"Tell me, Mrs. Harvell, did your husband ever bother to pay attention to this perfect ass?" He circled my clit and I lost the ability to answer. The pull was there; I was close.

"Answer me!" His hand blistered the inside of my thigh and I screamed out, "NO!"

I saw the light flicker as he picked the candle up and jumped when I felt its contents trail down my back. HOLY FUCKING SHIT.

I felt the lava on my back cooling as he blew across it and massaged it in. It smelled amazing and I moaned as he rubbed it all over my ass.

"Hmm, pity. He missed one hell of an opportunity." He opened my backside and I felt more wax hit the top of my ass and cried out.

"Careful, we wouldn't want to singe my pretty pussy. Don't move." He poured even more, and I gripped the sides of the chair so tightly the leather gave and I had to adjust my grip. He smoothed the oil onto my skin then moved his finger down to my tight hole, massaging it while rubbing in the sweet scented oil. I became terrified at the thought of his huge girth and I tensed. I saw the flicker again and then he was under me, his head resting on the seat and nestled between my thighs. Rhys pulled my legs further apart as he sank his tongue into me. He circled my entrance, darting his tongue in and out and then wrapped his arms around my thighs, pulling me closer as he buried the length of his tongue inside of me. His moan was guttural and animalistic and I almost came with its arrival.

Pressing my lips together so not a single word had a chance of escaping, I began to move along his tongue slowly. He swallowed my sex whole, capturing it with his mouth, sucking my clit and dipping his fingers in and out. I looked down as I rode his mouth and saw his eyes were black in the candlelight. I slid my ridge along his tongue as I watched his eyes close and open with desire. I felt the pull and moved my hips faster as he twisted his fingers, tugging and pulling the orgasm from me. It started at my core and burst through every single pore I had, sending me reeling and shaking uncontrollably.

He didn't stop the lap of his tongue and I quickly pulled my hips up, trying to keep his tongue away from my sensitive clit. He smacked my ass, pulling me back down, plunging a finger inside my sex before moving it to my ass and pushing it in. I burst in his mouth, bucking and drowning in the sensation.

Defeated, I buried my head into the top of the chair. He rubbed my juices up and down my pussy, soaking me with it while keeping his finger moving in my ass.

"I'm going to fuck this ass tonight, Mrs. Harvell," he said, coaxing me with his skilled hands, challenging me with his eyes as I peered down at him. Panic seized my chest as he slipped another finger inside my ass fully, thrusting them both and stretching me. He slipped out from under me, keeping his fingers inside as his cock brushed my ass. The candle flickered again and I braced myself. The hot oil was less intense now and I reveled in the feeling. My senses reeled with the movement of his fingers. He pulled them out, covering me with even more oil mixed with my juice, and I felt his fingers deep again. He leaned over me. "Now I'll own all of you."

Moaning at his touch, I began to come undone. The intensity of his voice had my clit throbbing again. I heard a package rip and looked behind me to see him roll a condom on. He removed his fingers quickly and replaced it with the head of his cock and I screamed out.

"Oh God." I gripped the leather again, trying to acclimate to him. I moved my ass forward as I scrambled to get away from the pain.

Rhys stilled me, soothing me with his hands. He slowly slipped in further, taking care as he let me get used to the new feeling.

"Fuck," he spit out, moving gently, not giving me more than I was ready for. Hearing his arousal sent me over the edge and I gripped the top of the chair again, slowly moving with him, taking him in one delicious inch at a time. He stood there as I slid onto his dick and I could hear his breathing increase as he caressed my back. The minute he reached around and rubbed my clit, I slid back onto him completely. And this time we both gasped.

"Fuck, fuck!" Rhys hissed as he stood unmoving, patiently waiting for me to adjust to him. Feeling so full, so incredible, hardly able to speak, I pushed out the only word I could. "Please."

He pumped into me slowly and I clawed the chair desperately until the pain became more pleasurable than I'd ever imagined. I saw the flicker again and felt the wax hit my back as he rubbed it over my ass with one hand while massaging my clit with the other. I felt the pull come and pushed it away, savoring every single bit of pleasure and pain coursing through me. My whimpers turned into moans as he found a slow rhythm. My heart was beating out of control as he took me away with his strokes. I felt it then, a pull unlike any other I'd ever felt. My chest was heavy with emotion. I let it go. I didn't know if they were tears of pain or pleasure and why they belonged here, but they were silent, and for that I was thankful. I started to move against him, encouraging him as the foreign feeling came over me.

"Fucking perfect," he said, picking up speed with each thrust of his hips. I pushed my ass back, giving him more, making him moan in appreciation. He concentrated on my clit, moving his fingers quickly as he started to pound into me. Sensing my release, Rhys reached around and gripped my throat, squeezing hard. A feeling of complete ecstasy came over me. This time, I didn't have a choice. I came hard, every fiber of my being releasing and pulsating as a layer of sweat formed on my skin and I shook beneath him. I let out an intense wail, clawing the leather as I the rush continued to shake me. Evidence dripped from my sex and ran down my thighs. With a growl, he pulled out of my ass and I heard him rip the condom off quickly before he plunged into my drenched pussy.

In that moment, Rhys lost his control and I pushed back as he thrust forward, his strokes coming fast.

"Fuck yes!" His voice was hoarse with desire. His hand came

down hard, blistering my skin repeatedly, and this time I reveled in the pain, my moans matching his. I felt him growing harder inside me as he hit the need in me, and as soon as I let go, I felt another hard slap, driving my orgasm on as I screamed for him.

With the last ripple coursing its way through my limbs, he turned me over in the chair, laying me back down on the flat seat then pouring wax all over my chest. I savored the sensitivity as my breasts were covered in the hot oil that he rubbed in, taking special care to cover the valley between them.

"Push them together," he ordered, breathless. I had never seen his face so full of intensity, never seen him so hot for me. I grabbed my tits and squeezed them together as tight as I could. He pushed his cock between them, thrusting hard. After a few strokes, he pulled away, fisting his dick as he came all over my neck and chest. His entire body glistened as he threw his head back, teeth clenched. I watched his cock spurt more of his sweet liquid all over me. It was perfect.

He grunted with the last of his release, his legs shaking as he pumped the last drop onto my stomach.

The silence in the room was only interrupted by our heavy breathing as our eyes remained locked. His chest heaved in time with mine as he studied me. The connection between us was so powerful at that moment, I was sure that he would acknowledge it.

I sat up when he turned to leave me and felt the emotion come back tenfold. I covered my face with my hands and sobbed as I sat in the chair, terrified of what he would think, but at the same time not giving a damn. It hit me so suddenly; I had no choice but to let go. Rhys picked me up, sat me on his lap, and held me closely to his chest, stroking my back as I cried. I don't know how long it took for me to get it out, a minute or an hour, but he held me, pressing his lips to my forehead repeatedly. When I pulled away from him, I caught his eyes and saw the man I once had a chance with. He was still in there. He wiped the sides of my face and brought his lips to mine briefly.

We got dressed by candlelight, neither of us saying a word. I could tell he wanted to talk, that he had something he wanted to say, and I gave him an earnest look, hoping it was welcoming. The sex was incredible, we were amazing together, and this distance just felt...wrong. He watched me walk to the door and I turned back to him to give him one last chance, but he stayed silent. I walked out more sated and freed than I'd ever felt in my life. The only sadness left in the room was held in the gray eyes of the man who had truly freed me through pleasure and pain.

I stayed busy working and finishing the honey-do list around my house that Alex never bothered to get to. I hung shelves, raked leaves. Things that other people dreaded, I now looked forward to. I was completely independent. My mother would be proud. She always told me men weren't a necessity for any woman. When Alex and I had moved into this house and found the movers had left the couch in the center of the room and Alex was nowhere to be found, she picked up one end, gesturing for me to get the other.

"Leave it, Mom. We need a man to take care of that."

She walked over to me and firmly gripped my shoulders, pinning me with a seriousness I'd never seen.

"You don't need a man for anything. Especially for something you can do yourself, do you hear me, Violet?" I nodded, not arguing with her, and picked up the end of the couch.

I painted my soon to be ex-husband's old office and made it my own. It was progress.

I had found a small amount of normalcy and saw that I was losing the extra weight I had put on over the last year. My arms were leaner, firmer, and the small amount of pudge around my middle was disappearing.

I wouldn't change a fucking thing.

Remembering Rhys's words about my body made my chest heavy.

Rhys.

My heart squeezed. No matter how busy I kept myself, he was always in the back of my mind. Then thoughts of our last encounter would come flashing back. The room lit in a soft glow of orange, the feel of the leather chair, the scent of the oil, the sound of our moans mixed, all stayed with me.

He had raised my level of sexual awareness to the top in just over a month. I thought I would need a year to find out what I did and didn't want, but in a short amount of time he had shown me a little of both.

But nothing was off limits when it came to him. I would do whatever he wanted. His pleasure was my aphrodisiac. It was him that I craved most.

I didn't need a man. I wanted one. I wanted Rhys.

He doesn't want you anymore, Vi.

I needed to accept it, I just couldn't. And there was no way I could give him up. Not yet. Maybe our time was short. Maybe his intention was to end things. He said he was a relationship type of guy; maybe he would meet someone and end our sessions. That thought alone had me working longer hours, running in circles in my mind while I kept busy with my body. I would wait and endure his distance until I couldn't do it anymore.

I just couldn't give him up.

⚜

Brunch with my mother that Sunday proved to be a difficult task. I was anxious about the outcome of my divorce. I should have just

91

taken the money. Being free of Alex would be the best part of it. Brunch with my mother had sounded like a good idea at the time. She had driven me to The Carmine House, a beautiful three-story mansion nestled in the heart of Carmine Plantation. It was my favorite place to dine, and on that particular day, I had no desire to appreciate it. I sighed looking over my menu.

"What is it, Vi? You haven't said three words since I picked you up." My mother leaned over the table, concern in her eyes.

"Nothing, really, Mom. Don't worry," I said, motioning for the waiter. I wanted a Bloody Mary and fast. I just wanted to enjoy this day with my mother, but for some reason, I couldn't stop thinking about the gray-eyed man who had been punishing both my heart and body. I had two men fucking up my mojo. This was unacceptable.

"Mom, I'll be honest. I've been seeing a man who is absolutely beautiful. He's smart, funny, sexy as hell, and seems to have a good heart, but I've ruined my chances with him." I closed my menu, my appetite gone, and took an olive from the Bloody Mary just set before me and popped it into my mouth.

"Well, what happened?" My mother was on the edge of her seat. I never gave her dirty details, but I had a feeling all through high school and college and even after, she lived vicariously through me. Having found my father at such a young age, she didn't have the chance to really date around. Although she seemed content, she stayed curious. And she never pushed me for details, either.

"I lied about living with Alex." I saw her about to comment and waved my hand quickly to interrupt her. "In my defense, we had only been dating a few weeks and Alex got really sick, delaying me ending it and making him leave. I should've done it sooner, but I screwed up." I shook my head back and forth slightly and closed my eyes briefly. "He found out and was not happy."

"Can't start a relationship based on a lie, Violet." I nodded, wondering why I told her in the first place. I'd condemned myself enough.

"The thing is, we didn't know each other that well." Only he'd had his fingers, lips, and mouth on every inch of my flesh.

"Well, did you apologize?" she asked as I noticed a familiar movement from the corner of my eye. I straightened in my chair when my eyes caught a glimpse of the rest of him. There was no mistaking my lover. He had an air of confidence about him. I could *feel* his presence. I took a long sip of my drink and watched him.

Rhys was being seated in the corner facing away from me. He was with an older couple. I sucked in a breath and my mother noticed my sudden intake of air.

"What is it, Violet?" I quickly averted my eyes, not wanting to give anything away. "Nothing, Mother. Yes, I apologized profusely and he wouldn't accept."

"Well, then," she said, eyeing her menu, "his loss."

"Yes, I guess so," I replied, letting my eyes wander again as I held my menu high, covering my face. The couple smiled with apparent adoration on their faces at Rhys. These were his parents. My eyes widened when a very pregnant woman joined them, and I felt my chest fall as Rhys embraced her. I pulled out the straw and swallowed my drink in a few gulps, my face on fire.

Of course he had a wife. Why would he bring me to his home? She must have been out of town or something. We fucked in practically every room, where she lived, in her bed! He'd probably hid all of her clothes somewhere in the house. *What an absolute piece of*—

"Violet, if you are going to burn the man's head off with your stare and murder him secretly with your assumptions, at least go over there and introduce yourself to his wife to be sure." My mother, the absolute she-devil and epitome of an intuitive woman, could not only read me, but could read anyone. This is why I trusted her whole-heartedly with advice and…well, everything else.

She raised a brow at me. "I'm assuming that is the man you were speaking of?"

"He's married. This can't be happening." I looked over to see Rhys putting his head to his wife's full belly, sweetly rubbing his hand back and forth, the gesture of a man in love.

He'd just humiliated me for lying to him, given me the silent treatment, and made sure I'd paid with my body, though I really couldn't argue that point.

I couldn't stop the heat surging through my body.

Temper, temper.

I would kill him, of that I was sure. I stood quickly, pointing to my empty Bloody Mary, and my mother nodded. I walked over as casually as I could, thankful for the vodka coursing through me.

You have the upper hand, Vi. You can do this!

"Hello, SIR!" I spouted in a melody, placed my hands on Rhys's shoulders and squeezed quickly before removing them. Rhys stiffened in his chair, his head snapping to. I walked around so I was wedged between his parents' seat and his so I had a full view of the table. He got his eyes from his mother, his build from his father. Both of them smiled at me with a small look of confusion. I looked to the devastatingly beautiful woman on Rhys's right and smiled.

"Rhys, aren't you going to introduce us?" his mother asked, shaking her head at her son. "I'm Irene and this is my husband, Hugh." She held out her hand and I shook it with a smile as the Bloody Mary made its way back up to my chest and lingered.

"Violet Hale," I said, extending my hand, noting Rhys's jaw twitch in reaction to my maiden name, "it's a pleasure to meet you."

His mother shook it sweetly and I accepted Hugh's hand as well before moving it toward the woman next to him, smiling as my heart beat in my throat.

"Heidi Volz," she said, reaching out her hand.

Oh God, he is married!

"Nice to meet you, Heidi! Rhys never told me he was married, but we'd just met in passing, anyway." I was leaving and fast. I didn't care that violence wasn't the answer. I couldn't take it, not from Rhys. I could just picture the massacre now.

"No—" she laughed "—not his wife. His unwed, knocked up sister. I'm the black sheep. Thankfully, he has two of us. At least *she* made the family proud." She caught her mother's glare and I laughed a little too harshly at the exchange, letting the ten tons of relief fall away from me.

I'd not bothered to look at Rhys fully until that moment, and what I saw was surprise and anger.

"Rhys, a quick word?" I didn't give him time to answer before addressing his parents and sister. "I know how rude this seems, but do you mind if I steal him for a minute? I'll be quick."

"Of course." His sister beamed and his parents agreed easily.

The nervous laughter that bubbled in my chest was almost too much, but I maintained. Rhys got up from his seat and started walking toward the French doors that led to a wraparound porch. He only hesitated when he realized he looked absurd leaving me in the dust and turned and smiled, waiting. His sister winked at me as if to say "Go get him." I had a feeling they were close. I winked back, taking Rhys's offered arm. We walked out onto the porch to a beautiful but chilly fall day. He pulled his arm away, walking toward the railing. The Spanish moss covered trees swayed in the cool breeze. There was a green field ahead with a butterfly garden. It was absolutely beautiful. Rhys stood looking at the view in front of the porch rail, his back to me. I stayed silent as long as I could. He gave me nothing.

"Rhys, come on, just talk to me—"

"You think this is funny?" He was beyond angry. I had just poked the bear, and at this point, I didn't give a shit.

"Yes, I do," I said defiantly, a smirk on my lips.

"This is over, as of now." I stopped my walk toward him and had to fight to keep my wits. The feeling of rejection was so familiar now, I couldn't escape the pain of it. Instead of filling me with despair, it angered me.

"Fine, throw me away just like my husband did. Fuck you both." He turned slowly, pinning me with his stare. I stopped with my hand on the door behind me. He was angry but he wanted me, just as much as I wanted him. I was sure of it.

"You want me. I can see it. You can hide behind your words and turn your back on me all you want, but you want me." I crossed my arms. Still, he gave me nothing. "He was my damn husband, Rhys. I'd given up a long time ago. What you saw wasn't what it looked like. But I lied. I get that. So if you are going to end it, end it. But don't look at me like that and tell me you don't want me and that this is over. Clearly there is something here." I gestured between us.

"That's my family you introduced yourself to, Violet," he snapped, holding a finger up in the direction of his table.

I took a step forward, narrowing my eyes. "And what? I'm not good enough to meet your mother? Besides, it was the only way to get you alone. I've never met a man so relentless in his pursuit to turn away from someone so quickly."

"I have a bad history with liars," he said, holding his hands up, frustration on his face.

"I lied, and you've crucified me for it." I took a deep breath. "Fine, we are no longer more than fucking, you've made that clear. I'll accept that now, but can we at least be civil or are you going to act like a damn child much longer? Because if not, I can't deal with this animosity. If it doesn't bother you that we won't be together more intimately, you shouldn't be holding such a grudge."

"What do you want, Violet? And just what do you consider civil?" He took a step toward me. "You see I can't be *civil* around you because all I want to do is fuck your mouth, lick your pussy, and pound my dick into you so hard that you forget to fucking breathe." He made quick strides toward me. My legs trembled knowing what he was capable of. I couldn't hide my arousal. He watched my resolve crumble as he stood a foot away.

"You are a lot of talk, baby." He lifted his hand and wrapped his fingers around my wrist to test my pulse point. "But you aren't in charge here, are you? Your heart is beating so fucking fast for me. I bet that pussy is pulsing with my every word. Don't corner me, sweetheart, and demand anything. You get what I give. It's my cock that fills you, my lips and tongue that make you scream, not your husband's. I already own your body. I don't need anything else."

His words stung. I was his toy. He was supposed to be mine. I just had to accept it.

"I told you he's gone, Rhys. My husband is gone. HE. IS. GONE. And screw you for thinking I'm not good enough to be introduced to your family." I turned away from him but he held my wrist.

"Stop it, you know damn well I don't think that of you. I was bombarded. You are married, Violet. It isn't right. Do you think they buy the fact that we are friends? You are so fucking beautiful—" He stopped himself, his emotion taking hold as he looked down at the porch between us.

"I miss you," I said. "I've spent so much time thinking about you, I don't even know if I was beginning to fall for you or who I thought you might be. I just wanted another chance. And now I've embarrassed myself...again." He hadn't let go of my wrist, his eyes reaching mine the moment I said I missed him.

"Violet, this isn't just about me and what I want. My family—"

I yanked my wrist away and glared at him, my resolve coming back in waves. "You know what, Rhys? You want to punish me, go right the fuck ahead. I love every single punishment you deal out. That was the purpose of all of this, anyway. You're right. I am dripping and I'm dying for a shot at that cock, but I don't need to be judged and dismissed. You keep that shit to yourself. I'll be your sub when I'm supposed to. But out here, in the world of people like Alex, this bitch will dish it out as much as she takes it. Good day, *sir*. Have your cock text me. If not, it's not the only cock in the world."

Fury, fire, possessiveness, all of those things flooded his eyes instantly. He wasn't done with me. If I didn't have his heart's attention, I had his dick's.

With that, I walked into the restaurant. Seconds later, he grabbed my arm in a friendly gesture as he walked with me. "Who are you here with, Violet?" I looked to see amusement in his face as my face paled. "My mother," I said completely confused.

"Well then, let's meet Mommy and tell her what her little girl has been up to." I studied his face, but he gave nothing away. I began to panic. "Rhys, you wouldn't," I said, terrified.

"Of course I wouldn't," he whispered deviously.

"Mother, this is Rhys Volz, a friend of mine," I said quickly and loudly before Rhys could introduce himself. Terror crept up my spine as I thought of the thousand things he could say or insinuate in front of a woman who knew everything about me intuitively. Like the day I started my period, the first time I snuck out, even the first time I had sex. I used to think she had a camera in my room and a tracking device in my car. The fact was the woman could have been a spy, and a damn good one.

My mother spit out a small amount of her drink but recovered quickly. She stood slowly and grabbed his hand. "I can see why my daughter fancies you." I turned bright red and looked at Rhys who shook her hand and smiled, releasing it slowly.

"Your beautiful daughter was just telling me about her husband, Alex." He snickered and my mother caught it.

"Oh dear, Mr. Volz, I sure hope she did tell you the truth on how she kicked that piece of shit out of their home for cheating a few weeks back." I stiffened as Rhys stood there in shock before laughing loudly, drawing attention to us. He gave me a wondering glance and I could tell then he forgave me just a little. I sat down, red faced, and grabbed my watered down Bloody Mary.

"Come to think of it, Mrs...?"

"Hale, darlin'," she said smartly.

"Mrs. Hale, she did mention it." He looked over to his table. "Ladies, if you'll excuse me, I need to get back to my family. Enjoy your brunch. You should try the buttered lobster. I'm told it's quite good." He winked at my mother, kissed my wrist, and was gone.

Touché, Rhys.

"Holy hell, Violet, he makes Alex look like the garbage man."

"I know, Mom," I said with a sigh.

"Good Lord, I need another drink." She fanned herself with her hand and I just shook my head. If she only knew what the man could do with ten minutes and his tongue—okay, five...hell, three.

"That's the kind of man that would make you happy, Vi."

I saw my phone light up and read the message.

RHYS: My club. Two hours. RED.

"No, Mom," I said as my eyes followed Rhys as he took his seat, "that's the kind of man who could truly ruin my life. Shall we order?"

❦

I was shaking as he surveyed me from head to toe. I rubbed my hands together before covering my lower half, but he smacked them away.

"Don't you dare cover that pretty pussy," he growled, circling me as if stalking his prey. We were in a smaller room covered wall to wall with plush black carpet. "Did I hear you right earlier, Violet? Did you say there was more than one cock in the world?" He gripped the back of my neck. "Get on your knees."

I dropped instantly, the heat building inside me. I was breathless and near exhaustion from the rush of adrenaline that had been coursing through me the last two hours. He leaned down behind me as his hands covered each shoulder before sliding down my arms. My eyes fluttered shut with the pleasure of his gentle touch and then opened when he suddenly pushed me down on all fours. I was bared to him now and felt his thick cock brush my center. He dipped the tip of himself into me and removed it quickly. I shuddered with need, swollen and desperate for the attention he could give. Tonight he wouldn't be playing nice. I'd made sure of it.

"Rough day?" I smiled knowing I had just asked for the pain. I wanted to provoke him. I wanted punishment. Instead of getting what I hoped for, I heard the door click shut with his departure.

Well, fuck.

I was on all fours, naked, swollen, without a damn clue what to do. I should have kept my mouth shut. I slid my hand between my thighs, but knew I couldn't get relief that way. I had never been able to and envied the women who could. I circled my clit, drawing moisture from my middle, and brought it up. I was hot, bothered, completely consumed by the man who had just deserted me when I needed him most. I circled myself over and over, unable to get the pulling feeling I so desperately needed. Tears sprang to my eyes as I thought of the steps I had taken to be here, the hurdles I had jumped. I had made peace with my sexuality. I had made peace with my body. I had new cravings that could no longer be ignored. Rhys had brought them out of me and was denying me what he knew I needed. Furious and turned on, I was completely fucked and not in the sense I wanted to be.

I breathed a little easier when I heard the door open again, until I heard his voice. "You NEVER come until I make you." He pulled my hair roughly so my neck was exposed to his mouth. I felt his breath coming out hard in my ear as he gripped my hair and met my eyes. "Did you come?" he gritted through his teeth, his beautiful features contorting in anger.

"No, I can't. I need you," I begged. His lips traced the curve of my neck, landing in the divot. He used his tongue then and let it glide up my neck. I panted heavily, my hand gliding back down between my thighs to touch the pulsating need in me.

"What the fuck are you doing?" he said, releasing my hair and standing in front of me. I jerked my hand away.

"I didn't even realize I was doing it." He was fully dressed now, and I felt the tears coming heavy. "Please, I need this. I want this so bad. Don't leave me here like this."

He looked down at me without empathy and shook his head. His smirk was menacing. "You defy me and still beg for my dick, a dick you could so easily replace."

"Yes, I'm begging," I said, looking into his gray depths. "I'm begging," I said, ashamed of my behavior. He remained standing in front of me, a tower of strength, his eyes piercing mine. The longer I waited, the more furious I became. I could get laid. I didn't have to act like a dog in heat for this shit. What was I doing? I rose to my feet and gave him my famous death stare.

"You know what? Fuck you. This isn't worth it. Go find another whore to play with." I turned to walk away and was thrown against the wall, my palms flat. I cried out in pure fury and was instantly filled with his cock from behind. I screamed out in pleasure and began sliding down the wall as my limbs betrayed me. He gripped my wrists, holding me tighter while he took me roughly. I was completely full and felt every grinding inch as he took me hard and vicious. His strokes were filled with anger and lust and I felt my body tense. I was in flames, completely covered in sweat as I heard his grunts and felt his breath on my neck.

"This body is mine as long as I want it. As long as I want you filled with my cock, you will be. Do you hear me?" He stopped his strokes, pulling out of me and I immediately let out a protesting scream.

"Yes, yes, I hear you!" I was almost there and he knew it. There was no way I would let him out of this room until I got it. I whirled on him, slapping his face. I was wild eyed and determined to get what I had rightfully earned. He stuck his thumb against his lips and pulled away a small amount of blood. This seemed to excite him as I stood there, chest heaving, staring into his heartless gaze. "What the fuck are you doing to me?" I said desperately, trying to get my emotions in check. "I thought I made it clear I wanted pleasure. This is not pleasure!"

He gripped my neck with both hands, covering my lips with his, our first kiss in weeks. I opened my mouth without protest as he slipped his tongue past mine to taste my mouth. I moaned and he immediately relented.

"Your moaning and screaming when I taste you, fuck you, that's pleasure." I glared at him.

"You know what I need!" I said, pushing his rock hard chest, unable to move him at all.

"I know you aren't listening to your body. Your fucking tits are drawn up so tight they probably hurt."

He flicked my nipple with his fingers and I nearly dropped to my knees. He pinched the nipple he had just punished, making it even more painful. Before I could jerk away, his mouth was on it. I tilted my head back, burying my hands in his thick black hair. He released my nipple from his teeth and licked around the peak repeatedly, showcasing the skilled movement of his tongue until I felt my core clench. He smirked as he watched me react and slid his hand down my stomach until he reached my aching clit. His eyes grew tense with desire as he slid his finger along my pussy in a punishing stroke.

"I listen to your body," he taunted as his fingers slid inside me. I bucked into his hand, crying out. "Your body tells me what to do." He turned me to face away from him and bit my shoulder while still sliding his fingers in and out of me. He trailed my wetness to the top of my ass, sliding a single finger in my puckered hole. I moved my hips, grinding into it, loving the feel.

"Hmm, tempting, but I want to fuck that pretty pink pussy." He cupped the back of my thighs, spreading me wide, and with one deep thrust was inside me again, keeping his finger darting in and out of my now slick ass. Every single inch of my skin was peaked with each stroke. The fullness of his cock, the finger penetrating my darkest place, it was exquisite. I felt the pull again as he bent me over further, hitting me deeply and drawing out my moans. I lost it minutes later, screaming and coming, screaming and coming, until all that was left of me was a shaking mess. I still felt the rhythm of his pounding though it was slowing. He pulled out of me and turned me quickly, taking my mouth in a tender kiss filled with everything it hadn't been minutes before.

It was amazing and genuine and filled with so much. I was too scattered to even wrap my mind around it. I kissed him back, his cool tongue putting me at ease. The next thing I knew, I was straddling him on the floor, slowly riding him. He looked up to me and kept my gaze as I slid on top of him, completely dazed and fucked out of my mind.

"So fucking beautiful. I'm going to make you come again, Violet, nice and slow." My chest tightened at the way he said my name. I fought the emotion as my eyes bore into his. He reached up to my still throbbing clit and pressed hard as he pumped his huge cock into me from beneath. I felt that pull again and roamed his chest with my hands as he thrust up, moving both of our bodies, circling my clit. "Eyes on mine," he commanded. "Those fucking gasps belong to me, and you give them to me when I give them to you."

The minute our eyes fully connected, I came again. Leaning in, our lips met, our tongues thrust together. He pumped furiously into me, making my orgasm last. When I felt his hotness spurt into me, I reached below me and circled the base of his cock with my fingers, pumping hard while I moved up and down his shaft quickly with my body. He let out a grunt as I watched him come, staring directly at my parted mouth.

"I'm not done," he said, lifting me from him abruptly and placing me beneath him so I was on my back. I looked down between us to see him half-hard and became wide-eyed when he brought himself back into me, growing harder with each thrust. I tilted my neck up with my moan and felt his lips cover it.

I heard him whisper, though it was faint, "I missed you, too."

An hour later, we were tangled on the floor, his mouth covering mine in a slow kiss that had my toes curling and my body aching for more. He leaned in, taking my mouth and tasting me, my arms and legs wrapped around him. It was as if we were making up for lost time. He pulled away, placing small kisses on my nose and chin before devouring my mouth once again. When he pulled back, I noticed the small place on his lip with broken skin.

I brushed my finger over it. "I'm sorry."

"For what? I've been dying to get the best of your temper since we started this." He grinned and licked his lip. "Tastes like sweet victory." He removed himself carefully from underneath me and I mourned the loss of him.

"I've never hit another human being in my life," I said, sincerely saddened that was no longer the truth, and even more so about the fact that the first human being was him.

He gathered his clothes and turned to me as he started putting them on. "These things we do, they bring out the best and worst in us, Violet. There is a balance and a morality you have to kind of follow. Otherwise, the lines get blurred, and that can lead to a ton of shit." He buttoned his shirt, eyeing my body.

"Like what?" I asked, curious, hoping he would change his mind about the last button. He didn't, and I sighed at the loss.

"Like ménage, and the third person brought in and becoming an affair for one of the partners," he said, turning to look at me. "That's just one of a thousand things. I have to go."

"Well, I am good on ménage, if that's what you're wondering. The only reason I liked Tara was because your eyes were on me. It wasn't her turning me on." He looked touched and I almost laughed.

"Good to know. But you know that's not the only scenario," he said, his eyebrows lifted in challenge.

"I'm good on that, too. As far as I'm concerned, your cock is the only one in the world."

He gave me another breathtaking smile as he began to walk away. Seeming to think better of it, he turned, kneeled down, and kissed me. I took his tongue, sucking it sweetly and giggled when he groaned, collapsing on top of me to taste my mouth further.

"Does this mean you forgive me?" I asked as he held his lips an inch from mine, hovering over my face.

"I'm trying. I have to able to trust you, Violet."

I nodded as I tugged his bottom lip with my teeth, my mouth full of it as I mumbled, "Go, then. Wait...where are you going?"

"Family stuff," he said, nodding toward my naked body. "Are you planning on getting dressed?"

"When I'm good and ready," I said, challenging him.

"Violet, don't make me bring down the hammer. I can't ensure you're safe when I'm not here." I didn't say a word and got up, putting my clothes on.

He grinned as he watched me slide on my panties. "You know,

KATE STEWART

you may be the worst sub I've ever had. I saw where you got that sassy mouth from today."

"It's an art us Hale women have perfected. Don't try and change it."

"Why change it, baby, when I have a cork that fits it just right?"

"Ha ha," I said, pulling my sweater over my head. "So why are you selling?" I knew I was pushing it. I'd barely made my way back into his good graces.

"I never wanted this club. I might enjoy the lifestyle, but I do not want to host it. That's not me. That's...just not me," he said, turning off the light and opening the door as I grabbed my purse.

"So how did you end up with it?" He gave me a hard glance. I had a feeling his reluctance to answer had more to do with his stubbornness than his grudge against me.

"I'm late, Violet."

He held my hand as he walked me to my car. He wrapped his arms around me and pulled the collar of my jacket so we were a hair away from our lips touching.

"My cock will text you." He graced me with another slow and devastating kiss. This man had moved me. Pulling away from his kiss, I saw it in his eyes. I mattered. To Rhys I still mattered, and that was enough.

"Bye, Rhys." It was the first time I said his name without consequence, and he gave me a knowing grin. I was pushing it again.

"You know why I wouldn't let you say it?" He still held my collar and his scent was stirring me again.

"Why?" I asked as he noted his effect on me. I was dizzy at our proximity.

He leaned in closer. "Because the first time you said it, I knew no other woman could ever compete."

"I knew you loved the way I said your name." I smiled. "If I say it again, will you come home with me?"

"I can't," he said, giving me one last kiss. "Goodnight, Violet."

"Night, Rhys." He groaned playfully as I opened my door. This time he pulled out and gestured to me with his hand to go in front of him.

I slept better that night than I had in years.

☙

HALLOWEEN

RHYS: The Barracks 10 p.m. Ladies' choice.

I read the message as I gave the last of the candy bowl to the neighborhood children. If they only knew their neighbor was a sex-crazed nymph, they would more than likely snatch them away with a look of judgment on their faces. What exactly was I doing again? Didn't I want to be a parent? Weren't my dreams tied into a nice neat bow along with the rest of the world? My priorities were simple as a young adult: win the love a good man, have a successful marriage, and a child to go with it. It wasn't exactly original.

I had plenty of time; I knew it. Today was a day that reminded me that time was of the essence. I was thirty-three. I took a hard look in the mirror after my shower. A slight touch of crow's feet, a little dimple in my thighs here and there, I could live with that.

"Overall, you still look good, girl." I laughed as I jiggled my butt a little for effect. "And you are slightly insane too, Vi."

Then again, no one makes it out of this life unscathed. Normal was an illusion, and every single person on earth had flaws and idiosyncrasies, no matter how well they were hidden. Why I was suddenly ashamed at my increase in libido and blatant sexual appetite was beyond me. There were millions of people out there who daydreamed about the way I'd been fucked in the last two months and never had the guts to actually ask for it.

107

Not to mention you swore you wouldn't beat yourself up about it, Vi.

Also, it'd opened a whole new world to me, which led me to my current happy place: Rhys. We had started texting again regularly and he promised that as soon as he could he would take me out and we could start fresh. He had some interested buyers in the club. Between his day job, his family obligations, and trying to get out from under the club, his time was limited. I told him that was fine as long as he made my birthday memorable. Clearly, he intended to.

I pulled up the black stockings and attached them to the garter belt. I'd gone all out tonight. I found a set of really interesting leather lingerie, and while it wasn't exactly comfortable, it looked hot! I hoped to make him squirm a little, though my beautiful man rarely did. My stomach fluttered with anticipation. This might be my best birthday yet. I pulled out a simple dress, knowing it didn't matter what covered what lay beneath, and some sassy red heels and I was ready.

I was making my rounds in my house to turn the lights off and went to shut the front door. I'd left the screen door open all night due to the large amount of trick or treaters. I heard a shuffle of footsteps in the dining room next to me and gasped when I felt a hand cover my mouth.

"Don't you fucking scream." I saw a dark silhouette raiding my dining room and realized quickly I was being robbed while I had been shaking my stupid naked ass in the mirror. I lived in an amazing residential area that hardly had an ounce of crime. Well, until...until, now.

Terror raced through me as I realized just how bad the situation was. My phone was in my purse that was being removed as I thought of it by the man gripping my mouth.

"Where's your husband?" He lifted his hand briefly and I spoke softly, not wanting to rock the boat. "He'll be home soon."

"Well then, we better hurry." He dug his erection into my back.

I felt my eyes well. "Don't worry, baby. We don't have time for that. I'll come back for it later." His smell was putrid and I gagged against his hand. He slapped the side of my head with an open hand.

I heard glass breaking all throughout the house and felt the rage build. I hadn't realized the man held a knife to my throat until I protested his hold and felt the sting of it. The blood seeped slowly out and I whimpered.

God, no, if he is going to kill me, please make it quick.

All I could think of were those trick or treaters and how I would leave this world without ever knowing what it was like to be a mother. The only people who would attend my funeral would be my parents, maybe a few realtor acquaintances, and Molly.

And Rhys.

My chest heaved as I panicked. Rhys was waiting for me. I'd just gotten him back. If I didn't show, what would that tell him? Would he even bother to find out why? I heard more glass breaking as I stood still, listening to the pig behind me breathe as he held my life in his hands. I couldn't move my neck to get a better look at him. I heard a loud crash in the kitchen and jumped, feeling the knife go deeper. I held my whimper in.

I had done nothing in my life but live for a man for the last few years. I had nothing to show, no legacy to leave. What could they say at my funeral? What had I done that truly mattered? In that twenty seconds of rational thought, I'd come to two conclusions.

One, I didn't want to die.

Two, if I lived through this, I would have new priorities.

"Stupid bitch doesn't have anything here worth shit!" His partner came in and pulled up my left hand. I tried to take inventory but it was impossible besides height and weight due to the fact he was wearing a Halloween mask. He leaned in and I flinched, even more terrified as his disfigured clown mask inched closer to my face.

"Where's your wedding ring?" The truth that set me free might get me killed. I leaned into the man holding me prisoner as the knife dug in deeper.

"I sold it," I said truthfully. He didn't like my answer. I got back-handed and was unable to recover before I felt the next blow. The man released me from his grip and I felt the warmth spurt up my cheek and no longer had any clue what was happening as I took blow after blow. I refused to beg for my life. Somehow, I knew it wouldn't help.

And then everything went black.

I came to on the floor, noticing my purse had been ransacked and was a few feet away on the floor. I moved toward the blue light as my head pounded. I felt the moisture on the floor and raised my hand to see it was blood. Fear raced through me as I reached my phone. The black was creeping back in. I fought it hard, sliding my thumb across my phone to open it. A text message came through as I grabbed it. I swiped the screen with my thumb again, trying to see through the streak of blood that I'd just put on it.

RHYS: I'm leaving. I can't stay.

He'd just sent it at midnight. It was 12:01 a.m.

I only managed to type one word and hit send.

VIOLET: Help.

I knew the minute Rhys was by my side. He pulled me into his lap, then I heard cursing and his call for help before I was out again.

"Home invasion...didn't take much...big items...neighbors saw nothing." I heard the words coming from an unrecognizable voice as I faded in and out. I tried to open my eyes at the prodding of the voice directly above me.

"Violet, can you hear me?" I moaned and reached for the top of my head and my arm was brought back down.

"Listen to me, Violet, I'm going to get you to the hospital. I just need you to tell me you can hear me."

"Yes," I said, growing cold suddenly. I looked amongst the people crowding my entryway, searching for the pair of eyes that could make me forget, just for a second, the pain I was in. As soon as I wished for them, they were there. "Rhys," I said, pleading for him silently not to leave.

"You're going to be okay, Violet, you are." His voice was hoarse and his shirt covered in blood—my blood. His kiss on my wrist had tears coming down fast.

"Rhys," I croaked, unable to keep from shaking.

"Violet, honey, I know you're upset, but you can't do that now."

Another paramedic spoke to me now, waving her hands in front of my face to catch my eyes. She was a beautiful black woman with short hair and kind eyes. I gave her my attention.

"You have lost a lot of blood, baby. You need to stay with me, okay?" I looked back to Rhys and realized the woman above me was pressing hard on my neck. I felt the pinch of the pressure and winced. I fought the pain and turned to look at him again.

"He knows you love him, honey. If he didn't before, he knows now. Don't you, Rhys?" He nodded quickly as tears streamed down his face. "I do."

"See, he knows. No, Violet, stay with me. Stay with me now—She's crashing!"

I went in and out, thankful for every uncomfortable situation I was in, every bit of sleep that was interrupted, because it meant I was still here, still alive and fighting. I felt hands grab mine at times and then it was silent. I had no sense of time, only the bright light that greeted me each time I was interrupted from my slumber. I felt a warm soothing sensation flow through me from time to time and basked in the feeling, letting it warm me and take me to a more peaceful place.

I opened my eyes, letting them adjust to the light in the room. I awoke knowing what happened, but jerked anyway with the amount of activity I had to absorb since I'd been out. I heard my mother's voice instantly.

"Oh, shit. I swore to your father I wouldn't start crying when you woke up. Please forgive me." My mother howled as she buried her head in my stomach and gripped my hand tightly. I wanted to laugh at her but knew how badly this had scared her. I lifted my arm that felt like lead and rubbed it against her hair. She dug in, causing one hell of scene for the people who passed by the room with curious looks on their faces.

"Mom…" Oh shit, talking hurt. My throat was sore and there was no way I was risking that pain trying to talk again. I tapped her head lightly and she looked up, ten years older than she was the last time I saw her. I gave her wide eyes to indicate her mere presence was hurting me. She seemed to get the clue and I thanked God as she removed herself from the bed, apologizing and crying.

I winced and my mother pushed a button connected to what I assumed was my pain medication. I felt the rush and suddenly felt like I could sing a musical.

Good shit.

"How bad?" I asked, pointing to my neck and head.

"You look like you've been hit by a Mack truck and drug down a gravel road, but you'll make a full recovery."

I chuckled at my mother's antics. She was never one to sugar-coat anything, but laughing hurt.

I tried to keep my questions to one word. "Mirror?"

"Listen," she said, rummaging through her purse, "your throat looks much worse than it is."

Vanity had never been an issue or a flaw in me until that moment. I nodded, knowing I probably couldn't handle what I saw.

Still, I had to know what I had left to work with. She held a compact away from me and I motioned with my hands that I wanted it closer. I had blood stained hair, that's what I noticed first. It was streaked pink and I let my eyes drift. The entire right side of my head was swollen and bruised and my eyes were black. Underneath my left eye was a series of cuts that had been stitched. I assumed that was where they had kicked me.

"He nicked your artery. The son of a bitch who cut your throat nicked it. You lost a lot of blood and Rhys found you just in time." She was texting as she spoke. I pointed to her phone.

"Who?"

"Rhys. Oh, honey, Rhys has been here day and night for the last three days. He's only gone now because he's at your house having a security system installed."

I moved the mirror down to my busted lips and then to my neck and let out a small cry. It was so much worse than what I had expected. There was a thin red line covering my throat that got thicker as it circled toward my ear where it was covered by a thick bandage. I closed the compact and nodded. I was alive. No matter what, these would just remain scars, not my cause of death, just nasty scars reminding me I had lived. My mother held my hand as I cried without sound. She stayed silent and my father came in shortly after, grabbing my hand on the other side of the bed. His eyes filled with tears.

"I knew you would make it, my little fighter. I knew it." I nodded as my father's soft cry filled the room and he held my hand tightly.

I got tired suddenly as the doctor came in to check me out. I drifted off to sleep minutes later.

⸎

I woke up well rested and saw my mother stir from her sleep as she noticed I'd awoken from mine. I was dying to see Rhys, to thank him. And as soon as the thought crossed my mind, he walked into the room and the air shifted, as it always did.

"Hello, Pam." His smile was for my mother and she embraced him as if they'd known each other for years. How long was I out?

My mother beamed at him. "Rhys, you are a damn dream to look at. I swear, if I was twenty years younger and I knew you weren't crazy about my daughter…"

Nice, Mom. I watched them go back and forth and he seemed as amused with her as he was with me. I noticed Rhys hadn't looked my way one time. I cleared my aching throat and they both turned my direction, though my mother was the only one who was truly looking at me.

"Hi," I said simply. "Mom, go away." She and Rhys chuckled as she leaned over and kissed my cheek.

"I'll be right outside." She grabbed Rhys's arm and caught his eyes then whispered to him. He nodded and turned my direction.

"Eyes on mine, Rhys." It wasn't the best time to use his words against him. His was clearly tortured by having to look at me. "I need to see them, please." He looked at me then and I saw a man destroyed. He roved over my face and the cut on my neck and expelled a harsh breath.

My words came quickly. "So this happened and I'm not going to freak out. I'm alive and that's what matters most, right?"

"Yes, yes, of course," he said, staring at the monitors.

"I'll heal, Rhys. I won't always look like the bride of Frankenstein."

"I'm so sorry. It's not that at all. I guess I'm just feeling a little guilty." He met my eyes again. "I haven't been very good to you lately." He sighed, taking a seat next to me.

"Says who?" I asked, sitting up straight. "For who we are to each other for now, I'd say you have been giving me a dose of everything good." I adjusted myself again on the bed, irritated with the limitations of my body. I was getting out of this bed by tomorrow if it was the last thing I did. "Speaking of dose, have you ever had morphine?" I clicked the button and the warmth spread through me. "I'm thankful for this experience alone. Whoo, baby."

He chuckled then and looked up to me, his eyes stormy. His hair was a mess and he looked like he hadn't slept in a month. I reached out for him and he grabbed my hand and stroked his fingers on the inside of my palm. That gesture alone had my heart pounding.

He looked so crushed, I felt like I had to comfort him.

"Shit like this happens to people all the time. The police have been there. Did you know they caught the one who slit my—"

He tensed, his body instantly alert, and his eyes even more cloudy.

"Rhys, this stuff happens, right? When they called me a victim, I almost laughed. It's unbelievable that it would happen to you or me; it's just on the news and in the paper. I mean, he almost killed me and for what, my grandmother's silver?" I thought back to what happened with indifference and I was sure I was still in shock. "It was so strange, the whole thing. I was alone and on my way to see you and then...they were there, tearing up my house. I was scared because I didn't want to die. I was more afraid of what I hadn't done yet. There's a bucket list I haven't made that I think I'll start today, and I'm pretty sure now I want kids."

He reached out and ran his hand through my hair.

"Don't, save yourself. I'm pretty sure you could fry chicken up there. I am a greasy mess." He laughed nervously and then leaned in, pressing his lips to my forehead.

He pulled back so we were face to face. "Violet, there are so many things I want to tell you, show you. I just don't want to do it because this happened. It's not right. It's not the way it should be. I will tell you this, finding you lying on the floor was the worst moment of my life." I pushed my tears down. I didn't want him to see me cry.

It seemed I'd found Rhys's weakness...and that weakness was me.

"I know we were getting somewhere, Rhys. Save your words. You are here, right, and without your little black bag. Unless—" I looked around the room "—it's here somewhere? Sure could use a good session with those ribbons."

"You are incredible." He squeezed my hand a little tighter, his softened eyes piercing my heart.

"Oh, don't stop being the unbearable bastard you are because of this. I was just getting used to it." He laughed again, and this time when he leaned over, his kiss was for my lips. I pulled him to me and choked on emotion. He stood, planting soft kisses on all the un-damaged parts of my face. He sat with me and held my hand, telling me that they had smashed a good amount of valuables and weren't sure what had been taken, that I would have to do inventory when I was well. He'd had the house cleaned and explained that he knew it was presumptuous, but he wouldn't dream of letting me go back home without having a system installed, and my parents agreed.

"Your door was unlocked?" he asked as he kissed my fingers.

I shrugged my shoulders. "I was giving candy out. I had the screen door closed and I guess I forgot to lock it before I got in the shower. Bonehead move, I know. I was just so happy when I got your text." I paused, thinking how those words would affect him. "Really, I'm not sure how careless I've been. I probably leave it un-locked all the time." I braved a look at him. He wasn't buying it.

"Don't lie to me," he said sternly.

"Fine, but don't feel guilty. It's pointless. You had no idea this would happen and it's not something you get to feel guilty about. Besides, it's the truth. You have firsthand experience of how easy it is to get into my house."

"I know, Violet," he said, standing quickly. "Still, I can't even begin to explain the thousands of thoughts that have raced through my head in the past four days, and not all of them were ones I could tell you." His face went dark and I knew he was thinking about the men inside my house. "Did they touch you?"

"No."

He let out a long breath and relief flooded his features. Even a disheveled mess, he was absolutely stunning. I loved the amount of shadow on his face. His black wavy hair was unruly and his clothes were wrinkled. My eyes ran from the top of his head down to his shoes and up again. His mouth twisted into a smile.

"And just what are you thinking about right now?"

"I had on the hottest outfit for you, a leather thong." He raised his eyebrows to that and I continued. "Yeah, baby, it was awesome. And my thirty-three year old ass looked smoking...Oh my God!" I said, covering my mouth.

"What?" he said, racing to my side.

"They saw it. The hospital staff had to have cut it off me!"

He chuckled and shook his head. "I'm sure they were more worried about saving your life, Violet."

"Well, at least I gave them a good water cooler story, right?" I said, my face heating.

"I wished I could have seen it," he said with melancholy.

"You will. I bought one in red, too," I said, giving him a wink. He gave me my first big smile and my heart flipped at the sight of it.

"Violet, I don't want to, but I have to go make sure the install is finished and—"

"Yeah, yeah, go. It's boring in here right now, what with the bedpans and all. We have no potential for bondage." I smiled and it hurt, but I didn't let him see it.

"Oh, Violet, I can think of a thousand scenarios right now. You underestimate me. I want you walking out of here whole. I just want you to be okay. And the next time I take your body, I will make love to you in my bed."

"Sounds good to me," I said as he leaned in one more time. "Text me?"

"Call you," he said, lingering on my lips. He passed my mother on his way out, who turned to me with a knowing look. She closed the door with a whistle.

"Go ahead and say it, Mother," I said, rolling my eyes as she turned to me with a smile.

"Told you so. He is your match, Violet, in every way."

"Honestly, you probably know him better than I do. And if that's the truth, Mother, why do I feel like I am always on the edge of losing him?"

"He feels the same with you. God, you should have seen how destroyed he was when they brought you in here. I don't think I've ever seen a man lose his mind quite like that."

I studied my mother for a few moments. "Mom, I don't want to go back there." No matter how strong I'd tried to be for Rhys, I didn't want a damn thing to do with that house.

"You don't have to. Come home; stay as long as you want. Hell, sell that house."

"No, it will be home again, just not yet."

<hr>

Settled at my parents' the next night, I got a text.

RHYS: How are you? Better I hope?

VIOLET: I thought I was getting a phone call.

RHYS: Sorry, it's noisy here.

I hesitated, not wanting to ask, but did anyway.

VIOLET: Where is here?

RHYS: Home. Family over.

VIOLET: Oh. Well, why are you talking to me?

RHYS: Because I miss you.

My heart filled instantly.

VIOLET: I miss you too. You and your family sure do get together often.

RHYS: Yeah, we're close. What are you doing?

VIOLET: Taking numbing amounts of Vicodin, eating chocolate, and watching cheesy romantic movies. You know every girl's dream.

RHYS: So you are lying when you say you miss me?

VIOLET: Yes.

RHYS: Ouch.

VIOLET: Sorry, they say chocolate is a good substitute for sex, so I'd say I'm breaking your rules.

RHYS: You will be punished.

VIOLET: Can we please keep the punishments to your club? I never want to go to The Barracks again.

RHYS: I know. I regret taking you there. I was angry. But we had a little fun :)

VIOLET: That wasn't fun.

RHYS: No?

VIOLET: No.

RHYS: What was it?

VIOLET: Indescribable.

RHYS: Agreed, I think about it every day.

VIOLET: What do you think about?

RHYS: The way your hips curve when you wrap your legs around me. How beautiful you are when you come. I love the shape of your mouth.

VIOLET: Will I ever get you alone again for more than an hour?

RHYS: Yes, I promise.

VIOLET: Good, I hope so.

RHYS: I wish I was there now with you wrapped around me, kissing every inch of you that isn't bruised.

VIOLET: What's stopping you?

RHYS: Well, for one, I don't think your parents would appreciate the things I want to do to their daughter.

VIOLET: Silly me.

RHYS: Soon.

VIOLET: I'm sure you'll be in touch.

RHYS: Shut up.

VIOLET: I'll wait patiently for your next cryptic text.

RHYS: You'll pay for that.

VIOLET: I'm counting on it.

RHYS: Now it's going to be worse.

RHYS: Goodnight.

VIOLET: Goodnight.

An hour later, he wrote back.

RHYS: Now I can't stop thinking about your legs.

VIOLET: :)

By Monday of the following week, I felt amazing. I had stopped my meds, and though I still had a set of stitches in my face and the side of my neck pinched and itched at times, I was able to move around freely and without pain. I decided to make a house call to Rhys. We hadn't spoken every day on the phone, but he'd made sure to text me or call me at least once a day. He seemed to have the bedtime of a ninety-year-old and I constantly made fun of him for it. He seemed distracted and I knew he was busy catching up on the work he had missed when he was at the hospital with me. He had shown the club a few times, and though his schedule was full, he always seemed to end his night with me with a phone call or a text telling me how much he wanted to see me. It seemed pretty obvious that we both wanted to resume what we had started.

Meanwhile, my mother held me hostage, refusing to let me join the online world on my laptop to look for new listings to show, although I'd secretly found a few on my phone. She was constantly checking on me and it was starting to drive me up the wall. She refused to let me leave the house.

I'd had a few nightmares, but nothing I couldn't handle. I'd had a moment or two in the bathtub alone at my parents' where I was filled with sheer terror, so much so that I couldn't move. I managed to make it through the first one, but had to call my mother the second time, making an excuse for her to come in and talk to me. Seeing her soothed me, though she could sense she was in the room for much more than handing me some shaving cream.

Fucking clown mask.

It was if he knew what the scariest mask to terrorize a person with was and pre-ordered it to make sure I would never forget an already terrifying event. Then again, they'd left me for dead. The stupid sons of bitches didn't stop at my house, either. Hours after they attacked me, they were caught two neighborhoods over. The one who raided my house was shot dead by the homeowner who had a gun, and the one who had used the knife on me was arrested after the man held him at gunpoint until the police arrived. He would never be getting out of jail. He was a convicted rapist and was wanted for several other crimes, including my home invasion and attempted murder. I dreaded the day I had to face him in court, but that day wasn't today.

I didn't want the therapy my mother suggested. I wanted to deal with it and get over it. I wanted to resume my life, not dwell on it.

It had only been a week, but I was dying to see Rhys, to touch him. I was nowhere near ready for the physical activity he could put my body through, but I damn sure would take him up on the making love in his bed he had promised me. I needed to be with him, to feel him, to know he was real.

I stopped at the store first and smiled as I carried my packages up his seven billion stairs. I knocked on the door excitedly, knowing he was home from work because I saw his car in the drive. With a plant in one hand and cucumber bath salt in the other, I was ready to resume some small sense of normalcy. I just wanted to see him, to thank him for being there for me, for my mother.

Fuck it, I loved him. I wanted to see him because I loved him. It was way too soon to confess this and I understood that, but I was in love with Rhys.

He opened the door and two sets of gray eyes peered back at me. Rhys looked devastating in his work suit, holding a toddler carbon copy of himself wrapped in an oversized towel. I looked at the baby who was opening and closing his hand at me in hello. I had no idea what my expression was.

He had a son. I was sure this was his son.

His expression was one of utter shock at me darkening his door. He sure had not expected it to be me. I stood there completely dazed.

"Down, down, down, Da Da, down." I looked at Rhys who was clearly struggling with his words. He looked at his son then at me and started to open his mouth when I stopped him.

"You weren't ready to tell me…then. I understand that." Tears blurred my vision as I studied his beautiful baby who was struggling to get away from his father, making "eh, eh" sounds. I watched him squirm as Rhys held him tightly in his towel, trying to keep him warm.

"Da Da, down!"

"God, he's beautiful," I said, his tiny hand opening and closing it at me, "just like his father." I looked at Rhys, still struggling with what to say. "What's his name?"

"Bryce," Rhys whispered, opening the door further, ushering me inside.

"Kind of a moot point now, don't you think? You clearly weren't ready to invite me into this part of your life."

"Violet, I was. I really was." I nodded just to be agreeable. I would never really know if that was the truth. I didn't want to argue with him and scare the baby, and to be honest, the fight had left me. Once again, I found myself in love with a man who was a stranger to me.

"I'm just the crazy lady on the porch with her heart in her hand looking completely idiotic with a plant…again," I said, setting it down with a humiliating chuckle. "I brought you this, too." I shoved the bath salt into his hand and he struggled to grip it while he held a wiggling Bryce to him.

"Don't, don't go. I can't come after you. And it will kill me if I can't. Violet, you mean…so much to me. Please don't go." The pleading in his voice caused my eyes to well with tears, but I couldn't trust him.

"Da Da, down!" Bryce was no longer happy with the situation and grabbed the bath salt out of his hand and threw it on the floor behind them.

"How do I know this is what you really want, Rhys? You never even told me. I lied about a situation. You omitted a whole person." I couldn't help the amount of hurt I felt. I knew I was openly crying and felt the tears burn the stitches on my face. He took a step toward me with his squirmy bundle tight in his arms.

I took a step back and shook my head. "No, you kept this from me. I can't stay." My eyes wandered to Bryce, who had tilted his body toward me with his arms out, opening and closing both his hands. His eyes pleaded for me to take him and free him from his father's arms. I studied his sweet cheeks, the dark curly hair still damp on his head. I was taken with him. He was the mirror image of the man I loved. I kissed his hand and addressed him. "I would love to hold you, sweetheart, but it's cold." My voice was shaking. I was going to blow. I turned quickly, walking down his first few steps.

"Violet, please stay. There was just never a good time. The way we met, I needed time to—"

"I get it. I really do get it. I can't tonight. Not tonight, okay? I'm trying to be cool here. I'm upset—" I held my chest "—and I don't want to scare him." I turned on the steps, my eyes swimming as they slammed into his. He nodded. "Take him inside, Rhys, it's cold."

"Please answer when I call," he said, watching me walk down the steps. I walked to my car, a shaking mess. I thought we were becoming closer, but what the hell did I really know? I had no idea what the man was like in his everyday life. I was his sexual partner. We fucked, and we did it well. In that way, we were compatible. I still hadn't learned much about him since our one day alone. He'd kept me at a distance this whole time. The more I thought about it, the more I realized why he did things the way he did. Always a text once a week, rarely twice, and always when it was convenient for him. He was a single father. Everything began to click as I thought it over.

Click. Click. Click. Click.

All of it made sense now, the texts instead of phone calls, the need to constantly leave for family gatherings. His family was his son! God, he had a beautiful baby boy. But where was the mother? Was she still in the picture?

Rhys was a father. That had to be why he wanted to sell the club. He wanted to wash his hands of that part of his life. It was understandable, and actually, I loved that he was doing it.

I was so blinded with lust and my own agenda, I hadn't realized he had his own. He was done with the life. He was leaving it and I had just begun. It made perfect sense for him to keep me away. He didn't know me well enough to introduce me to that part of his life. He was being protective, as he should be. And at the same time...I was pissed.

I made it to my home in record time. I walked through the house with a broom in hand, checking closets out of pure paranoia. Once I was sure I was alone, I set the security code and called my mother.

"Are you insane? What the hell are you doing at home alone!"

"Well, Mom, when a woman grows up and gets a job—"

"Don't you take that smart ass tone with me, young lady! I'm coming over."

"No, Mom, I want to be alone."

"TOUGH SHIT!" The line went dead in my hand, and as soon as she ended the call, I jumped as it rang in my hand.

Rhys.

The bitter bitch in me let it ring. I had suffered because of *my* unfortunate circumstance. Not that having a baby was unfortunate.

That baby. God, he made beautiful babies.

I popped a bottle and poured.

I had been busted in the same way. This was irony at its finest, an unexpected house call that led to the discovery of a family member dwelling in the home that wasn't expected. I voiced the end of my internal rant, screaming at my missed call.

"Sound familiar, asshole? Now you can sit and think about how your intentions were nothing but good and you were doing the right thing and are now being punished for it! Maybe I should fucking make you call me madam!" I chuckled as I poured more wine. What a week. I downed the first glass and poured another.

He sent a text.

I was pissed. He shouldn't have.

> **RHYS: Please talk to me.**

> **VIOLET: Oh, this situation is so familiar. Shall I ignore you for weeks and only demand sex when I see you?**

> **RHYS: That's not very fair.**

> **VIOLET: No, it's not. My husband was half dead when I found him on the floor after our night together. You never really let me tell you that. I rushed him to the hospital to make sure he stayed alive—although between you and me, I could be a millionaire now if he hadn't survived—but hey, them's the breaks and that's the wine talking.**

> **RHYS: No, I never let you tell me.**

> **VIOLET: That's right, you didn't. So against my better judgment, I nursed his stupid ass back to health so I could ask him for a divorce. I planned on getting him out sooner. I didn't want to lose you, so I lied. I wanted you too.**

This is where I started glass number three.

> **RHYS: I swear even though we are texting I can hear you saying this to me, telling me off.**

VIOLET: Does my pain amuse you?

RHYS: I'm grabbing Bryce and I'm coming over to your mother's. I can't take this. I need to see you.

VIOLET: I'm at home.

RHYS: What?

VIOLET: I'M HOME.

The phone rang in my hand and I screamed out a little. Okay, maybe I *was* a little freaked out.

Rhys didn't give me a chance to greet him. "Are you insane? What the hell are you doing there alone!"

"Did you call my mother before you called me? Damn, she said the exact same thing." I waved him off, although he wasn't anywhere near me, nor could he see my gesture.

"Maybe we said the same damn thing because we both know it's dangerous!"

"Being in this house alone is the story of my life, Rhys. Nothing new here, and quit screaming, you'll wake your beautiful baby up! Besides, they caught the assholes that did it to me. I'm fine."

"Not physically dangerous, Violet. What happened to you was horrible. You can't be there alone, not yet." His voice was ruining me by the second.

"My mother is on her way." I hiccupped and he heard it. He stayed silent. I was buzzing and a little bit horny, but even more pissed off.

"I'm sorry, Violet."

Sighing with sarcasm, I let my anger through. "I am too. I'm out of wine, and I was really looking forward to a bath in that claw foot tub and your cock. But seeing as how you are up to your ears in dirty diapers—" I hung up before I could do any more damage. I was angry and full of wine. Calmer and clearer a few minutes later, I decided to text him.

> **VIOLET: Anything I say for the rest of the evening isn't going to be nice. I'm pretty sure I am in love with you and the Hyde to your Jekyll. And also, that baby that was squirming on your hip tonight, I'm pretty sure that was love at first sight with him. But I can't right now. So don't make me.**

I turned off my phone and waited for my mother.

I stood staring at the bloodstain on my hardwoods. It was time to face what had happened to me. I didn't need to keep hiding behind my parents. It was time to really think about what I was doing. I needed to process and move on. Get divorced, get on making that bucket list. I had no idea what would happen with Rhys, but I needed to start today. What I was sure of was there couldn't be anything more surprising than the last two stunners I'd just had thrown at me. I was robbed and left for dead. And my beautiful demanding Dom was a loving and doting father. Nothing could be more bizarre than this.

But you know what they say, everything happens in threes.

VOLUME THREE

THE LAST DANCE

RHYS

had just hurt her, and it was the last thing I wanted to do. She had already been through enough.

Pulling up to her house, I was determined to make things right. I parked across the street behind a Lexus, recognizing her husband's car immediately. I'd seen it the last time I was here. I stamped my rage down as I stepped out onto the street. Noticing that the car was still occupied, I approached it quickly. He was staring at the house as if he were afraid of it.

He should be.

I had no time for this bullshit. Violet was inside, alone for the first time since she was attacked. Although she told me her mother was coming, I was unsure if it was the truth or an excuse to keep me away. The look in her eyes when she realized Bryce was mine, the way she studied me as if I was a stranger, had me dropping Bryce off with the neighbor and racing here. I was a man possessed and so close to claiming her, there was no way this clown was fucking it up.

Alex jumped when I tapped on his window. He opened it, eyeing me carefully.

"Can I help you?"

"Yeah," I said, bending down eye level so he could see me clearly. "You can get the fuck out of here."

"Pardon?" He looked completely confused as he studied me.

"Alex, right?" I snapped.

"Do I know you?" Alex wiped his face with both hands to cover the fact that he had been crying. I didn't give a shit.

"I'm Rhys, your replacement."

Alex looked stunned, and at the same time, a little affronted. My gaze surveyed the inside of his car, noticing a half-empty bottle of bourbon in his passenger seat. His voice was a whisper as he stared at the house. "Is she okay? I saw on the news and I knew her mother would never let me see her in the hospital. They almost killed her?"

"Yes," I said, my agitation growing with his concern.

"I have to see her." Alex's voice shook and I took a step back as he got out of the car. Grabbing his jacket collar, I slammed his body against the car to help him close the door.

"You lost that privilege the day you left the house. You weren't there to protect her that night. What gives you the fucking right?"

His face contorted in anger as he tried to pull away from me. "She is still *my* wife. I have things I need to say." My blood boiled as I tightened my grip.

"I should pound your pretty fucking face in for what you did to her. She's moved on. Let it go. It's not your job to look after her. You gave it away. I took it." I saw the fear in his eyes as I shoved him back against the car again, his body sinking against my hold.

"You're right. I have no right to be here." His face twisted painfully and I let him go.

"I just wanted to see her, make sure she is okay," he said in his retreat, putting his hand on the car door. He gave up so easily.

He didn't deserve her.

"You don't get to want anything when it comes to her. I'm all she needs," I said possessively.

He simply nodded in agreement and I shook my head in disgust.

Fucking pussy.

I wanted him to do something stupid; any excuse at this point would be a good one.

Alex looked back at the house. "She didn't deserve what I did. I know that," he said in a whisper.

"And that's your cross to bear, not hers," I said stiffly. "She's been through enough."

Alex simply nodded with defeated features as he took one last look at the house.

I felt my phone vibrate as Alex slid inside his car and pulled away. After checking my text, I quickly walked to mine, cursing in frustration. It was late. I had to get back to my son. Relief washed over me when I saw her mother's car approach and pull in the drive.

Alex didn't want her; it was his guilt eating him alive. He didn't deserve her forgiveness and I wasn't about to let him try for it. He'd never earn it. I would erase him from her completely.

She wouldn't be alone tonight and that's all that really mattered, that and the fact that she loved me.

❧

VIOLET

RHYS: I need to see you.

It could have been worse. He could have not responded at all. Then again, needing to see me might not be promising, either. I had told Rhys that I loved him in a text while drunk and angry. Not my finest moment. The problem now was that I was in love with a man I hardly knew. The feeling of unfamiliarity had a great deal to do with the omission that he was a father and had hid that fact

131

from me. I wasn't sure if I was longing more for the man who, until recently, seemed to be an open book, had an easygoing demeanor and a matter of fact look at life, whose eyes were filled with sincerity, and had a gentle touch and endless patience. Or if I was pining more for the man whose voice consumed my every thought, sent a shiver down my spine, filled my body with longing and had a hard edge and seemed unreachable. Rhys was both of these men, but how much did I really know about him? I needed to know more before we went any further.

I kicked my mother out early this morning and kept busy by circling my house, taking inventory of the things that were missing as a result of my home invasion. I went shopping and bought a rug to cover the huge bloodstain in my entryway until I could get the floors replaced. I was in the middle of writing a list in the kitchen when I heard a knock at my door. Startled, I jumped where I stood, dropping my list, instantly terrified.

Snap out of it, Vi.

Taking deep breaths, I grabbed the closest thing I could to arm myself—a meat mallet—and walked to the door.

"Who is it?"

"Crete's Messenger Service."

Cautiously, I opened the glass door between us and stared at the seemingly harmless man.

"Who is it from?"

He glanced at the package then eyed the meat mallet before turning an irritated look at me.

Yeah, buddy, I'm crazy.

"Alex Harvell."

I opened the door wider and signed where he indicated. Not wanting to see his expression as he took in the bruising on my face, I shut the door quickly. I'd made the mistake of thinking it would be an easy trip when I'd gone shopping earlier for the rug, but had caught the attention of everyone there. I was overwhelmed with the help I received while deciding on my purchase, which normally would have been appreciated, but I just wanted to be left alone. After locking the door, I walked into the kitchen then stood staring at the package for a few minutes before quickly making the decision that whatever I was offered, I would accept. I didn't want a messy divorce. The marriage had been enough. It was a complete and utter failure.

I opened the envelope and saw that the official papers had been drawn. That was fast. I read it carefully. The house would be mine and would be paid in full and titled to me along with my car, and in lieu of alimony, I would get a lump sum. I had to turn the page to see the figure and when I did I froze.

Seven hundred and fifty thousand dollars!

Well, a house and car, and close to a million dollars would do, I supposed. I was happy, more than happy, but I couldn't bring myself to get excited. I called my lawyer and sent him the signed paperwork to be reviewed, with strict instructions to have it completed within the next day or two. I had been toying with an idea and I was now sure I wanted to see it through. I called Molly to ask a favor. I also called my regular doctor and made an appointment to have my neck and face checked the following day.

I had just finished inventory and was folding clothes when my phone pinged.

RHYS: Hi.

VIOLET: Hi.

RHYS: I can't stop thinking about you.

VIOLET: I was sure you would have your number changed.

RHYS: Don't regret telling me how you feel.

VIOLET: Right now I don't trust how I feel.

RHYS: I'm calling you.

My phone rang and I picked it up, dreading the conversation.

I didn't bother with pleasantries. "I was upset, Rhys. I was drunk, emotional, and scared last night."

"You can't take it back and I don't want you to." My heart plummeted at the sound of his voice. His effect on me was overwhelming.

I sighed at the thought that with Rhys, I may never have control. "Fine, I wasn't taking it back, anyway. I was more or less explaining my behavior."

"I happen to like it when you get a little crazy. It means you care," he mused.

"I do, but, Rhys, is this really what you want? I feel like I forced myself into your life. And honestly, I feel a little pathetic," I said, my voice shaking slightly.

"You forget that *I* started this, Violet. *I did,* not you. I need to see you. Can I come over after work?"

I closed my eyes, picturing his hands on my face, feeling his kiss on my lips. I wanted that more than anything.

"Rhys, I'm leaving."

"Leaving?" I could hear his voice twist as he became upset.

I took a deep breath. "Before I passed out last night, I was thinking about the way we started and because of the way I've acted, you have every right to keep him from me. Bryce is your priority, as he should be. I'm not upset anymore."

"And I'm happy about that, but what I'm really interested in is the leaving part," he said gruffly, becoming more agitated.

"Not for long. Just a week. My friend Molly's parents own a house in Grand Cayman and I want to get away and...I want to start dating you while I'm gone."

"That's kind of difficult, Violet."

"No, it's not actually. We can talk every day."

A long silence followed before he spoke.

"What are you doing? Running?" he snapped. I could tell he was pacing.

"Please don't get upset. I'm trying to get to know you. If we were in the same room right now, what would we be doing?"

"Fucking...and only because you would beg me to. You don't have to leave to start dating me. I can keep my hands to myself, Violet. I'm actually quite disciplined in that department."

My whole body heated at his dismissal of his own need for me. Instead of being perturbed by his statement, it turned me on. I was officially a sick woman.

"I don't want you to keep your hands to yourself. I just really want to go to the Caymans, and according to my lawyer, when I get back, I will be a slightly wealthy divorcee. I need this trip. I want this trip. I think I deserve it. I have a bucket list to write. I want to come back healed and divorced. I don't want you to look at me now and see that night. I want you to see me whole and without another man's last name attached to me."

"I'll take you the way you are and here," he insisted, his tone more of disappointment than annoyance. I understood it.

"Sounds like a sweet response, like the right one...but really, you are being selfish," I noted.

"Fucking A I am," he said testily. Silence lingered between us. He couldn't exactly be the demanding beau he wanted to be and I had to keep from chuckling at the thought.

He let out a long breath. "I'll date you, Violet. I'll do whatever it takes to get you back on my porch, because next time you are there, I won't let you leave." The defeat in his voice tugged at my chest.

"That porch is cursed for me as far as I'm concerned. Rhys, I don't expect you to be a Casanova. I just really want to know the basics like your middle name, favorite football team, and about your son." I took out my large suitcase and started packing.

"It's not like we wouldn't have discovered these things if you weren't leaving." This time I let my chuckle break over the line.

"You find my pain amusing?" he bit out, using my words against me.

"Yes, Rhys, I do, but only because I know it's killing you not to order me around. Though I'm sure if you wanted to order my pussy around right now, and you said it just the right way, I might not have a choice."

I let the invitation sink in. I was testing him, and with his groan, I knew he had passed.

"I know better. I will give you what you want. I would've given it to you anyway because I want it, too."

"Then we agree," I said, hopeful.

"You aren't giving me much of a choice, but yes," he said grudgingly. "You're punishing me."

"Maybe...a little," I said truthfully.

"I had every intention of telling you. I never meant to hurt you."

"I want to believe you, Rhys."

"You will…and, Violet, you are going to pay for every single fucking hard-on I get in the next week."

"Make it RED," I said sweetly then hung up. Minutes later, after my suitcase was zipped, I got a text.

RHYS: Just come back to me.

The tears fell and I wiped them away. There was no need for them. This wasn't the end. It was just the beginning.

DAY 1

VIOLET

Molly's parents had agreed to let me pay for a week, at my insistence. It was the only way I would agree to stay. I'd left Savannah without seeing Rhys, because if I had, I wouldn't be standing at the entrance of the most breathtaking villa in the Caymans. The house was large, a two-story stucco with a Spanish style roof that sat oceanfront. The views in every room held me captive for minutes at a time as I walked around the house. The windows were all open, offering a panoramic view of the property, making it feel almost as if it existed within a tropical rain forest. A mosaic of dark blue and aqua tiles lay at my feet and spread from corner to corner. I chose the largest bedroom with a huge, king-sized canopy bed and the best view of the water. It was magnificent. I unpacked quickly, getting the burden off my shoulders so I could go put my toes in the sand. The breeze was warm, light. I put on a large hat to shade the newly unveiled scars on my neck and face to protect them from the beaming sun, then made my way out onto the sand from the back porch. I took in a deep breath as I listened to the lulling of the waves. Peace was what I felt here. It was what I longed for, what I needed.

This is the life, Vi.

I spent the day rubbing on sunscreen and reading my first book in months. I kept the book clean, keeping to the rules Rhys had set early on in our relationship. When the sun set and I had soaked in as much soft, white sand and aqua blue water as I could get, I went into the house, realizing I had nothing to eat. After freshening up, I called a cab and made my way to a local restaurant the cabbie suggested. It was there, sipping a mango margarita, that I sent my first text.

> VIOLET: It's so beautiful here. The longer I'm here, the more I know it was the right thing to do. I'm just missing one thing.

> RHYS: I come with a party of two.

> VIOLET: I know. You can join Bryce if you like.

> RHYS: Cute. What did you do today?

> VIOLET: I spent it by the water.

> RHYS: What color is your bikini?

> VIOLET: Red.

> RHYS: My favorite. I can picture you there.

> VIOLET: No need to.

I sent him the selfie I had taken and a few others of the water and the house. I waited forever for his response.

> RHYS: Do you have any idea how hard it is to tote a baby around with a hard-on!

I burst out laughing as my plate was served and apologized to him quickly.

> VIOLET: I'm sorry.

> RHYS: Don't be, I just really don't want anyone getting the wrong idea.

> VIOLET: What did you do today?

RHYS: Worked, picked up Bryce and took him to the fountain in Forsyth Park where he ran away from me as I screamed for someone, anyone to stop him. The kid is lighting fast and I swear he ran before he walked.

VIOLET: How old is he?

RHYS: Fifteen months.

VIOLET: And the mother?

RHYS: Is not and will never be in the picture. I come with no baby momma drama.

I laughed as I forked some enchilada and took a huge bite. Then the thought occurred to me.

VIOLET: Deceased?

RHYS: No, and I will tell you everything but only when I can see you.

VIOLET: Okay.

RHYS: No more secrets or lies between us.

VIOLET: Never again, not of any color.

RHYS: I'm going to get him fed and put him to sleep then I'll call you.

VIOLET: Sounds good to me.

RHYS: Violet, you in that bikini. There is a place I want to lick.

The throbbing began at my core and I swallowed hard.

VIOLET: Hurry up. I want to hear your voice. Kiss him goodnight for me.

I finished my plate then headed to the local grocery store for odds and ends before returning to the villa. There was plenty of time to sightsee. For now, I was more fascinated with the house. As I sat in a cream-colored lounge chair on the back patio, I listened to the ocean, trying to write a bucket list. I sat for an hour, coming up completely blank. It wasn't hard. There were a million places I wanted to see, a million things I wanted to do, but it all seemed so... unimportant. Travel wasn't what mattered most. The thought hit home for me because, although I was wrapped up in the arms of paradise, the arms I craved were in Savannah, Georgia.

I just didn't want to depend on those arms so quickly.

I'd meant what I said to Rhys. I didn't want to be Mrs. Harvell the next time he saw me. I wanted to be free of the name and the scars, and anything else that could taint my new beginning—*our new beginning*. An affair of the heart was not what I had been after, but it's what I ended up with, and I wouldn't change a second of it. After another hour of staring at a blank piece of paper, I gave up and was thankful when my phone rang. I smiled and slid it to open, his voice greeting me instantly.

"I keep staring at this fucking picture and I want you. Fuck, I want you!" I squeezed my thighs together so tight I nearly fell off the chair. I dropped the phone and scrambled to pick it up. My breathing was erratic and I couldn't stop picturing the things he could do to me. The way his eyes closed when he plunged his tongue inside of me. Calming my breathing and letting out a nervous laugh, I finally responded.

"There is a way to get even with me," I rasped as I fought for control.

"Oh yeah?" His voice spiked slightly. "How?"

"Take a picture of Bryce and send it to me," I murmured.

"Should I be jealous of my son?" he asked, amused.

"Yes, it took you a few months, it took him ten seconds," I scolded playfully.

"Wow...maybe I could learn a thing or two from a baby who was playing in pigeon shit earlier. You know that stuff is toxic, right? God, I don't think I'll be able to sleep tonight."

I burst out laughing and he chuckled.

I loved this side of him. And then I thought of the passionate and disciplined lover who commanded my body. I stayed silent and he sensed my hesitation.

"Violet, what is it?"

"Rhys, we can have both, right? This and...the other. Don't get offended—it's just, am I wrong to want both? We—you and me—when it comes to the bedroom, we—"

"Absolutely," he confirmed before I could finish.

"How?"

"Better leave it to me," he said, a slight hint of arrogance in his voice, and God how I loved it.

"How long have you been in this lifestyle?"

"I started when I was twenty-one."

Whoa. That gave him over thirteen years of experience. And man did it show. Jealousy coursed through me and I had to push it down. He had to have been with hundreds of women.

Don't ask, Violet. It's none of your business.

"So you have slept with hundreds of women?"

SHIT, Violet.

"You are a shitty phone date." He sounded amused, but I knew he was on guard.

"Sorry, I've never dated a Dom before," I said playfully.

"All the questions can't be yours, anyway. I plead the fifth on my number. And you are the last and only woman I want to be Dom to. I mean that." I sat stunned at his admission. It was the first time he had ever referred to a real future with me.

"Rhys, why were you in the chat room that night?"

"The same reason you were. It's been a busy first fifteen months. I was bored. My days are pretty boring sometimes. You can only watch so many episodes of Bunnytown before you start to sing along then slowly plot the damn puppet's death. I couldn't exactly bring a sub home. I'd been a good boy."

"But you managed to see me?" I asked, interest piqued.

"I can honestly tell you, I had no intention of doing anything but browsing. I was on my couch screening new members for the club. I saw you check in, a few hours later you hadn't typed a word, so I spoke up."

"And then?" I asked quickly.

"And then curiosity got the best of me. We were kind of in the same situation. We both needed the same thing at the same time. You wanted the experience, and I needed a sub without long-term expectations."

"So, I kind of fell into your lap?"

"At first I was going to let you seek out your own partner by using the club. It's not something I've ever done. I just knew you were lost, and I was just as lost at one time. I felt I was leading you to a safer place."

I thanked the stars that aligned for me that night then asked, "Why leave it? I mean, you just told me we could have both."

"I couldn't own that club. Like I said, it was never something I wanted. And honestly, no subs were interested in dating a single father. I wasn't exactly interested in dating them either at that point. Some of their needs are…insatiable. I couldn't run out at all times of the night to fulfill those needs. I couldn't really justify doing or starting anything with you the next day. I was determined to leave it behind until I could find a woman more suitable. And then, I saw you on the security screen."

I stayed quiet. I wanted to hear more. He had no idea what he was doing to me. I was on fire and so wet I could have slid off my lounger. The mere sound of his voice triggered every nerve ending I had.

"And?" I prodded.

"You are just dying to hear this, aren't you, Violet?"

"Yes," I said, breathless. "Please tell me."

"Are you wet now, thinking of me sucking and fucking you? I know you are. I won't let this go there tonight."

"Damn it to hell." I was gasping as he chuckled at me.

"I can control your body from Savannah. Tell me, is my pretty pink pussy aching for me? It's probably throbbing right now, swollen and needy, hungry for me to push in."

"God…please…shut up." I stood and walked to the bathroom to splash cold water on my face.

"You shouldn't have run away," he taunted as my limbs fell heavy with need.

I stood in the bathroom, seeing firsthand what he did each time he aroused me. My nipples were drawn tight, my cheeks flushed, my skin blistering hot.

"Rhys, I'm completely ready for you. How do you do this to me?" I leaned in to look at my pupils, which were dilated.

"Don't touch, Violet," he commanded, his low growl only making my need grow.

"I can't, Rhys. I've never have been able to do that," I whispered, breathless.

"You can't come with your fingers?" He sounded truly shocked.

"No, I've tried. God, like a sixteen-year-old boy I've tried. I've just never been able to," I admitted.

"Oh, baby, that's a fucking tragedy," he murmured. I sighed in reply before smiling at his term of endearment for me. Rhys had been the only man who could get me off, and so easily. I knew it had a great deal to do with our chemistry. All it took was one look from him and I was a willing participant in any game he wanted to play. The feelings I had for him now magnified it to make something that used to seem so impossible…simple, intimate, addicting, fucking perfect. Rhys didn't just have the right set of skills. He was the right man.

"And that's why I had a toy." I sighed as I turned off the bathroom light and wandered into my bedroom, listening to the ocean waves, inhaling the breeze while staring at the full moon. It was spectacular. I laid down in the bed, drawing the covers up over me.

I heard Rhys moving around his house. "Toys are fucking sad excuses for men who are too lazy to do their damn job." He sounded disgusted and I laughed.

"Well, sorry to disappoint you, *baby*," I playfully added, "but it's the only way for me…alone."

"That's bullshit, and I'll prove it." He sounded convinced. "Fuck, this is a nightmare. Is it too late to demand that you get your pussy back here right this minute?"

"Yes." I chuckled. The sight of the moon, the smell of the ocean, and the beautiful house I was surrounded by did little to stop the next thing I told him. "But I left my heart there, Rhys."

Silence. Shit.

What the hell are you doing, Vi?

I offered an excuse quickly, my face heating and my heart racing. "It's really romantic here, Rhys, and I told you I love cheesy romantic movies. Can we just move forward here? Better yet, I'll let you get some sleep."

"Violet, stop it." His voice was firm. "You can't keep saying shit like that to me then take it back. If you could see me when you said it, you would know I closed my eyes and smiled. Don't hide from me. I've given you no reason to."

I lay in bed picturing his eyes closed, his smile, and sighed. "Tell me about you. Tell me about your childhood, about your parents, your sisters."

"What do you want to know?"

"Everything," I said wistfully.

We spent hours talking about our childhoods, laughing at the similarities in our upbringing. I told him how I wasn't very popular, and though sad but true, aside from Molly, my mother was my true best friend.

"I just kind of blended in."

"Violet, I highly doubt that," he remarked.

"It's true, even in college I was just kind of a homebody. Never really that reckless. I'm pretty boring, not too much of a colorful past."

"You are more to handle than any other woman I have ever dealt with," he said with certainty.

"I'll take that as a compliment."

"I'll let you," he rasped playfully.

His mother was an art dealer and currently owned a gallery in downtown Savannah. His father retired several years ago as a banker. Rhys now lived in his childhood home, which he bought from his parents when they moved to their new home on Tybee Island, less than an hour away from the city. He said that house would stay in his family as long as it was in his power. He was a bit of a traditionalist.

We moved onto dating. I was more curious than ever about his past. He had the typical high school experience that included losing his virginity to a steady girlfriend, but after her he had never stayed with one girl for long. He discovered his thirst for kink with a partner in college when he was at his sexual peak.

"The more painful it was for her, the harder I got and the more excited she became, and so we sought out to find others who were into the same thing. We experimented a lot. I took it to the extremes until I found someone who taught me what I needed to know."

"And your extreme side now?" I asked.

"Still there and is your red," he stated plainly.

"Have I seen it all?" I asked, hoping for the answer he gave next.

"Not even close," he said, his voice low, causing a tingle to spread down my spine.

I quickly changed the subject. Only a day apart and I was about to lose my control.

He had two sisters, Heidi and Hillary, who he nicknamed big H and little H, and he was the youngest. His sister Hillary watched Bryce once or twice a week so Rhys didn't feel so overwhelmed. She had young children of her own, and Rhys felt guilty that his son had no one to play with. He said they used to switch out until her family multiplied to four. Heidi, the one who I had met at brunch, was a photographer and a free spirit. I could tell she was Rhys's favorite by the way he spoke. He said she was a reluctant mother, but would be fantastic at it.

"So why the vasectomy?" I asked, curious.

"It was more at the insistence of the mother when she got pregnant. I knew it was reversible, so I did it. I don't regret it. It's actually great to not have to worry about it. I'm concentrating on the one kid I have for now."

"Rhys, do you want more?" I asked, hopeful.

"Do you want another proposal of marriage, specifically from me?" he said in a mocking tone. I couldn't tell if he was testing me or laughing at me, and I hated it.

SHUT UP, VIOLET. SHUT UP NOW.

"I'm sorry. I…you should get some sleep." His laughter echoed through the room as I'd had him on speaker for the last hour. "Stop laughing at me! If this was a first date, you would NOT get a kiss goodnight."

"No, I'd already have you gasping and coming and naming our future children."

My entire body lit up like a Christmas tree at his words and I groaned in frustration. "Ugh, you are such a conceited ass," I said, frustrated at his playfulness, my heart beat spiking at the truth of his words.

"You are so cranky when you are horny. I would love to put

you out of your misery. It's a little late for a plane. Are you a good swimmer, Violet?"

"Rhys," I said, now standing at the window again, stunned by the beauty of it. "If we...make it, I want to come back here to this very room and not talk at all for days. I can't even explain to you how beautiful this is. A picture won't do it justice. Just know the moon is full and the water is sparkling like it's covered in diamonds. It smells amazing, ten times better than your bath salt. I'm standing here right now, surrounded by a room of white, a cool breeze blowing through the curtains, and all I want is you to be behind me. Promise me, if we make it as a couple, we will come here one day together."

I got nothing.

"Rhys?"

"I'm here. Jesus, what your voice does to me. I can't even explain the fucking spell you just put me under. I promise."

"Go to sleep. Same time tomorrow?"

"Yes, goodnight."

"Goodnight."

RHYS

She was killing me. I couldn't even stop myself from staring at that damn picture. She had covered her bruised eye, her fingers pulling her hat down over half her face, and all that was left was the fullness of her lips, the hollow of her chest, and the round fullness of her perfect tits I couldn't touch. As if that wasn't enough, it was followed by her beautiful belly and thick hips. Those legs hurt to look at; they physically *hurt*. I would never tire of her smart mouth and sexy ass.

She was an answer to a prayer I had never asked.

I heard Bryce call out to me and walked over to his room then waited outside the door.

"Da da da da da."

He wasn't crying, he was just talking to himself. I looked at the clock. Midnight, shit.

Go back to sleep, little man.

My phone vibrated in my hand. I looked at the ID.

The Devil.

I stood stunned as I stared at the phone in my hand. I hadn't heard from her in almost a year.

"I told you to never to call me again," I snapped.

"You miss me and you know it." Her voice used to get me hard in seconds, now it was like nails on a chalkboard.

"The hell I do. I told you I don't want or need anything from you." Bryce was getting louder, so I walked down the hall to the bathroom so she couldn't hear. This wouldn't take long.

"I think about you all the time. There is no way you have forgotten me." She sounded so smug, so damn confident. It disgusted me.

"I can't really say the same. What the fuck do you want?"

"So, who is she?"

"What do you want?" I gritted out, irritated.

"You, your cock filling me, right now," she said in a seductive tone I was all too familiar with.

"Ship has sailed. Sailed fifteen months ago. I've gotten all I've ever wanted from you," I said, matter of fact, my boredom clear over the line.

"I think we both know that's not true, Rhys."

I never used the word hate, and I never thought I would feel it toward someone I used to care about, but I was sure in this case, I hated her. I stayed quiet, having no desire to entertain her at all. I should have never answered the phone.

"And how is he?"

"Seriously, you will never know good or bad. Are we done

here?" I couldn't even handle her with care anymore, the way I used to. I had no intentions of ever treating her like she was important ever again.

"Rhys, please at least come soothe me."

I laughed at her. She had actually assumed I would go aid her in her sexual depravity. "Why don't you ask the idiot who flogged you? Seriously, is there a mental illness in your family? Not a chance. Don't call me again."

"What's her name? This has to be because of a woman. You were always a bit soft on your subs. Too soft to be a good Dom," she hissed.

"Fuck you. You can't, nor will you ever know *her* name, and she will never know yours. Neither will your *son*."

I hung up. Things must be going horribly for her to have graced me with that phone call. I didn't know why I was so surprised she had the audacity to call me and beg for it. When it came to her, nothing surprised me.

"DA DA DA DA DA!"

"Okay, son," I said, walking into his room. He smiled so wide, I couldn't help but return it. He was trying to hoist himself from his crib as I approached him. Soon he would figure it out.

"Young man, go back to sleep," I said, feigning a command. He giggled and reached for me, opening his hands. Even my son knew I was a sucker for him and didn't take me seriously. Some Dom I was. I couldn't even get a baby to obey me.

"Come on, big boy."

He pointed to his diaper and I nodded as I picked him up. I shook my head as I grabbed him.

"You are the only baby I have ever heard of that summons his father to clean the crap off him. You are either really smart, which I'm thinking you are, or very OCD, which could be a problem."

He studied me as I ripped open his diaper to change him. "You know, I'm thankful every day that you look like me, kid." He smiled again and pulled at my nose as I leaned in. "You're a handsome devil. You sure have worked your magic on my girlfriend."

I sat with him in his rocking chair with the light dimmed and pulled out my phone. "Want to see Violet?"

"Tet," he said, attempting to say her name.

"Yep."

"Tet."

I pulled up the picture. It wasn't exactly age appropriate, but I was sure my son could appreciate beauty when he saw it. "Violet."

"Tet."

"Good enough." He looked up at me then back at the phone, picked it out of my hand and threw it to the floor.

"I may want her, kid, but I'll always be your daddy. Now, do me a favor and pass out." I covered his eyes with my hands and he fought viciously to remove them. I chuckled and brought him to my bed with me and we both fell asleep looking at the world's most beautiful screensaver.

DAY 2

VIOLET

"People should be ordered to get one of these once a month," I grunted to my current therapist, Alana. I continued, "Crime would be lower, the world would unite as one. I'm telling you, this could solve any crises." Alana chuckled as she leaned in, working my lower back. "Oh God, oh, that's...fuck that's great. Whoops, sorry about my mouth."

"It's okay, Violet. I've heard the word." I looked up to her and she winked at me.

"Ahhhh..." I belted out for both our benefit. She had a velvet voice and nice brown eyes. She was tall but slender, and had hands that could melt a statue.

"I don't see a ring," Alana said, working my arms. "Are you here with someone?"

"No, I'm alone, though I am regretting that right about now. It's been a crazy few months. I just needed a break."

"I can feel the crazy few months in your shoulders," she said, soothingly working the hard knots out with ease.

"You have no idea," I said, pressing my face tighter into the cushion as she rubbed in more scented oil.

"You have twenty minutes," she said, her voice lifting in curiosity.

I thought about confessing my sins. I was alone in the Caymans. Chances are she would never see me again. I had never been able to open up to another woman about Rhys, but still couldn't bring myself to tell the whole truth.

"The cliff notes version is I am days away from a divorce, I was recently robbed and beaten then left for dead, I became involved with a man that has completely ruined me for all other men, but is right now a little bit of a mystery. He's kind of perfect, but has...a dark side, I guess."

Understatement of the year, Violet.

"Wow," she said, digging her elbows into the hard tissue just above my ass.

I chuckled. "All that just in the last *two* months. *That* might be one reason I'm here." I shook my head with wide eyes as I glanced at her over my shoulder. "Anyway, I wanted to make sure I am in love with the dude not the dick, even though I'm sure it's both."

"Well, honey, it sounds like a win-win to me. Love a little mystery in a man."

My phone vibrated and I grinned back at her. "This is him. Let's make him jealous."

I let out a moan as I slid my phone to answer. "Rhys, oh GOD, the hands, mmmmmm."

"What the hell are you doing?" he chuckled as I moaned in his ear.

"Mmm, oh, yes! Don't stop."

More chuckling from him.

I deadpanned, "What? No jealousy for me? I'll have you know I'm being rubbed down by a set of hot hands right now."

"Those better be the hands of a woman, or maybe I should warn you what happens when I get truly jealous." His tone was deadly. I got hot immediately.

"That's more like it," I said instantly, no longer interested in the hands that were touching me.

"Violet, I'm warning you now, you moan in my ear one more time, I'll make your homecoming painful."

"Mmmm," I said, thinking of the ways it could be.

"Was that for me or her?" he said, his voice rough and laced with want.

"You, always for you." Alana tapped my shoulder and smiled. I waved her a 'thank you' and sat up. "I like your hands more."

"Then come back." His words were harsh. He wasn't enjoying the distance. My heart tugged. I knew he wanted me without a doubt. I was sure I wouldn't last the week.

"I'll be divorced in two days," I piped happily.

"Good, I'll see you then?"

"I'm thinking about it," I said seriously.

"I have to get back to work. Tonight, same time?"

"Perfect."

You will write one damn thing on your bucket list before you go back to Savannah, Vi.

DAY 3

RHYS

"Bryce, please, son. Keep them in your tray." I stared at my bullheaded son who insisted on throwing his Cheerios on the floor. To spite me, he looked up at me with another handful and emptied it onto the floor. I grinned, shaking my head. "Fine," I said, pouring half the box on his tray. "Try to get some of them into your mouth."

The doorbell rang, and for a second I got my hopes up. But it couldn't be her. Damn that woman. She had no idea what she was doing to me. I opened the door and immediately my blood boiled.

"Rhys." She smiled sweetly. I knew that smile. Not a chance in hell.

"Look, if I have to get a court order, I will," I said, taking an aggressive step toward her.

"Tsk, tsk," she said, waving her finger arrogantly. "I just stopped by to say hello."

"Because you thought I would take one look at you and come undone, right?"

She crossed her long legs as she leaned against the door, her smile wicked and her intentions worse.

"I had hoped for a better reception," she said, leaning in close, too close.

"Listen to me. I want nothing to do with you. I tried with you. I did everything."

"Everything I wanted you to do," she fired back, clearly shocked she hadn't made a dent in my resolve.

"I'm getting a court order. You can't do this. I was never as weak as you thought I was. You were just fucking delusional. Leave." I pointed behind her and she snatched my finger with her mouth, sucking it slowly, making a popping sound when she let it go. I heard Bryce knock off the tray from his high chair—a skill he had learned recently—and ran into the kitchen to grab him before he fell out of it.

I got to Bryce just in time and heard her behind me.

"He looks just like you," she said coldly. I stiffened as I held him, knowing I had no choice but to face her. I turned with Bryce in my arms and saw her take in her son for the first time since his birth. I never wanted him to lay eyes on her. She had just taken that away from me.

"Get out. I'm not even joking; I will fucking throw you out. You can't do this!" I felt Bryce shaking in my arms from my hostility. Looking down at him, I smiled and rubbed the top of his head. "It's okay, buddy."

"Don't you miss it? The way we were? How hot it was?" she said, completely ignoring the baby in my arms.

"No, I've moved on. You should, too. I don't want you coming here. It will only confuse him," I said evenly, hoping to keep the conversation civil. She glared at Bryce, as if he was the reason for our separation, and then turned to walk toward the front door.

"He will always be the abortion I should have had."

I saw red at her words. "If you ever come back here, I'll have you arrested. You'll be served with a restraining order, bet on it," I said, hot on her heels as I followed her out.

"Don't flatter yourself, Rhys. I won't be back."

I slammed the door on her back, eliciting an enraged scream as it hit her in the ass. Violet was right, the porch was cursed.

Fuck. Fuck. Why is she doing this?

I felt my phone vibrate.

VIOLET: I am sitting in the tub and could use a war story.

I had been telling her tales over the phone last night that I'd heard over the years of BDSM scenarios gone wrong. They seemed to fascinate her. She had laughed hysterically. I loved that sound.

RHYS: Now is a bad time.

VIOLET: Everything okay?

RHYS: Yes, just perfect. Enjoy your soak.

I was too angry to think about my response to her until later that day.

The more I thought about my behavior, the more I thought about her—Violet, not the evil bitch that showed up at my door. She was non-existent and I refused to entertain her. If she wanted me thinking about her, she'd failed.

My thoughts were of the woman who had captured me completely with her body first and then her words. I wanted to apologize to her but disliked the idea of doing it over the phone. She'd put up with much worse from me, but she didn't deserve it this morning, or then for that matter. How the hell could I make it up to her if I couldn't see her, touch her?

The image of the night I found her on that floor covered in blood flashed through my mind. I got her *help* text and made it to her house in fifteen minutes. I should have called the police, but I didn't know where she was, so to be sure I went there first. The rest repeated on an endless, slow motion cycle when I thought about it. The door was open, the screen closed, and I immediately felt a heaviness in my chest I never knew was possible. I opened the door while dialing, afraid to touch her. There was so much blood. There was no way I would ever recover if she were dead. I knew then I would never be the same without her in my life. When I reached her, I knelt down, checking for a pulse. It was there, weak, but there.

I scooped her up in my arms, applying pressure to the source of the blood escaping her neck.

She was alone in a house in Grand Cayman. Fuck.

If she only knew how that affected me every day she'd been gone, how worried I was about her safety, she wasn't concerned about it in the least. Or, if she was, I couldn't tell. I didn't want to scare her by voicing mine. Then again, I had gotten into her house through an unlocked door the night I confronted her about her husband.

I'd never been anywhere close to doing anything like that with anyone else. I should have given her a chance to explain. Then maybe she wouldn't be off on some island wondering where the hell my head was at and why I didn't tell her what I should have a month ago.

The guilt I felt while she lay in that hospital bed consumed me. I wouldn't fuck up like that again, not with her.

When I had laid Bryce down for the night, I called to apologize.

"I'm sorry. I had a bad morning." I didn't even let her finish her hello.

"I figured. What happened?" I could tell she was on edge. I'd probably done that to her. She didn't deserve it.

"Can we not talk about it right now?"

"No secrets," she reminded me.

"This isn't a secret. We can call it a delayed conversation," I gritted out.

"Nice. I can tell you are still angry. I wish I could serve you some ass to take it out on." I could practically see the smile she was wearing and groaned in reply. Fuck, she was perfect.

"And this is why I couldn't get anything done at work today."

"Tell me about music," she murmured, her voice putting me at ease.

"Music?"

"Yeah, tell me what you like."

"I have a thing for good guitar solos," I said, my mood evening out for the first time today. I climbed the stairs and checked on Bryce then went to my room to strip and bathe.

"Hmm, interesting," she said, playing along.

"No, it's not really," I mused at her reach for small conversation. "I'm taking a bath. Why don't you join me?"

"I took one today. I was in the tub when I texted you, remember?"

"Take another one," I said suggestively.

"Okay." I heard the rush of water as she readied her bath, and minutes later, we both sank into our tubs.

"Kind of a feminine habit you have here, Rhys." She laughed and I joined her.

"Baths are relaxing. I don't drink when I have Bryce, so this is what I do. Don't hate on Daddy's bath."

"Not hating, just an observation. Don't forget to sprinkle your salt." She laughed again and I heard her water splash.

"Cute, really you are adorable. In my mind, I have blistered your ass about a hundred times since you left." I knew I had her attention.

"Well then, I guess I'm thankful my ass is safe." She sighed and I could picture her beautiful hazel eyes peering at me, mouth parted.

My bath was no longer relaxing.

"Tomorrow is Thanksgiving, Violet. I don't like that you'll be alone."

"I have a chicken to cook," she said, upbeat.

"I'm cooking my first turkey." I laughed at the thought.

"What's so funny?" she asked, her silky voice making it hard for me to concentrate on her question.

"Me, Bryce and a raw turkey. I can't wait until you get a chance to know him. He is a twenty-eight pound Godzilla."

"Tell me more," she said sweetly.

"What do you want to know?" I asked, rolling up a hand towel with one hand before sticking it behind my head.

"Everything," she sighed.

"Before I brought him home from the hospital, I Googled everything and I mean everything. I watched a few videos to get the gist of it. There was a lot of trial and error. I had help from my family, but I've been pretty much alone the whole time. I thought it would be easier than it was. Feed him, clothe him, change him. I didn't put much weight on sleeping schedules or an extra set of clothes just in case, or the croup or baby reflux." I paused. "I really never thought I would be a dad. I've been pretty selfish with my freedom my whole life. I liked just worrying about me. And then I found out he was coming and I couldn't handle the thought of not keeping him."

Thinking about the lengths I had gone to be his father, I admitted the truth to her. "You know I had to beg for his life. I had to beg every day for her to keep him until it was too late and she had to carry full term." I thought about my son and smiled. "He's the best thing that ever happened to me. I really do love it, being a father. I'm not resentful I had to give up my freedom, because honestly, I realized I wasn't too happy with it. Things changed for me so drastically, I didn't even realize that I'd become a father and nothing else. You were the first thing I had for myself since he was born. I guess that's why I waited to tell you; I was being selfish." There was nothing but silence on her end of the phone.

"Violet?"

"Can I call you right back?"

"Sure, is everything—"

VIOLET

When I was done sobbing into my washcloth, I waited a few extra minutes to call him back to make sure my emotions stayed in check.

This *woman,* who he referred to so carefully, intrigued me. What kind of a woman wouldn't want to have a family with Rhys? I was in no place to judge and I had agreed to learn more, but I already knew I didn't like her. And from what it looked like, she had abandoned them both.

I had to get a grip on these feelings. But in truth, when he spoke about his struggle and his love for his son, it left little room for doubt.

I shook those thoughts away and dialed him.

"Sorry, I had to use the restroom," I said, the only decent excuse for my quick withdrawal. I was all for heavy conversation but I feared I couldn't take much more, so I started where we left off on a light note.

"So tomorrow you and Bryce are going to cook a turkey?"

"I'm cooking one of four," he said casually. "Thanksgiving is kind of ridiculous at my parents."

"Yeah, it will be the first one I've spent without mine, ever," I said softly. "I wasn't thinking about the holiday when I booked."

"You do deserve to be there. You do deserve this break. Please tell me you are locking the house every time you go in and out?"

The worry in his voice gutted me. Fuck, I hadn't thought about him having to worry about me, but I was touched that he was.

"I am, I promise. I actually carry mace with me everywhere. I get a little afraid sometimes, but it's gated and I feel mostly safe here. I have a hard time some days. I'll be honest, feeling safe was something I took for granted."

"I'm sorry I brought it up," he said, his voice low.

"No, I mean it's valid. I'm in this big empty house, I didn't think about how that would bother either of us. Honestly, I came to think about my next step, to get my shit together, but I kind of did that before I left. I'd stopped drinking as much, started working and working out," I said, defeated. "I haven't written one thing on my bucket list." I sighed, getting out of the tub. "I mean, don't get me wrong, it's beautiful here and I have a nice tan."

"You ran away," he stated firmly.

"I ran away," I conceded. I was thankful when he let the subject drop.

"Tell me what you look like right now in the mirror." His voice instantly put me on edge and made my pulse kick.

"Naked," I said slowly. "You aren't going to try to have phone sex with me, are you?"

"No, but if I was there right now...Fuck, the things I would do to that mouth and pussy."

I was wet, so wet, and I'd already dried myself with a towel.

"Tell me one thing, please," I said breathlessly, feeling my pulse pick up as I watched myself aroused in the mirror.

"I would open you up and lick you smoothly, but only once, from bottom to top with my whole tongue."

My nipples peaked with that one sentence.

"Okay, a little more," I begged.

"I would hesitate, because you would be so close to coming. I would work around your clit then plunge my tongue inside of you so you wanted it more...but you wouldn't have time to ask because as soon as you opened wider for me, I would lick your tip so fast and then drive my fingers in, fucking you until you came hard, closing your legs around my neck. You do that, you know? You close your legs around my neck and squeeze when you come."

"More?"

"No." His voice was firm. "Tell me what you are doing."

"Watching my body respond to you. Should I touch?"

"That's for me to do. Come back. I'll do it all in that exact order." His voice was heated and hungry.

"I will. I just...I hate that house now, Rhys. It's not a home anymore. It's a graveyard of bad shit. I think I just figured that out. I'm going to sell it."

"I'll show you where home is." His voice was ragged and I knew he was just as turned on as I was.

"Rhys, I need you inside me so much," I breathed.

"Fuck, come home now," he commanded, no longer playful.

"I am. I'm packing. I swore if I could write one thing on my

161

bucket list, something worthy of doing before I die, then I would come home."

"What will you write?"

"Go back to Savannah. I'll call you with my flight info. No more unannounced visits."

"Violet," he paused.

"Yes," I said, half packed and dying to get back to him.

"I'm in."

I took a shuddering breath at his words as he paused. I wanted more, so I waited.

His voice was silky smooth as he spoke to me. "I know that's what you are afraid of. I know why you ran. I should have told you about Bryce, but I wasn't as sure then as I am now. I know this is all really soon and I know you will barely be divorced, but this is something we both know is worth taking the risk for. There's no question of what's going on here. Come back, come fall in love with my son like you want to. He will love you back. There are two men here that could really use you around."

I sank to the bed next to my open suitcase. "I couldn't handle falling in love and pushed aside like that again. I don't think I can go through it again. And with you—with you, Rhys—I know how much it would hurt," I admitted.

"I'm in." Those two words were all I needed.

"Okay," I said hoarsely.

"Okay."

I hung up with him then called the airlines. I was scheduled to fly out first thing Friday morning, unable to get an earlier flight due to the holiday.

I quickly texted Rhys my flight info and told him I would be at his house by noon on Friday. I couldn't handle hearing his voice any more tonight and not being with him. I went to sleep dreaming of two sets of gray eyes that held my heart.

DAY 4

RHYS

RHYS: I burned my fucking turkey. How is that even possible? Don't these things have to cook for hours?

VIOLET: I'm sorry. I just pissed in my bikini laughing at you. I'll have to get back to you on that one.

RHYS: It's only noon and this day is a disaster.

VIOLET: If it makes you feel better, I forgot to thaw my chicken and have to eat a frozen burrito.

RHYS: No, it doesn't. It makes me sad. There are three other turkeys left for us. I'll save you some. We can have a picnic in bed.

VIOLET: A picnic in bed sounds kind of romantic.

RHYS: I can be romantic. I can do one even better. I heard a song while I was cooking and thought of you.

VIOLET: Really? You have a song for me?

RHYS: Yeah, with a kick ass guitar solo.

VIOLET: Uh huh. Send me the link.

RHYS: https://open.spotify.com/track/5gbxzSqAB-ThINGDb7vIiwe?si=386af290749a4f6f

Oh God, I was pretty picky with my music. I sat staring at the link, wondering what kind of music he could possibly be thinking of me to. I bit the bullet and clicked the link and damn near had a heart attack on the beach.

The man was a fucking miracle.

It was Thanksgiving and I couldn't get to him fast enough. Halloween—aka my birthday—had sucked as well. Christmas better damn well be good to me. After another day of sunbathing, I took to my favorite chair on the back deck and called my mother.

"Hi, Mom. Happy Thanksgiving," I said, hoping she didn't hear the sadness in my voice.

"Baby girl, I sure hope you are relaxing and enjoying yourself."

"I am. It's beautiful here, Mom," I noted, staring at the ocean as the waves rolled in and the sun blazed in the background, making it's descent.

"Good girl. Have you talked to Rhys?"

"Every day for hours. Mom, he's wonderful, like a truly amazing person." I felt my voice shake. Why the hell was I getting emotional?

"He is," she agreed, waiting for more.

"He has a son. A baby named—"

"Bryce, I know, honey. He told me in the hospital. He showed me a picture. He's got to be the most beautiful baby I've ever seen, aside from you, of course."

"Wait," I interrupted, "you knew about his son?" My whole body came alive in a jolt as she confessed to me.

"Yes, he told me he hadn't introduced you yet but would remedy that when you got home in one piece. That man is in love with you, Violet. I got to know him pretty well. It can happen when two people are worried sick and stuck in the same room together for hours."

He'd told my mom, which meant he had every intention of telling me. My heart filled then burst.

"Mom, remember when you told me I didn't need a man for anything?" The quiver in my voice returned, along with a burn in my throat.

"Of course."

"I think I need him," I said, wiping tears from my face. "That's why I'm here. I can't *stop* needing him."

"Oh, baby, you are in love with him. You *want* him. But if you had to do it alone again, could you?"

"Yes…no…I don't know. When it comes to him, he's got me pretty good," I said, burying my head in my free hand and trying desperately not to fall apart on the phone with her. She would only worry, when the truth was they were tears of relief.

"You are coming home early, aren't you?" She was smiling. I could tell.

"Yes, Mom."

"See you soon."

VIOLET: I'll be at your house in twenty minutes.

RHYS: Jesus, did you just send me another picture of you half-naked on the beach?

VIOLET: I took it yesterday.

I got no response.

My heart was pounding out of my chest. The entire plane ride all I could do was think about his smile, his laugh, his kiss, his touch. I knew so much more about him, and yet it seemed like useless details compared to…simply…the way we felt. When he and I were together the world fell away and I knew for certain this—*this*, what I was feeling right now—was the way you were supposed to feel when you fell in love. I pitied the previous me who had lived so long without it.

I all but ran through the airport, dragging my luggage like it was a nuisance. I couldn't remember ever wanting someone this bad. I had proven to myself that I was capable of being alone the last year of being married to Alex.

Now the truth of it was, life was just much fucking better with Rhys.

I would do this for me. I would allow myself to be happy. I would take a chance with Rhys and I would do it afraid.

I parked on his pavers next to his sedan and flew up his steps, running my fingers through my hair.

Suddenly the door was open and there he was. My chest was rising and falling as I took in Rhys. His forearm rested against the jam and he was leaning casually as he studied me. I heard the song he sent me playing in the background and my eyes filled. God, I was gone on this man. He took me in from head to foot and I couldn't move as he drowned me in a sea of gray.

"You're becoming very cheesy and romantic, *Sir*," I said, my voice raspy and breathless.

"What do you say we break the curse of these steps right now?" He took two steps forward and I was in his arms, his mouth covering mine with his kiss. We both moaned, desperately pulling and pushing with tongues and hands. And then I was in the air with my legs wrapped around him, holding on tight as he carried me into the house and up the stairs. As the music grew more intense, I buried my head in his neck, breathing him in. I had listened to the song at least a hundred times by now and felt every word. Soap and spice filled my nose and I moaned a hello as I welcomed it. He put me down on my feet at the top of the steps and stood back, taking off my shirt slowly. I stood with my breasts exposed and peaking for him as he slowly unbuttoned my jeans, keeping my eyes on his.

My lips parted as he slid them down my legs along with my panties and removed my shoes. I waited naked before him as he perused my body. He cupped a breast and moved his hand slowly up to my face, tracing the scar under my eye with his thumb. I let a tear escape me as his thumb slid up and down my cheek gently. He moved his other hand to my face and pulled me to him, capturing my mouth, thrusting his tongue deep. My knees buckled and he caught me, hooking my legs with his arms and taking me to his bedroom. He laid me on the bed and spread my legs, eyeing my drenched middle as he pulled his shirt over his head with one hand. Moving slowly, he tugged his jeans and briefs down, and then I was covered by his sculpted chest, his broad shoulders, and the face that had ruined me for all others. He slid his fingers inside me and I heard his groan. Grazing my clit lightly, his eyes filled with lust and I mourned the loss of his fingers as he pulled his hand away to remold and shape the contours of my body. His lips traced my front half, covering every inch of skin; then he turned me over and repeated his explorations with his lips and tongue. My limbs hummed as he turned me again, pulling me under him, spreading me out and massaging my thighs as he dipped his head and licked the divot in my neck. His tip was at my entrance and I gasped at the feel of him. He put my hand over his chest.

"This is home."

With one thrust I was gasping his name. He moved inside me, grinding his thick cock so hard I dug my nails in his shoulders roughly, wrapping my legs around him tight as I pulled him deeper. He traced the scar on my neck with his lips as he circled his hips, making love to me slowly but with so much friction, I was on edge. I ran my hands over his chest and down his arms as he lifted me with his strokes, his eyes telling me everything.

"Rhys," I whispered as his lips hovered above mine, my whole body shaking underneath him. He kissed me deeply, capturing the gasp from my orgasm and not letting me free. When my spasms subsided and he had no more breath to steal, he tore his mouth from mine. I looked up at him with everything in me and said the words that had been on the tip of my tongue that I could no longer keep inside. "I love you."

He closed his eyes and came.

RHYS

I had exhausted her last night before we finally took a bath together, passing out just before dawn. When I opened my eyes this morning, she had stolen my breath. I traced the curve of her hip with my fingertip. The scar on her cheek had healed beautifully. If I didn't know it was there, I might have missed it. The larger one on her neck was a beautiful shade of pink. I moved my fingers over it gently. I couldn't stop touching her. Her tan lines had me hard again as I traced every single one. Her hair was a little lighter than it was the last time I saw her. Her breathing was sweet and even, passing through the most perfect set of lips possible on a woman. I knew she was sleeping well and had to resist with everything I had to keep from waking her. I trailed my finger around her nipple and it pulled tight for me. She moaned before her lips slowly formed a smile.

"You were faking?" I said, smiling down at her as her eyes fluttered open.

"Only for the last few minutes," she whispered. I was instantly on her.

"You aren't tired of me yet?" She grinned as she opened up for me, wrapping her legs around my hips, urging me to sink into her.

I looked down at her beneath me and pulled her bottom lip into my mouth as I mumbled around it. "I really hope you don't have any other plans this weekend. Come here."

I pushed my need away and sat with my back to the headboard and pulled her onto my lap.

I placed her between my legs, facing away from me so I cradled her. Her breath hitched as I rubbed her nipples with my fingertips, burying my head in the side of her neck, tonguing it and pulling at the skin gently.

"Rhys," she begged as I opened her legs between mine, lifting them at the knee. I smoothed her stomach with my hands then brushed her sides gently with the backs of my fingers. She tilted her head back and moaned as she looked up at me. I took her mouth, thrusting my tongue in slowly. She kissed me more aggressively and I dipped my finger low and felt her growing wet. I grabbed her hand and brought it between her legs, tracing the tip of her clit lightly back and forth with her fingers. She gasped in my mouth then pulled away.

"Rhys, I can't," she said as she attempted to pull her hand from my grasp. I kissed her deeply and brought it back down, dipping her fingers inside and pulling it back up to her clit, making slow circles and pressing it tightly just where I knew it affected her the most. She gasped again and I knew she'd felt it. Her breathing picked up as her perfect breasts rose and fell with her spike of desire.

"Right there, move your fingers like this." I circled her fingers and she dropped her head back against my shoulder and started moving them as I'd told her. Her moans increased as she was pulled in by her own touch.

"Feel that, right there. Faster," I whispered in her ear as I guided her fingers, seeing the goose bumps form on her arms. She called out to me and I nearly lost my shit as my cock twitched. Fuck, this was perfect. I felt her legs begin to shake and let her hand go, rubbing up and down her sides and laving her neck with my tongue.

"Oh God, Rhys." Her voice was hoarse, letting me know she was on edge. I felt her body start to break. I bit her shoulder gently and she came, by her own hand, in my arms. I gripped the side of her head with my hand, pulling her hair and trailing kisses down her neck as she shuddered. She looked up at me, her eyes dazed.

"Do it again," I whispered to her. "For me, do it again." She lowered her hand and licked my lips as she continued to work her pussy. I felt the flex of her thighs as she moved her fingers faster and once again came apart in my embrace.

"Now let me drink it," I said, moving her off my lap and turning to hover above her. She looked up to me, wide-eyed.

"I told you so." I grinned before making my way down between her thighs to lap up her handiwork. She smiled and nodded as I kissed my way down, sucking and licking her until there was nothing left while she writhed beneath me.

VIOLET

I sat up in bed and stretched fully, my limbs weak from two days of endless lovemaking with a side of vicious fucking.

"Good morning." I looked to see Rhys staring up at me as he adjusted his head on the pillow to get a better look, gripping it behind him.

"Hi," I said, leaning over to kiss his beautiful face. He pulled me to his chest and ran a hand up and down my back.

"Stay another day. Bryce is coming home in a few hours." He held me close to his chest, caressing my face, my shoulder, and my arms.

"I want to, I do, but I need to get home, unpack. I promised my mother I would come have a late Thanksgiving with her. I don't want to interrupt your routine, either."

"You wouldn't be interrupting," he whispered, taking my mouth.

"Morning breath, Rhys, jeez, doesn't it bother you?" I covered my mouth with my hand.

"Nah, I like it dirty." He moved my hand and plunged his tongue into my mouth as I pushed at his chest, caving to his tender kiss.

An hour later, we were at his front door, and I was having a hard time keeping my clothes on. Every time I reached for my coat, we kissed again.

"You know you want to stay," he whispered as he brushed my hair away from my face.

"I feel like we've had this conversation before," I said, pulling him closer. I couldn't get close enough and it seemed neither could he. He smiled and reluctantly let me go.

"Be careful, and tell Pam I said hello."

"Yes, your new best friend and my mother. I'll make sure to let her know." I stood there as we grinned at each other and then I remembered my conversation with her. "You told my mother about Bryce, before you told me. Why didn't you mention that? I would have been a lot less hurt."

"I want you to believe *me*, especially when I tell you something important, Violet. *Me*. Not anyone else."

I nodded and turned the knob, looking back at him. "Why do I feel like if I leave the bubble will burst?"

"We had a rough start, but now we won't let anything shake us, right?" He leaned in and pressed a quick kiss to my lips.

"Right." I made my way down the steps, practically dancing, and gave him a wink as I turned to walk to my car. I got behind the wheel and buried my forehead on the top of the steering wheel, saying a late Thanksgiving prayer. I prayed like I was accepting an academy award. I couldn't believe my new reality. I heard my phone ping.

RHYS: What in the hell are you doing?

171

I looked up and saw him watching me from the porch. I turned crimson.

VIOLET: Gathering my thoughts, Rhys. A little privacy, please.

I watched him look at the message and smile.

RHYS: Were you talking to yourself?

VIOLET: No.

RHYS: I saw you talking to yourself.

VIOLET: If you must know, I was praying.

RHYS: Praying in my driveway?

He was laughing hysterically now and I laughed with him as I replied.

VIOLET: Don't you have anything better to do than spy on me?

RHYS: No, there's nothing better to do than you.

VIOLET: Cute. I'm leaving.

RHYS: Bye, beautiful.

I made it to my mother's and had the turkey and dressing I'd loved since I was a kid. It was amazing and a perfect end to my weekend. My all-knowing mother beamed at me throughout dinner, and questioned me in her roundabout way.

Thoughts of Rhys and our picnic in bed kept me warm on the drive home. Truly comfortable in my own house for the first time since my attack, I settled in that night, heart and stomach full. Right before I drifted to sleep, I got a picture.

It was of Rhys holding his sleeping son. Rhys was grinning, though he looked exhausted. Bryce had his little hands gripping his t-shirt, his eyes closed and mouth open, his long dark lashes covering half his chubby cheeks. The message attached said "Godzilla for sale."

⊗

RHYS

Caring for a woman was easy for me. I had always cared for different women for different reasons.

Loving a woman had always been quite a bit harder.

Doms don't have to say I love you.

I got my companionship and sexual satisfaction through my relationships with my subs, but in truth, I could never really classify them as *real* relationships. I had heard the words I love you out of a woman's mouth on more occasions than I'd ever cared to, mostly in bed. Making a woman come repeatedly had its disadvantages, especially if her feelings got involved and it wasn't mutual. And up until this point, it never had been.

Often they confused sexual chemistry with love, and I would have to break it off carefully once they confessed their affections. There was a fine line. I used to think I wasn't capable of loving a sub, until her...but when it ended the way it did with Bryce's mother, I was sure it was just poor judgment. She fascinated me with her wicked ways and what I once thought was so intriguing became what I was most disgusted by. Three years wasted on a woman who had almost taken my son's life before he'd had a chance. She was my past.

And that wasn't love.

Violet was my future and had given me a clear definition of how the real thing felt, though she was not at all the definition of a sub. She was a woman who was curious, much like I had been. I'd dated numerous women in my lifetime. Well, maybe dating was not a good word. I put my destructive demons to rest when I was twenty-one, learning the art of discipline and what coupling plea-sure and pain could do, how it could free you and if you weren't careful, how it could enslave you.

I never could kick the habit of being interested in the women I brought to valleys and peaks through sexual acts. I liked learn-ing what made them tick. I did the same things with Violet that I had with any other partner. I started off slow as I was taught, The Waltz. A little give and take, something to test the hard and soft limits, and Violet had loved every minute. I knew then I wanted her for my own. There was no way I was letting her go. And be-fore I knew it, she had gotten under my skin and crowded my thoughts more often than I was comfortable with. I became ad-dicted to her moans and smart mouth. I didn't want to see her, but I suddenly *needed* to. When we moved on, The Tango, I tested her hard limits. She seemed to have none, which shocked me. I was sure at times I would hear the word stop pass her lips. I spent long nights thinking about how a woman who had never experienced anything like what we were doing could endure so much. It was then that I realized she loved me and I prayed for the words not to come, because I wasn't sure where her head or heart was, or if we had a future at all.

Now those words were all I want to hear from her, and once she'd said them, I knew I had everything.

With Violet, it didn't matter how simple her reasons were. I was more fascinated by her than any other woman I'd ever met. She had no real demons to fight, no dark secrets. She just craved it, and I understood that craving. It used to drive me. Now I had another driving force: my son. And Violet was becoming a part of it all.

I was on my way out of the life when she came barging in with her new appetite and unrealistic expectations of what a Dom should be. I was selling the club, unattached, and completely free to be the respectable father I'd hoped to be.

All I had left to do to break free was sell the club and walk away. Now I found I had something to walk toward. And for the first time in my life, I hoped I'd be enough for a woman.

I started out her master, but I had already become her slave.

⊗

VIOLET

Christmas shopping with my mother was a nightmare. Thankfully Molly agreed to accompany us today to distract me. Mother was insistent on getting all her shopping done in a day. I found myself looking at items for Rhys and searching through the toy aisles in the store for Bryce, but had no idea if it was even appropriate at this point.

Last week had been a dream. I had spent a few days with Rhys, getting to know his son. Though Bryce seemed a bit weary of me at first, as if I was an intruder, he warmed up to me quickly.

I couldn't help but smile at the fact that the last time I left them Bryce's lip quivered slightly, as if he didn't want me to go. I refused to stay the night, though Rhys objected.

Sunday afternoon, Rhys had fallen asleep on the couch as Bryce and I played on the floor with his new Lego set. We spent the afternoon pulling out his arsenal of toys from his toy box as his father lay practically unconscious in a deep sleep he looked like he so desperately needed. When he woke, he looked up at us and shot to a sitting position, completely disoriented and started apologizing quickly.

"Rhys, we are fine," I insisted as I nodded over at Bryce, who was telling me about his very important plastic hammer. Rhys lay back down, watching us play, his hands on his chest with his head turned our way, looking to me then his son. His gray eyes told me he was hungry and I shook my head with a smile, giving my attention to the other new man in my life. I looked up every once in a while as

he watched us play, catching his stare and smiling. I knew for the first time he was thinking what I was.

This is happy.

"Earth to Violet," Molly said, holding up two pairs of earrings, to which I wrinkled my nose.

Buying a tie for Rhys seemed *too* impersonal, and though I had let the L word cross my lips, I wasn't sure how he would receive a Christmas gift. He had a completely different way of showing his affection that didn't involve sex. He never really vocalized his feelings and had only really opened up to me in my absence while visiting the Caymans. I had rushed into assuming he felt the same, and with each minute we spent together, I could feel his growing feelings, but couldn't be sure. I did purchase a few toys for Bryce, leaving the mystery of gift giving between me and my new beau open ended. I was going to see him tonight after a long few days of us failing to connect. I was kept late showing houses and Bryce had caught a cold. Rhys didn't want to chance us both getting sick. I eyed a bottle of men's cologne on the counter, wondering what type he used.

"So what are you getting him?" I looked up to see Molly smile at my mom who was questioning me and then eyeing me with interest.

"Mom, I swear, please go read someone else's mind. Does this ever bother Dad?"

"Are you and Rhys exchanging gifts? Are you thinking cologne? Is that his style?" Molly piped, amused at my discomfort. I looked to her with narrowed eyes. She knew more about the nature of my new relationship with Rhys due to a near full confession from me the week I got back from Grand Cayman, a confession I was regretting at that very moment. The tone in her voice mocked the manner in which her question was asked. What I heard from her was "Wouldn't he much prefer a new whip?" Molly was a petite brunette with big blue eyes. She looked far more innocent than she was, and played it to her advantage.

Molly smiled as she lifted a shirt off a rack and I shook my head at her. Her tiny frame glided quickly through the aisle as I picked up the remains of the end caps I knocked over as I passed through, my ass having a mind of its own. The store was a madhouse and I was thoroughly unnerved at the goings on. My mother seemed fit for the race, and Molly appeared oblivious. My mother lifted a man's sweater and I shook my head again.

"Mom, I don't really know if it's appropriate yet."

"It's a sweater, Violet," she said, giving me a strange look, "and honestly, I don't know why you mask your feelings for him. The feeling is mutual between the two of you."

"That's just it, Mom. I mean, I think so, but I'm not sure." I shrugged my shoulders as they both eyed me.

"Then take a chance and buy him a noncommittal sweater." She moved her eyebrows up and down as I yanked it out of her hands. It really was a nice sweater, gray to match his eyes.

"So what's the hold up, dear daughter?" she continued, plucking clothes off the rack to eye them. "At Thanksgiving you couldn't live without him."

"There's *no* hold up. He's just not very vocal with his feelings and I have been nothing but. It's humiliating but I can't shut up. I assume he will tell me how he feels when he is ready, and in a way, he already has—"

"In many ways, I'm sure," Molly added then held her hands up defensively when I took a step toward her, my eyes saying as much as my body language. I sighed as I addressed my mother again. "Anyway, I would just feel better if I knew for sure he was feeling the same."

My mother looked to Molly then to me, as if she needed back up. "Men are always slow to come around. You have only been dating a few months. He loves you, and I know it. Just give it a little time."

I put both hands on my face, embarrassed by the conversation. "God, it's disgusting. I'm being needy. Two weeks divorced and I'm needy."

"Your mom is right, Violet, but don't beat yourself up. You are a woman. The minute we meet a decent man and have a good orgasm, we start planning the wedding. Whoops, fuck, I'm sorry, Mrs. Hale."

"About which part?" she said, grinning at Molly. She knew better than to get through a day with Molly unscathed.

I shook my head at the both of them. "Let's talk about something else."

"No," Molly said, looking pointedly at me, her lips pursing. "You are the only one who has a new hot boyfriend."

"Amen," my mother said in agreement as they looked at me expectantly.

"I'm leaving," I decided quickly. "Why don't you too speculate on my life while I go live it?" I snatched Rhys's new sweater and Bryce's toys out of the cart as they both protested my announcement.

They shared a smile, and I knew the minute I walked out of the store that they would do just that. I had to let go of my need for constant reassurance. I knew where it stemmed from and I wouldn't let my past win.

A day of shopping, a sweater, and some toys richer, I had a date to get to.

I quickly texted Rhys.

VIOLET: I could use some RED.

RHYS: That could be arranged.

VIOLET: It can wait. I would rather hold that baby.

RHYS: Not tonight. He's at his aunt's until tomorrow morning.

VIOLET: Damn it, Rhys.

RHYS: Pussy here, now!

An hour later, I was at his door. We had agreed to meet at his house since Bryce would be delivered bright and early tomorrow. He opened it quickly after I knocked and pulled me to him. I wrapped my arms around him and kissed him hard on the mouth.

"Missed me, huh?" he said, his tone cocky.

"I bought you something," I said, thrusting the shopping bag in his face. Gift-wrapping—I had decided—would be over doing it, and since technically it wasn't Christmas, I had nothing to be worried about. I had covered my bases.

He looked at me with puzzlement as I reached in and pulled the sweater out.

"Violet?"

"If you don't like it, I can get you some cologne or bath salts... shit," I said, feeling embarrassed and racing to his kitchen to get some wine.

He chuckled as he followed me. "There's nothing wrong with the sweater. It's just the manner in which it was presented. You threw it at my head, are you sure you want to part with it?"

I pulled out a bottle and quickly served myself a glass as he studied me. He looked gorgeous in his dark jeans and black, fitted long sleeve t-shirt. His hair was perfectly styled. He was still holding the sweater as he perused me. His eyes held his question, not wavering as they blurred briefly through the lift of my glass. I swallowed more before I braved an answer.

"Sorry, I spent the day with my mother," I said, turning to his kitchen drawer behind me, rummaging through it to find a stopper for the wine.

"Uh huh," he said, inching closer.

"Well, she's crazy. She makes me a little crazy," I offered, waving my hands around like a crazy person.

"Don't need much help there," he said, stepping in front of me, stopping my fidgeting.

"Do you want to get laid tonight?" I said testily.

He paused, studying me, his eyes growing dark. "As if you have a choice," he said an inch away from me. His eyes were amused but his jaw was set. I felt a shiver run through me.

"How about a tour? I never really got one of upstairs. Show me Bryce's room." He looked back at me with confusion as I started toward the stairs, rattling on and on about my day.

My insecurity in the lead, I pounded up the steps and down the hall, searching for Bryce's room. I didn't want to spout off about feelings and the nature of our relationship. I wished I had never vocalized my concerns to my mother and Molly, leaving the thoughts in the forefront of my mind. I heard Rhys approach behind me as I turned the knob to a room, finding it filled with a queen bed fit for a guest. With the next turn of the knob, I found myself standing in the baby's room, surrounded by all things Bryce. I walked to his rocker and picked up his teddy bear, holding it in my hands as I studied the pictures on a shelf above his changing table. They were all of the two of them from day one. I envied Rhys being a parent.

I felt his hands on my shoulders.

"He was a pretty newborn. Most newborns aren't that pretty, did you know that?" I said, turning to Rhys who was watching me. He eyed the picture I was referring to and nodded.

"How old was he here?" I asked, taking a step out of his arms to scrutinize the next photo.

"Well, the frame says six months, Violet." He chuckled behind me.

"Oh, yeah," I said placing his teddy in his crib. "It's a beautiful room."

"Why don't you want me to touch you?" he said, turning me to face him.

"I just need you to take it tonight, Rhys. Can you do that?" He pulled me roughly to him, making me cry out.

"With pleasure," he said, his need growing evident against me. "Then again, what the hell is your problem?"

"Nothing, just do it, okay? I need you to not be the nice guy right now...Is that so fucking hard? Do you think you can handle that?" His eyes glazed as his jaw hardened. He looked down at me, the confusion leaving his eyes and his determination setting in. The air shifted and I was suddenly slightly on edge.

He turned me around and lifted my skirt, tearing off my panties in one swift movement, his breath on my neck sending a shiver down my spine. "You seemed to have forgotten who you are talking to. Go to my room, undress."

Naked in his bed, I waited. I heard nothing, which worried me. I should apologize. I didn't want to ruin our night with my nervous shit. Things were going so well between us; I didn't understand why I just couldn't embrace it.

I'd been bold with him before, rude even, and each time my reception was met with the same distaste and amazing payback.

You lost your cool, worried about his reaction to a sweater, jackass.

"Turn over on your stomach and put your face in the mattress." I jumped at his voice and looked up at him. He had taken off his shirt but kept his jeans on. He looked ridiculously sexy, but the air of him had changed into something I was familiar with, something I hadn't seen in a while. Leaning against the door, he held his black bag.

"Rhys, I'm sorry. I shouldn't have taken my day out on you."

A slow, sardonic smile spread across his face. "No, you really shouldn't have."

I rolled over on my stomach as I was told, my pulse kicking out of control. This could go really bad for me...or the opposite. I buried my head in the mattress with a groan. The silence in the room was suddenly filled with music as Rhys cradled his iPod in the station on his nightstand and busied himself around me. I lay waiting and naked, not saying a word. Anticipation fluttered around in my stomach, every nerve in my body coming to attention.

I felt the bed sink with his weight, his breath hot on my neck. "You are going to watch me fuck you tonight, Violet, so you remember—" He leaned down closer to my ear "—that I'm the man who makes you come." The words rolled off his tongue like a threat made of silk. "And I'm the one who can take it away." I felt the bed dip again as my flesh became covered in goose bumps. If he'd wanted me on edge, I was there.

"Get on the table." I looked up from the mattress to see he had set up a black massage table at the foot of the bed, except this one was much larger and had straps at the top and bottom of it.

Restraints. Oh my!

"Face down," he said as I rose slowly from the bed. I immediately did as I was told as I took in Rhys's naked form. I admired him for mere seconds when his hand came down hard in a punishing slap on my backside, fire in his eyes. I shifted my eyes from his and got on the table fast. When I put my face into the headrest, I noticed a screen the size of a small TV beneath me and on it my bare ass on the table. I raised my head quickly to see Rhys behind me holding a small camera and setting up another.

Oh my God.

I planted my face back in the rest, watching Rhys as he dug a small tasseled whip out of his black bag.

He strapped in my wrists as I stared at the screen, watching his beautiful body as he hovered over me.

"You make a sound and you don't come," he said, firmly trailing the soft leather down my ass to my toes. He did this repeatedly for several minutes as I watched, trying to stifle my moans.

A shift on the screen let me know he grabbed the camera again as he ordered me to spread my legs. Once I did, I saw my whole sex on screen as his tongue met it. I was on fire immediately, unable to make a sound as I watched my lover eat me, lick me, slide his fingers inside of me. Watching his lips pull at my clit, his tongue cover me, it was the most erotic thing I'd ever seen. My chest heaved as he teased my pussy, darting his tongue in and out until I was clawing the top of the table in an attempt not to make a sound. He pulled his mouth away as I again saw the tassels of a tiny whip trail down the back of my ass. Before I could register the sound, the sting hit me and I screamed out.

"One minute, Violet," he chided as the whip came down. "It took one minute for you to take your own pleasure away."

Another switch on screen had me seeing the both of us, Rhys behind me, pumping his cock with his hand. "You wanted me to just take it." My mouth watered as he pumped his fist around himself, taunting me.

"Is this what you want?" he hissed and I moaned in response. "Lucky for you, I'm feeling generous."

Unhooking my straps and pulling me to the end of the table, he put the small screen in my hands. I watched as he stroked himself while smoothing my skin with his other hand.

"Taking it means it's all for me, Violet." With that, he slammed his length into me as I gripped the monitor. He pulled out to the head as I protested. "This cock does not take orders, Violet." He pushed in again all the way as I watched him bury himself in my folds then stopped again suddenly. Swiping my wetness with his fingers, he held it up to the camera. I moaned as he reached around, shoving his fingers in my mouth. I bit down on them as he thrust back inside, ramming me so hard my eyes watered. My swollen pussy protested as he again took his dick away, making me beg.

"Don't beg tonight, won't work." He parted my legs further and I saw my swollen backside as he took special care to angle the camera on me. He brought the whip down again and I screamed out in pleasure as one of the tassels hit my sex. My adrenaline running high, the sensation completely foreign to me, I pushed my ass out to urge him to do it again.

"Can I fucking handle you, Violet?" he brought it down again, gentler this time, landing it right on my sex as my head slumped and perspiration dropped onto the screen.

OH MY GOD.

He leaned in then and licked and sucked and teased my clit, never giving me enough to let go as I pumped my hips up and down in a vain attempt to help myself. As I was close, the whip teased me again with a sting.

"Greedy little pussy," he growled as he traded his whip for his hand that now came down hard on my ass. I moaned at the arrival of more heat, helping to ease my frustration. For the first time ever, I wanted more of his hand. I pushed my hips out as I watched his hand come down again, leaving a bright pink mark on my already sensitive skin.

In my mind all I could do was think 'please do it again,' although I couldn't utter a single word.

He buried his face inside me then, his nose nudging my puckered back entrance as his tongue lapped me up. I shook with anticipation but he refused to take me there. I screamed out in frustration as I rolled my hips.

"I think I can fucking handle you." Another slap had my insides coiling. I almost came then and was shocked at the sudden realization that another slap may be the very thing to set me off. His huge shaft bobbed at my entrance again as I clenched in anticipation, knowing that the first thrust of his cock would ignite me. He took his time sliding into me as I watched us connect, completely consumed by his dick filling my pussy. Once buried, he reached around and pinched my nipples. I came so hard that tears sprang to my eyes and my voice went hoarse with my scream. Rhys dropped the camera and pulled my hair hard, using it to center himself and ram into me.

"Again!" His hand came down in a series of hard slaps as I bucked beneath him, succumbing to his will, pulsating and squeezing his cock. I was dizzy with lust, completely drunk on the sensations as he took me higher and higher, slamming his hips against the table, his girth into me.

"Fuck yes," he hissed as he gripped the top of my shoulders, pulling me to him hard, his fucking vicious and unforgiving. I felt his dick twitch as he spilled himself onto my back and branded my ass with one last hard slap.

⸎

"Rhys, please, please, please!" I begged as he put the piece of ice inside me, letting it melt and numbing me further. I was on my back now, completely strapped down as Rhys hovered above me. I couldn't stop shaking, the numbing sensation keeping me from letting go. As soon as he licked me enough to warm me back up, he was rubbing another piece onto my clit to keep me numb. I was spread wide before him as he teased me with his mouth. I could only twist and writhe underneath him. As the numbness wore off, I begged again.

"Rhys, I can't take it," I said, meeting his unforgiving eyes.

"You know the word, Violet," he murmured, taking another drink from my insides as the cool juice from the ice leaked out. He held the cup in his hand, shaking the ice that remained, his beautiful naked chest hovering over me as he alternated using the ice between his teeth to numb my nipples and then drifting down to my clit. He thumped my numb center painfully and I screamed out in fury, knowing I would never say the word. I knew relief was coming as he knelt before me, sucking my lips and warming my center with his tongue. He spread me wider as he tasted me and I pulsed with pleasure. When he pulled away, my arousal on his face, he licked his lips clean. "Delicious."

I would never ever say the word.

Hours later, in his arms and in bed fully sated, I looked up to see him smiling.

"What the hell are you smiling about?" I said, smiling with him though I didn't know the reason.

"That was more than I have ever put any woman through in one night, and you," he said, lifting me onto his chest, "Violet, you should never have been able to endure all that." He chuckled again. "I was determined to make you say stop." He laughed again as I punched his chest.

"I am sure that isn't true, I mean, come on," I said rolling my eyes.

"No, really, you are a true freak," he said, burying his face in my hair.

"You are such a bastard," I said, my face turning red as I thought of the hell I had to endure with the ice. Then it occurred to me to ask.

"How many pieces, Rhys, have the others stopped at?" He looked at me, fearful now as his chuckle slowed. "How many!"

"Two was the most, until you."

"And how many did you use on me, Rhys?" I asked, my voice a high-pitched squeak.

"Five," he said, bursting out laughing. I punched him hard in the chest as I tried to escape the bed. He pulled me back down, cradling my face as I cursed him for everything he was worth.

"Wow, you have got one hell of a mouth on you, sailor."

"I can't believe you did that to me!" I grumbled as he kissed my neck and nose and chin, chuckling.

He pulled back, incredulous. "I can't believe you let me!"

"Well, you are the one in control!" I said defensively.

"And I have never been so convinced," he said, hysterical as I pushed at his chest to break free.

"Not funny!"

"The word is submit, Violet," he murmured, laying me beneath him and positioning himself between my legs. "You don't get points for high tolerance." He rubbed his stubble over my already sore nipples as I sucked in air through my teeth, the pain subsiding when his tongue covered me.

"Please tell me you are going to erase that video," I said, suddenly terrified he might have more with someone else.

"That was Bryce's nanny cam and baby monitor. It was a one time only live show," he chuckled as my eyes widened.

"Wow, that's pretty creative," I said, lowering my hand and wrapping it around his thickness.

"Genius, if you ask me," he replied, his voice growing hoarse with his budding desire.

"I still can't believe you did that to me," I said, jerking his hard dick in my hand as he made his way between my thighs and I became lost in the circle of his hips at my entrance. "Make it up to me."

He lifted his head and met my eyes with a sincerity I now lived for. "Anything for you."

I felt pressure on my stomach and quickly opened my eyes. Rhys had sat Bryce on me, straddling me as he tapped on my chest saying, "Up, up." He looked at his father, who was encouraging him, and I laughed at them both. He was absolutely adorable. His hands were chubby and his knuckles barely visible except for the small dimples in between his fingers. He had on long pajamas and his diaper was sticking out of the back of them. His beautiful gray eyes matched Rhys's color perfectly. His lashes were long and black and made his eyes sparkle. He was a dream to look at. His cheeks looked stuffed and his voice came out in a squeak.

"Up, up, gee up," he said, bringing his tiny fists down lightly on my stomach, making me laugh harder.

"I'm up," I said, smiling at him as I put my hands on his hips to make sure he went nowhere.

Bryce leaned in with a smile and opened his mouth, a small amount of drool escaping him as he covered my chin in a wet kiss. I laughed with my whole heart and looked over to Rhys who was staring at us with a grin.

"Good morning," I said to Rhys, who was leaning in to do a better job of kissing me than his son. I gave Rhys my lips as Bryce bounced up and down on my stomach, jolting me quickly out of my bliss. I felt a tug on my hair and opened my eyes to see the baby had grabbed handfuls of my hair and was pulling it so hard my eyes teared up. I cried out, a little stunned, and Rhys pulled back with an, "Oh shit," and grabbed his son's hands and unclamped my hair.

"I told you. Godzilla," he said carefully, giving my hair back to me.

"No big deal," I said, grabbing Bryce's hands, terrified he would do it again. That shit hurt. I sat up, grabbed the baby and walked him down the stairs.

"You hungry?" I murmured to the top of Bryce's head as he jibber jabbered, waving to his father behind me.

"We ate. It's almost noon...loser," Rhys said behind me in jest.

"Well, I was exhausted. And I wonder why?"

"You will be tomorrow, too," he promised as we hit the foot of the stairs.

I went to the kitchen, set my buddy down, and grabbed some juice from the fridge. Bryce went straight to his toy box to destroy it.

I turned on Rhys as my eyes lingered on his son. "I think it's time you tell me." Rhys stiffened at my remark, but played clueless.

"About what?" he said, grabbing a glass from the cabinet and pouring his own juice.

"Her. I want to know."

He took a long drink and swallowed hard. "Nothing to tell. She isn't worth talking about."

"You promised," I warned.

"Okay," he said hesitantly. "She was dirty, conniving, and diabolical."

"More," I said, taking his glass from him so he couldn't cover his mouth with it.

He smirked and stood at the counter, legs crossed as he eyed his son over my shoulder.

"Rhys," I said, crossing my arms and jutting out my hip.

"The club was hers," he said, his attention on me, studying my reaction. When I gave none, he continued. "She was a matchmaker and opened it for that purpose specifically."

"She was like a madam of the lifestyle?" I asked, intrigued.

"Yes, but she did it for her own selfish reasons, too, the evil bitch. Crap," he said, lowering his voice so his son didn't hear him curse. "That's twice today." He sighed. "I met her at The Barracks. That was the original place that we had to go to. She was looking for new business. The Barracks was the place for most of the originals, and for a lot of years that was home to me as far as a meeting place for subs. When she opened The Rabbit Hole, a lot of the regulars from The Barracks flocked to it, but the reason I did was because of her. She intrigued me. She was very matter of fact, to the point. I knew she wanted me, but what I didn't know was the price I would pay for my curiosity."

"Okay," I said, having a hard time keeping the jealous edge out of my voice.

"You're jealous," he said, picking up on it immediately with a smug grin.

"You're stalling," I said, annoyed he knew me so well.

"I had been doing the Dom/sub thing for some time when I met her. I was kind of growing numb to some of it. I was—"

"Bored," I stated and he nodded.

"She was sick, and when I say sick, I mean she would make it her mission to ruin the lives of others. If she saw someone she wanted or someone else's sub she had her eye on, she would go all out to make it happen."

"Wait," I said, my mind reeling, "are you telling me you were her sub?" My eyes widened and I felt a little bit of my excitement for Rhys stifle.

"Fuck no," he said sternly, which tickled me and made me want to cross the distance between us.

I hopped on the counter facing him and started to pull my t-shirt down to cover my underwear.

"Don't cover it up. He can't see, but I want to," he said heatedly.

"Um, no," I said, pulling it down further as he rolled his eyes. "Okay, so she wasn't the motherly type?"

"You're skipping ahead, which is fine with me, but—"

"No, no, finish. I'm sorry. Shutting up now," I said, begging him to continue.

"She was versatile and I was pure Dom, so she insisted we work together to make the club better. We ended up tangled in a mess of our own shortly after the opening and kind of became exclusive."

"So you fell in love?" I said, my eyes hitting his chest. I couldn't look at him when he told me he loved someone else. It was immature on my part, but I couldn't do it.

"No, I fell victim." His voice was now low with a hard edge. "Remember the thousand ways I told you things could go wrong in this lifestyle? She made sure to cause nine hundred of them between us, between other couples at the club, before I finally broke free. She was so subtle about what she did, and I have to admit, I let myself get sucked into it for a while. When I couldn't handle her games anymore and I broke it off, she ended up pregnant and I had to—"

"What?" I said, praying he wouldn't stop.

He hesitated before he looked straight at me. "She was extreme and I mean extreme. She liked to be flogged, and often. It's not for everyone. She liked a lot of things that I had an issue with. She wanted to be bled, raped, tortured, beaten in different ways, and I didn't have the stomach for it. When I wouldn't do it, she would find someone who would. Basically, during the pregnancy, I found her in several situations that you would never want to see any woman in. When she was five months along, I found her gagged and beaten badly at the club. She was bleeding from every orifice of her body. The guy had pissed on her before he left. I wanted to finish the job he'd started and knew then I had to break free. That was the night I decided I wanted out of the club. I almost filed a suit against her and that's when we struck a deal."

"Which was?" I asked.

"I would have to take care of her until she delivered."

"Take care of her?" I asked, even though I knew the answer.

"Violet, don't make me go any further."

"I won't," I said, convinced I couldn't hear any more. "Sexually, you had to take care of her sexually. I get it. Why did you have the vasectomy?"

"She demanded I get one. I think she thought Bryce wouldn't make it to term. She wanted me sterile for putting her through the task of carrying him. I don't really know all her reasons, but they were always for control, the one thing she never really had over me until she got pregnant. I damn sure didn't want the procedure. She had me at her complete mercy. I guess she assumed that after the baby was born we would continue our situation. I had to look out for my son. She didn't care at all about his wellbeing. She moved in with me at my insistence, and I did whatever she wanted within reason to keep her sated enough to have him. When he was born, she didn't look at him, not once. She had moved out a week before she delivered, after I told her she would never have me again. I had my son and I didn't want a damn thing from her. He was healthy and I could finally breathe again. Her career was starting to take off and she had alienated most of the regulars at The Rabbit Hole, so she signed over the club to me as a kind of payoff. I didn't want it at first, but she insisted, saying I wasn't going to get her for child support later, so we made another deal. She signed away her rights and I would take the club."

"Jesus," I said, looking over at Bryce, who looked back at us as we stared at him.

"You would never suspect her to be this way in passing. The way people hide who they truly are sometimes is fascinating. She was beautiful, smart, articulate, and deep down, the most disgusting human I have ever known," he said, gripping the counter top behind him. "When he was born, I ordered a paternity test just to confirm. I didn't want to challenge her while she was pregnant and give her a good excuse to abort. I went through hell, but for good reason," he said, looking over my shoulder at Bryce.

"Oh, he's all you," I said, waving at him as he banged on his Play-doh workshop with a plastic hammer.

Rhys grinned. "Don't I know it." I turned to him and watched him watch his son.

"Whatever you had to do, you did good, and here he is," I said, beaming at Bryce as he banged away with his hammer.

WINTER

CHRISTMAS EVE

I t had been an amazing month filled with endless nights of laughter, sex, large amounts of quality time with Bryce, and we were just scratching the surface. We had started something real, something tangible, and something meaningful. I was becoming more and more comfortable with our unusual new dynamic, and Rhys made sure to shake things up a bit in the bedroom. He had finally sold the club and tonight was going to be his last night as the owner. He had found buyers who intended on taking it over as the kink haven it was meant to be. The older, experienced couple who frequented the club couldn't bear to lose one of the only available and safe places for those like me to explore their sexuality. I'd met them the day the sale closed and was thrilled about the fact that the curious, those who needed guidance and direction into the unknown, would find their refuge at The Rabbit Hole like I had.

I had come here for a sexual revolution and ended up with much, much more.

I had found refuge from my failed false start in the arms of a dominating and caring man. One I loved so feverishly, everyday thoughts of him were torturous. A man who had captured my heart, body, and mind, and I had no hope of fighting it. I didn't want to. It seemed like neither of our thirsts for each other would ever be quenched. We spent our days fighting the world and our nights taking our stresses out on each other in the most amazing way.

I had just received notice that I would have to face my attacker in court the first week of the new year, and other than the stress of having to face the monster who had almost ended the life I had just really started to live it, I couldn't be happier.

It was still light out when I entered the club to greet Tara. I knew that Rhys would be here for at least an hour or so before picking up Bryce and taking him to his family's house for the holiday, so I texted him to make sure he was here. This was our meeting place, after all; it held a small amount of sentimental value, though our relationship had developed beyond just sex. I told him I would be busy with friends and family on Christmas Eve to throw him. My intentions were to make his last night as the club owner memorable.

His reaction to my sudden appearance, the parting of his lips, let me know he was completely shocked as I closed his office door behind me. I removed my jacket, revealing the red leather lingerie I had purchased on Halloween. The one I promised he would see.

I had gone all out, crimping my hair and styling it wildly, painting my face like an old school pinup. My lips were a glowing red and my leather corset pushed my exposed breasts up, making my drawn tight nipples an immediate focal point. I had purchased some spiked leather heels and wrapped my neck in a thin strip of black velvet accompanied by small chains.

"Merry Christmas, Rhys," I whispered seductively as he took me in from head to toe. His gray eyes sparked with fire as his gaze started at my eyes then drifted to my lips, then down to my spiked feet. A slow smile spread over his face as he watched me. He made no orders, and I knew then I was in control. He was going to let me have it.

Merry Christmas to me!

"Sit the fuck down. I want your cock in my mouth," I ordered without hesitation. I was all too ready to run this show. He lifted his brow, a small smile forming on his lips, but obliged by sitting quickly, his eyes trained on mine. I walked over to his seat and stood in front of him, barking my next command. "Don't touch me, not once or you won't get my pretty pink pussy tonight."

He smirked as I stood before him, pulling at his pants roughly to free him. He was rock hard and I saw his tip glisten as I pumped it with my fist and licked the moisture, leaving the rest of him throbbing.

"I need this hard cock inside me, but maybe I should show you first what you get." His eyes widened as I pulled the bottoms down, revealing my bare, soaked center to him. I spread my folds with my fingers and gilded them up and down. I was drenched in anticipation and brought the moisture up to his mouth. He opened wide and I took the fingers out of his grasp.

"Why should I give this to you? You think you deserve this?" I sneered, standing closer to him, my swollen middle inches from his face. I heard him groan and saw his cock twitch. I became more excited as his breathing picked up.

"You want this?" I held the slickness of my sex under his nose and saw his eyes meet mine with fury for teasing him. Rhys loved my scent, my taste, and told me daily. I was sure this was the first time he had ever been dominated. I was taking my gift seriously. I shoved my fingers between his parted lips.

"Suck it good or you don't get anymore, Rhys." His tongue darted out, capturing my fingers and pulling them into his mouth, sucking mercilessly. I tapped his nose roughly when I almost lost my cool.

"That's enough," I said, surprised at the command in my own voice. Even he seemed a little surprised at my sudden niche for dominance.

"Hmm, what to do," I said, circling his chair, his cock now purple and pulsing, eyes fucking me with his stare. "Tell me, Rhys, am I the best you've ever had? We both know what a little whore you've been." I almost laughed at my own question but his gaze and next words only made me more determined.

"Why don't you bring it to me and I'll tell you." His voice was threatening and it took all my strength not to do what he asked.

"You don't make the rules here," I said, sliding off my top then pulling his body down so he was almost lying down in his chair. I straddled his legs as my pussy grazed his dick and my nipples brushed his nose, a breath from his lips. His breathing hitched as he licked his lips and his eyes rolled slightly at the way my wet pussy glided back and forth on his dick.

"Pretty vanilla, Rhys, don't you think?" I said, turning around so that my center was still touching the head of him and my ass was close to his nose.

"Fuck," he whispered as I rubbed the head of him between my folds and reached down to cup his balls.

"You want to touch me?" I said, losing myself as my center contracted at the feel of his thick head. "I'll give you an inch." I slid down, taking his cock in my hot middle, taking only the promised inch, and heard him curse more as he kept his hands to his sides. I reveled in the sensation as I rocked that inch in and out, teasing him.

"Nah," I said, pulling up and turning his chair so he was facing his desk. I sat on the edge, propping my feet up to give him a clear view of my sex. He looked on, his eyes tortured as I bared myself to him. "I don't think you're ready for me. I'm not *feeling* it, Rhys. Maybe I should just lie back and fuck myself." And I did. I spread my legs before his face as I lay on his desk. I heard another moan and knew I had him right where I wanted him. My heels looked wicked on the armrests of his chair as they supported my legs. I lifted my ass to bring my middle closer to him as I plunged my fingers in.

"Violet, fuck." His breath hit my pussy and I damn near went over the edge. I stopped my fingers and looked up at him. His eyes were deadly. I had brought out RED Rhys.

GO ME!

"Did I say you could fucking talk?" I smiled as he stared at my center and inched closer. "Don't move!" I licked my fingers and brought them back down to play with my clit the way he had shown me. I could hear the slickness as I moved my fingers in and out and up and down. I felt the pull and knew I was close. My chest heaved, my breast heavy as I moved my fingers faster, watching him take all of me in, his eyes on fire and turning black with his arousal. I stopped just as I was about to come and heard him growl in protest.

I was shocked as I watched his chest move up and down. I was completely floored at how much my little show had gotten to him. I sat up quickly, brushing my straining nipples across his face.

"You get what I give," I bit out as I kneeled before him, my own need beginning to interfere with my control. Our eyes locked and his pleaded with me as I grabbed his pulsing cock in my hands and stroked it. His breathing was erratic as I swallowed him whole and he jerked in my mouth. I moaned as I sucked hard, tasting another burst of pre-cum and pressing my lips hard around his thickness.

His breath hissed between his teeth as he held onto his chair arms, his knuckles white.

"I just want a taste," I said, taking him down to his base. I opened my throat, taking him deeper, and felt him stiffen. He was close. "Don't you dare come," I hissed as I worked even harder to pull out his release. A few strokes later, he was covered in sweat, having lost all control. I gave him a knowing smile. I released him from my mouth and heard him moan again as I stood.

"Fuck me," I ordered.

He stood quickly and grabbed my throat, squeezing roughly as his mouth came crashing down to mine. Our tongues thrust together as we fought a war for control and both lost. I gasped as he pulled my ass apart, separating and kneading me roughly, pulling my body to his erection. He let go as I strained to keep our kiss and put me back on his desk, laying me down and burying his head between my thighs, licking my ass repeatedly and devouring my pussy. I screamed out as he thrust his fingers in me, eating me like I was his last meal. He plunged his fingers in and out and fucked me ruthlessly with them as he licked and sucked my clit, drawing my orgasm quickly. I erupted, my legs shaking and my entire body exploding in sensation as he continued his assault well after I finished.

"Fuck, yes, Rhys, fuck," I screamed as I came again minutes later, feeling the warmth slide down as his tongue quickly lapped it up. When the wave subsided, he plunged his tongue in deep, pulling my ass off the desk as he swirled it inside of me. My ass fell back to the desk and I looked up to see him stand over me, his black eyes crazy with desire. He stripped off his shirt, revealing his glistening chest. Once naked, he used both hands, worked them over my body, touching every inch as I moaned and writhed beneath him.

"You're perfect, and you're *mine*, Violet." He pumped his dick with his fist and put it at my entrance, leaning over me to taste my lips. Once satisfied with my lips, he buried his huge cock inside of me, filling me so full my whole body seized. Hooking my legs over his shoulders, he took me roughly. His thrusts were of a man possessed as he branded my body with his hands, touching me everywhere.

Near his release, he pulled me onto his lap, never losing our connection. I placed my hands behind me on his thighs as my legs spread wide over his armrests. He cradled my ass as he pumped his thick cock inside and we got lost in each other. He leaned in, kissing my lips as he stroked my pussy with his length. I pushed off of his thighs, angling my hips so he touched me deeper and felt the tip of him stroke my g-spot.

"I'm going to come again, Rhys. Come with me," I pleaded as my body started to shake. One more stroke and I was convulsing, singing his praises as he licked my lips and spilled into me, pumping faster as we rode it out together.

I brought my legs down on either side of him, tucking them under my thighs as I buried my head in his chest. Minutes passed as we held each other, covered in the evidence of our need. I looked up to him, his lips smeared with red, his breathing still heavy as he smiled down at me.

"I hope you enjoyed your present because that shit is NEVER happening again."

"Aww, come on. You liked it," I said, running my fingers through his damp black hair.

"Never again. This is my body to touch, my pussy to lick, and these are my fucking lips to take." He leaned in again, drawing my bruised lips into his mouth and sucking.

"Fine." I pulled away as he dipped back in. "But, I know you liked it." He nodded his head yes then shook it to toy with me as I hugged him tightly. I looked at the security screen over his shoulder and froze.

Sensing the tension in my body, Rhys asked, "What is it?" He pulled back to look at my face. I locked my arms to keep him from doing so.

"Violet, what's wrong?" he asked again, concern in his voice.

On the screen, I saw Alex walking in with a couple, a smile on his face. He was taking off the woman's coat, and I narrowed my eyes to get a look at her.

Sandra.

Rhys stood still, locked in my grip around him as my legs hit the floor. He pulled out of my grasp easily and demanded an answer.

"Violet, what the hell?" he asked, jolting me out of my stupor.

"It's Alex. He's here."

Rhys stiffened at my confession and turned to look at the monitor. His eyes went cold as he studied the screen. I looked up to see his jaw twitch. His expression was murderous.

Baffled and beyond shocked, I quickly started rambling.

"I don't know how the hell he found this place, but this shit is not okay," I said, scooping up my jacket and fastening it quickly. "I'll take care of this, Rhys. Seriously, don't be upset. I can't even begin to imagine how he even knew of a place like this."

Rhys buckled his belt and smoothed down his tie, his expression unreadable, but his eyes holding more contempt than I'd ever seen. He moved to the door quickly as I straightened my hair. I barely caught the words as he walked out.

"It's not him. It's her." I looked at the security screen filled with Sandra and the realization almost brought me to my knees...Click.

VOLUME FOUR

CURTAINS

RHYS

The Barracks. Four years ago...

Perfect, another damn sub gone due to my inability to emotionally commit. My reluctance to be more intimate had ruined yet another year of training. I'd had her just where I wanted her. She was completely responsive and obedient. Just as my time and patience were paying off, she insisted she wanted more.

FUCK.

"You won't even try with me, Rhys!" she cried as she buttoned her blouse.

"Jill, I told you everything up front, made absolutely sure you heard and understood me, did I not?" I couldn't hide the irritation in my voice. This scenario, along with the rest of the past year, had become routine, mundane, and unfulfilling.

I would have to handle this situation the same way I had with all the women before her. When they looked at me, they saw a challenge, like a pawn that could easily be taken in a chess game with the right move, behavior, or sexual act. I was an emotional conquest to them.

She wasn't the first to dismiss my firm stance that the relationship would only remain sexual in nature. It wasn't about my lack of affection. I would compliment them on their beauty, kiss them tenderly, comfort them when they were upset, dine them, and then fuck them senseless. It was always about those three fucking words. The power they felt it gave them. The power I refused to give.

Though a few of them had sometimes charmed their way into getting more than I usually would allow, I always caught myself quickly. It was a conscious choice I made with each partner. I had been fair to Jill. I had been a committed lover to her and her alone. I had given her everything I promised I would.

She swept her long auburn hair into her hand and fastened it on top of her head as she walked toward me. "All I wanted was a chance," she whispered with pleading eyes, her tears falling down one by one. "I'm in love with you, Rhys." Her eyes told me she believed what she was saying.

"I'm not the man you need," I said quietly. "I can't give you what you want."

She had mistaken my kindness and attentiveness for weakness, as a sign I harbored the same feelings. She had decided to make me her project. She'd made a big mistake.

"You have no heart?" she asked, cornering me as she tucked her blouse in her pants. "You can't try or you won't? Why don't you need more?" She was beautiful, smart, a good sub, but I felt nothing *real* for her.

"It's just not who I am, Jill. Not right now." Her shoulders slumped as her body shook with emotion. Though I wanted to comfort her, I knew it would be a mistake. She would misinterpret it, and I didn't want to drag this out. "I won't ask you to stay, but I want you to," I lied as I pulled on my jacket.

She opened the door to walk out of the room then turned to me, regret clear in her posture.

"Just tell me what to do and I'll do it," she pleaded.

"Jill, I'm not the man you need. This doesn't have to end. We can continue—"

"I can't, Rhys. Goodbye."

Watching her walk out left me with a small sting. It was more out of resentment for the amount of time I spent with her. We'd never had a connection other than physical. Anything she was feeling was just due to the amount of time we'd spent together sexually. Of all my subs, she was the one I felt least strongly about. I was certain she was hoping I would go after her.

I wouldn't.

Once I'd situated my tie, I headed toward the door, but was stopped short by a beautiful woman filling the frame.

"It's a pity when they fall in love," she said on a sigh. "You know, fighting after fucking *is* a sign that you care for the person."

"I wasn't fighting," I admitted.

"No, you certainly weren't," she quickly replied with a smirk. We stood and stared at one another, both of us sizing each other up. It had been a long time since the sight of a woman made me hard. I appreciated that about her immediately. Her dark brown hair, closer to black, a sleek porcelain face and startling blue eyes made me want to fuck her right then. I imagined a few scenarios in my head as I perused her. She was far more beautiful than any sub I had ever had. Her body was made for sin and she was aware of it; her posture said as much with the way she leaned in the doorway confidently. This was a woman aware of her effect on men and comfortable with her sexuality. I liked her instantly.

"She looked like she was a lot of fun," she said, tilting her head quickly in the direction Jill left.

"Not today," I said, closing the distance between us. There was no denying the attraction we both felt in that moment. The air was filled with potential. She turned from me and opened the door at the opposite end of the hall. She looked back, catching my gaze

203

then giving me a knowing smile, which I returned. "Sandra," she answered my unspoken question before the door snapped shut.

It would not be our last encounter, of that I was sure.

Looking at my watch with a curse, I realized I had thirty minutes to get to dinner with my sister. I raced to the Olde Pink House, her favorite place to dine in Savannah. It was her birthday and she had just been released by her boyfriend, so I agreed to take his place. My dear sister Heidi was always throwing her heart out to the wrong suitor. I felt like a hypocrite stepping in when I had just hurt Jill. I had a heart, but Jill would never be the woman to possess it. Letting Jill walk away was for the best.

The Olde Pink House was located in Reynolds Square. True to its name, it was an old, pale flamingo, Victorian mansion that had been converted into a restaurant. Authentic to its historic bones, the décor was reminiscent of the 1800's and the rooms were quaint, each unique in setting.

Arriving on time, I spent ten minutes circling the square looking for parking. When I finally made it up to the steps to the entrance, I received a text.

HEIDI: Running late. Can you see if they can squeeze us in at the next available time?

Standing behind a couple waiting on the hostess, I was suddenly annoyed with my sister and her inability to be on time. I didn't want to be stuck in a romantic restaurant with my sister. I hoped they would nix the antique candlesticks on the table this time. I despised the bastard who had left her dateless and heartbroken on her birthday, and for the responsibility of salvaging her night. A night I was sure she had planned herself due to the type of man she usually adhered herself too.

I was definitely a hypocrite and this punishment was fitting. This punishment also reinforced the reasons why I didn't want to go further than sex when it came to a relationship. Clean lines were appealing; blurred lines were messy. End of story.

"It's perfect, thank you." The voice came from the woman who stood in front of me addressing her date and her sound instantly caught my attention. It was silky and raspy and her sentiment hung in the air. I watched their hands clasp and his thumb gently slide across the top of her skin. She looked up at him filled with longing and I had to take a step back. I felt like I was invading on a private moment, and yet I couldn't tear my eyes away from her. I took her in from head to toe. She was dressed in a long flowing red gown and her hair was styled loosely and fell sporadically around her shoulders. Her neck was statuesque and I suddenly felt myself wanting to touch it as I studied her profile. Her skin was perfection. Her mouth, from what I could see, was beautiful, and when she spoke I had to fight not to take another step forward.

What the fuck, Rhys?

It wasn't just her voice or beauty that captivated me. It was the way she looked at him. For just one moment in time, for one clarifying second of my life, I wished I was another man; the man who stood in front of me with the adoration of the woman next to him.

"I can see that," she said to him with a smile as I caught a small piece of their conversation. I felt the corners of my chest fold in painfully.

"Right this way," the hostess said to the smiling couple. A feeling of loss came over me in that moment, although I couldn't understand why. It was a pain that shook me fiercely and I had to put my hand on the wall next to me to steady myself. The hostess greeted me and I found my composure, though the ache in my chest lingered.

"Name, sir?"

"Volz," I forced out. "The other half of my party is running late. Would you be able to get us in at seven?" I asked, my gaze still focused in the direction of the woman who left me breathless that was no longer there.

"Sure," she said, eyeing me appreciatively before scribbling in her guestbook.

"I'll be at the bar," I said, ignoring her exaggerated stare. I walked downstairs to the basement bar I frequented often. It had an eerie, but at the same time, inviting feel. Savannah was infamous for modern décor in historic space, but this bar seemed completely authentic to the era of the house. The walls were lined with exposed brick and wood. The faint and familiar stroke of keys being played on the piano could be heard over the hushed conversations. The stone fireplace was lit, welcoming me as I sat at the small, formidable table next to it. I sipped two fingers of whiskey as I watched the red embers glow, thinking about the voice of the woman who had just unglued me in mere seconds. I had just fucked Jill for hours, and met a promising new prospect in Sandra. What I couldn't get my head around was the new crack in my once solid foundation. I was completely consumed by the way she regarded him. Did I want *that*? Why was I so envious?

Was Jill's outburst guilting me into wanting something more? This had to be guilt, pure and simple.

I shook my head in dismissal, drained my tumbler then nodded a thank you to the waitress as she replaced my empty glass.

I texted Heidi to let her know that I was at the bar but got a verbal reply.

"I see you, bonehead." She laughed as she joined me. Fresh martini in hand, she scrutinized me as she took her first sip.

"You look guilty. Whose heart did you break today?" she asked as she set her glass on the table. I studied my sister, whose eyes matched mine. One could easily tell we were family. She smiled at me, but I didn't let her question go unanswered.

"Another failed attempt at casual dating," I said dryly. "And I'm not sharing." Noticing the slight redness around her eyes, I realized the reason for her late arrival. "Heidi, why do you insist on entertaining every man that gives you a minute of attention? I told you this one was a total waste of time. I believe my words were, 'If in the first few months you have to fight for his attention in any way, he is not interested.' Not in the way you want him to be. "

"I know, I just..." She sipped her martini again, averting her eyes before meeting mine as she found her words. "Don't you ever get tired of being alone, Rhys?" I opened my mouth to give my usual answer, the one I was forced to give at every family gathering for the last ten years, but the words wouldn't come. Twenty minutes ago, my answer would have been a definite no. Twenty minutes ago, I had no issue stating that I would never settle down. When I didn't give her an answer, she smirked. "There is hope for you yet, brother."

"I'm rarely alone. I have girlfriends," I reminded her.

"You have dogs that bark and beg disguised as women. Really, Rhys, who the hell are you to give relationship advice?" She popped an olive into her mouth, her resentful stare showcasing her contempt for the harsh truth I just delivered. She didn't know about my lifestyle, but she had met a few of my subs and had realized quickly my relationship dynamics were different from others. Though I always treated my dates with nothing but the utmost care, it was easy to tell the relationship was purely sexual. Heidi was the only one I trusted to be social with that part of my life. I sipped my whiskey.

"I'm not in any position to give you advice, but since you decided to run to me with your issues instead of a more qualified girlfriend, I'll give you this. I'm honest. I tell them exactly what I want up front. Instead of planning your life around a kiss or a rare soft look they may gift you, why don't you try listening to them first? I'm pretty sure he was passive about dating. If he was more aggressive, we wouldn't be having this conversation."

"Rhys, just...let it go. I came for dinner, not a lecture from my brother who hasn't had a steady girlfriend since grade school." She swallowed the contents of her glass, looking as if she would rather be anywhere but at a table with me.

"Heidi, I'm sorry you're upset," I said, knowing I was being a dick. "Listen to me, you are worth it," I said, catching her eyes, hoping she would hear me. "You are. A man's needs are simple and yours will always be complex. Wait for your aggressor."

Her eyes were now full of tears as she looked at me, a picture of fresh pain with a ghost of a smile haunting her face. "How can you not want to experience *this*, Rhys? Doesn't it look like fun?" She laughed and I laughed with her as I ordered her a fresh drink for each hand.

After dinner, I watched my sister drive away, furious she hadn't let me call a cab or drive her home myself.

I was sure she was on her way to try and convince the object of her affection to reconsider.

Restless from the day's events, I made my way back to The Barracks, and gave pause when a pair of startling blue eyes greeted me at the bar. I sat next to her with a grin. "Sandra."

VIOLET

Present Day

Christmas sucks.

"Violet, come hang your ornament," my mother called to me from the living room as I stood in the kitchen staring at my phone. "Can you just do it, Mom?" I asked, pouring my fourth cup of bourbon with a splash of eggnog.

"No, ma'am. Thirty-three years, it's tradition," she said to me as I rolled my eyes. "Don't you roll your eyes at me!" I shook my head, my cup halfway to my mouth, knowing she hadn't seen it. She was a damn freak of nature.

"Call Rhys and have him come over and bring the baby," she

said, walking into the kitchen and grabbing my eggnog out of my hand and capping the bourbon. "What's the matter with you?"

"Nothing," I said, eyeing my father who was tinkering with a train piece from the set that toured the bottom floor of the house every Christmas.

My mother eyed me as I avoided answering her. "Fine, I'll assume Rhys has plans tonight. Come hang your ornament and stay out of your father's bourbon," she scolded.

"Here, here," my father replied, looking up at me through his glasses as he inspected his project closely.

Hmph, men and their toys.

"Fine, no booze, no boys. Let's party," I said dryly as my mother whisked me away to the tree. The house, as usual, looked incredible. My mother had always made it so during the holidays. But this year, I wanted no part of it.

"You want to tell me what stick has crawled up your butt? You usually love Christmas," she said, handing me my ornament. I stuck it on the nearest branch, my mother immediately catching it as it popped off.

"Whoops," I said under her heavy eye, hurt in her stare as she re-hung it carefully.

"What happened, damn it?" she asked in a harsh whisper, her hand on her hip.

"*I* happened, Mom. *I happened.*"

He happened.

She happened.

They happened.

I felt sick. Collapsing on the couch, I threw a pillow on my head to cover my face, feeling the burn move through me from the bourbon. I hiccupped as she pulled the pillow away.

"This is not how you act on a holiday, madam," she scorned, pushing me so I was forced to sit up then plopped down next to me.

209

"Mom, I'm thirty-three. I should have my own family now, not be bothering you two on Christmas Eve."

"That's the dumbest damn thing I have ever heard in my life," she huffed. "Even if you had a family of your own they would all be here. I'd make sure of it."

"Fine. True. Whatever. I sure hope I'm enough," I said, throwing my own personal pity party. I knew for a fact my mother wouldn't put up with it for long. So much so, that when her back was turned, I carried my bourb-nog up to my parent's guestroom—my old bedroom—and drank it until I felt comfortably numb. I stared at my phone, but I couldn't do it. I couldn't call Rhys when he was probably surrounded by family. What would I even say? What else was there to say? Tears fell heavy as I tossed and turned, thinking of how it had all played out.

At midnight, I sent him a text then passed out during my second viewing of *A Christmas Story*.

⁂

RHYS

I sat on the couch at my parents' house on Christmas morning as my son screamed "Vi tet, Da DAAA! Vi tet!" in delight at the TV. My sister Heidi heard him and came rushing in to see him wiggling back and forth as he watched the Christmas parade. The host did look a little similar to Violet, with long blonde hair and green eyes. My heart became heavier as his excitement grew with the thought it was her on screen hosting. She had invaded my every thought since the day I met her, and now she had my son's attention.

"Vi TETTT!" He shook animatedly to the music as the dancers surrounding the Snoopy float dazzled the spectators.

"Vi tett...Violet." Heidi smiled as she caught on, averting her

210

gaze from Bryce to me with a smug smile. "I knew it, brother. You are a true ass for keeping this from me, you know that?"

"Shut it, little H. I mean it," I said sternly. She waddled over to me, her belly completely full and near bursting and took a seat on the footrest in front of me, forcing my attention to her.

"Is this the one that will finally tame you, dear brother?" she asked, all smiles as she giggled at Bryce who was dancing his tail off, imitating the dancers as best as he could.

"Heidi, drop it," I snapped, unable to hide the grit in my voice.

"Not this time. As a matter of fact, I'll bring it to the table if you don't spill it." She nodded toward the kitchen where the rest of the family was gathered, prepping the day's feast.

"Okay, dear brother, so you introduced a woman to your son? Come on, Rhys, she must be important to you. I remember her from the restaurant. She was beautiful and seemed really nice." My sister refused to move from her spot, her expectation clear as she watched me.

I gripped the edge of the couch as I gave in. "She is important," was all I could manage.

"And Bryce, he seems to like her," she added, watching me carefully.

"He loves her," I said quietly.

"You love her," Heidi said, reading my expression.

"Can we please not talk about this here?" I pleaded with her.

"Oh my GOD, you do love her. Rhys, that's incredible!" My mother leaned back from her kitchen stool to look into the living room at the two of us talking, and I quickly stifled Heidi's excitement.

"Shut up right now. And anyway, I'm not so sure it's going to work out," I said, dismissing the whole conversation.

"Brother, I love you, but this time, I won't shut up." She looked at Bryce and then to me. "I never thought you were the type to settle down, but watching you with Bryce, I can't see you any other way. Honestly, if you have *finally* found a woman who will put up with your shit, and your son loves her and you love her, I don't see what the problem is."

I gave her a warning glare.

"Mom, guess what!" Heidi said, rubbing her belly as she eyed me with nothing but mischief.

"What, honey?" my mother answered from the kitchen.

"Fine," I gritted out. "What do you want to know?"

"Never mind," Heidi chimed in reply to my mother, victory in her voice.

I leaned in, ready to strangle her. "What, Heidi?"

"It's just...I want to see you happy. You've been alone for so long." She looked down at her stomach then back to me. "If you can find someone, it kind of gives me hope, ya know?" Once again, my sister had misplaced her affections for the wrong man and found herself alone, but this time with a constant reminder of the failed relationship.

I understood her need to see a different result for me. She was about to be a single parent, a predicament I was all too familiar with.

"She's everything I've ever wanted," I admitted. "I hate being without her. She's smart and so completely beautiful. She's real and raw and embraces her flaws, when to me she has none. Her vulnerability is refreshing and yet she has no issues calling me out on my shit or putting me in my place. You should see the way she looks at Bryce...She's not anything like the women before her and she makes me feel...everything." Heidi's eyes filled as she nodded. That's all it took to reduce my very pregnant sister to tears.

I didn't want to admit to Heidi that I was uncomfortable and felt helpless for the first time in my life when it came to a woman; that my past may have completely screwed up my future. That I had selfishly forced her from being my submissive into a relationship she may not have been ready for, then broken her trust repeatedly because I hadn't trusted her enough with the truth.

"He doesn't want anything to do with the baby," she said, her eyes reflecting her sadness. "I don't understand that, Rhys."

I put my hands on her full belly and her smile returned. "You've got everything you need right here," I said, rubbing her swollen stomach. "And you will always have me, I promise."

She threw her arms around me and gave me a quick hug. I braved a look at my phone as she went to join the rest of the family in the kitchen.

VIOLET: Merry Christmas.

⌘

VIOLET

"Take off your panties and hand them to me." Rhys had been waiting for me in his bedroom, his black bag on the dresser. The bed was covered in things I'd only read about and I quickly looked at him with wide eyes. I did as I was told as Rhys held out his hand, dressed in his unbuttoned, crisp white shirt that revealed his perfectly etched chest, jeans, and sexy bare feet. He took my hand and put it through one of the leg holes of my panties, twisting them until they were tight then pulled my other hand through, securing them until they were clasped at the wrist.

Bound with my own panties, oh God, yes!

"I still have a lot of work to do with you, Violet, so I need you to do as I say. No questions, or you will be punished. Do you understand?"

"Yes, sir," I said with a slight hint of sarcasm that he didn't miss. It was answered with the painful thump of his finger on my hard nipple. I glared at him in response and was graced with a seductive smile.

"Still so ready to defy me. Have you not learned anything by now?" He leaned in close enough that our lips almost touched and

213

I moved in to kiss him, but he pulled away. "That is where you fuck up, sweetheart. You must think I've gone soft. What do you say we remedy that right now?" he taunted as he pulled a black ribbon out of his magic black bag and secured it around my eyes. "Do yourself a favor tonight and don't think, don't speak, just obey."

I stood naked before him as I waited for his next order.

"So beautiful and such a sweet pussy," he growled, turning me away from him and pulling my bound wrists up to hook over the bedpost then sliding them down so I was forced to bend over, completely bared to him.

"Spread them wider, Violet. I want to see it all." I spread wider as my legs begin to burn under the strain. I waited patiently as my breath quickened with each passing second. I had been ordered all day by text to touch myself to the point of climax but never come. I'd almost given in as I stroked myself in one of the houses I was showing while I thought of him. In the end, I'd kept my part of the bargain, showing up at his house with a swollen and aching center, dying for release. He knew the minute he saw me I had obeyed him and promised me I'd be rewarded.

"I can smell how much you need me." My body jumped as his breath hit my center. I pushed it toward him in question. "Still giving orders, even without the use of that sassy mouth," he teased. I felt him set what felt like a stick on my back, balancing it just above my ass.

"If you drop the whip, you don't come. I really wouldn't test me this time."

I groaned in frustration, but it was cut short as I felt a slap on the inside of my thigh. I cried out but remained still and was rewarded with the feeling of the weight of the whip on my back.

I was completely wound up and ready to burst, sure that no matter what he did I would shatter in seconds.

"I'm going to fill every part of you tonight, and you will not come until I allow it." He spread my legs further apart and I gasped at the feel of his hands on my ass, smoothing it carefully, leaving the whip

undisturbed. He separated me and I felt his tongue touch my ring of muscle and gasped out, almost buckling.

"Careful, Violet. I need to eat your sweet ass. Don't fucking move." My sex pulsed out of control as I gripped the bedpost, my entire body shaking in reaction to the stroke of his tongue. I took in steady breaths, moaning loudly as he continued to lick me. I felt the whip shift slightly and quickly regained my stance as he filled my backside with his tongue. Without warning, I felt a cold probe replace his tongue and screamed out in pleasure when he slid it in.

"Oh fuck. Oh God, Rhys. Jesus, oh fuck," I breathed out, pleasure dripping from my shaky voice.

"I knew you would appreciate that." He chuckled. "Do I need to remind you not to come?"

He quickly pulled the whip from my back and struck me with it. The pain was all-consuming as I tightened around the metal; pleasure shot through me as I almost went to my knees.

Unable to speak unless I wanted to use my safe word, I praised him in moans.

"Taste so fucking good. I need more." He placed the whip across my back again and I felt his breath on my sex. He licked me once, turning the cold steel inside me as I began to beg.

"Rhys, I need to come. I have to come!"

"Violet!" I felt the absence then the lashing of the whip and fell to my knees. He quickly brought me to my feet, pulling me back further. I felt another sharp sting, then another and another. "You will obey me!" My legs shook uncontrollably as I moaned in response. He set the whip across my back again and thrust his tongue between my drenched pussy lips.

"You like it"—lick, lick, lick—"when I fuck you with my tongue." He sucked my clit hard as I gripped the bedpost, trying my best not to fall to my knees. "Maybe you don't need my cock tonight." I groaned in protest as he twisted the metal that stretched my ass and lapped me up furiously. I felt the orgasm push its way to the surface, no lon-

ger able to control my screaming. I held on, tears coming fast behind my blindfold as he pushed his finger inside me, twisting and stretching me, filling me completely. The sensation from the metal and his fingers sent me past my limit.

"Come for me." He pulled the metal out of my ass and thrust his tongue deep as I exploded, repeating his name with each shockwave, each pulse that poured through me. He took my release into his mouth and with one last lick, he swiped his tongue to the top of my folds, sucking them hard. I collapsed to my knees as he massaged me and released my hands from my panties then held me to him while I shook from the effect of what he'd done. I was covered in sweat and my heart was pounding as we locked eyes. The look of tenderness in his took the breath from me as he stroked my face, soothing me. He lifted me from the floor and carried me to bed, kissing me deeply.

"Can I talk?" I asked, wide-eyed when he'd taken his fill of my mouth.

"You said it all," he mused as he smiled down at me.

"Rhys, please...I want your—"

"Daughter! Just what in the *hell* are you doing?" my mother asked, making me jump out of my skin and stumble backwards only to fall over a stack of boxes before landing hard on my ass on the garage floor. My face was still flushed with arousal from my memory of that night with Rhys. He'd kept me tied to the bed while I slept so he could fuck me on his whim. I quickly started working again, grabbing a stack of old newspapers and throwing them into the trash.

"Jesus, Mother...I was...I am trying to keep you and Dad safe. There are enough old papers in here to set the entire neighborhood on fire."

"Did it ever occur to you that we might not want our garage cleaned out?" She put her hands on her hips and I mirrored her stance with an "Are you going to do it?" face. I ignored her for several minutes, trying desperately to calm myself as she watched me work.

"Mom, just let me finish this. I just need to keep busy right now. I don't want to talk. Just let me handle things my way, okay?"

"Fine, I'll bring you some iced tea and, Violet, as much as your father and I love your company, you have to go home sometime. You can't avoid life forever."

"Says who, Mom?" My voice cracked, though I hadn't let myself get upset since that night. "Reality, I have no use for it, *none*. You go live there. I'm happy to ignore it."

"Baby, I know you're hurting." She took a step toward me.

"*Do* you, Mom? Do you have any idea what *this* is like? I don't think so. You *got* the man you wanted. Me, I have to jump through a hoop of fire and swallow a pill of shit just to *date* mine."

"Violet, what are you talking about? Is there something you're not telling me?"

I sighed heavily, knowing I'd said too much. "I'm simply saying it's becoming more apparent that dating when you're thirty-three is not as simple as when you're twenty-three."

And when you're dating an ex-Dom who totes a diaper bag, has a split personality, and psychotic ex-girlfriend, it gets much more complicated.

Rhys's past gave a whole new meaning to the word baggage. Then again, I had severe trust issues and they were more apparent now than ever.

Oh, what a pair.

My mother watched me closely as I ignored her and took on a new shelf in her garage. I must have been a sight with my worn out denim jeans, grease covered white t-shirt, ratty hair and circles under my eyes from lack of sleep. I didn't want her to know that Rhys was anything less than the perfect man she assumed he was.

He was far too secretive, controlling, and infuriating at the moment.

And still I loved him. It was way too late to save myself from it.

Thankfully, my mother left me to my brooding to go get my tea while I collapsed on a set of boxes and buried my head in my hands. My pocket vibrated and my heart leaped as I looked at the text.

RHYS: Talk to me, Violet.

VIOLET: And exactly whom would I be talking to today?

RHYS: You don't want me to give up any more than I'm willing to.

VIOLET: Maybe you should ignore that fact. I can't trust you, Rhys.

RHYS: Maybe you could if you would stop fucking running away from me.

VIOLET: Maybe I would if you would stop fucking lying to me.

RHYS: Omitting.

VIOLET: Same thing. And I'm not running. My parents need me.

RHYS: For what…to clean out their garage?

I saw red as I realized my mother was texting him. "Mother!" She didn't answer and I knew she was cowering in the kitchen. Minutes passed as I waited for his next text. I knew he was angry with me as well. We were both hurt. If we were to go any further, I had to make it crystal clear I would no longer put up with lies and omissions. Even if he did it to protect me, even if it was for my own good, I wanted full disclosure. I never wanted to be put in the position again where she or any other woman knew more than I did. Not when I was the woman in his bed at night. My love and devotion now came with a price: honesty, loyalty and everything in between. I would get as good as I gave and I would never settle for less, ever again.

RHYS: I'll see you soon.

Even now, if he was willing to tell me everything, I couldn't forgive how he had broken a little piece of me with what he'd said. Even if he didn't mean it, even if he'd just said it in anger, I couldn't forget it.

Asshole.

Once finished with my task, I made my way to the backyard and sat on my old tire swing, replaying that night over and over. If I had only just once asked for a name…If I had only asked for Bryce's mothers name, we could have pieced this all together ourselves. Instead, I'd allowed him to stay secretive about his past, never willing to give me more than he felt he should. His vague answers to protect me had backfired and caused us more harm than good. If I'd only asked. If he'd only shared more, we would have both known our pasts were mutually bound by one fucking name.

Sandra.

"It's not him. It's her."

The weight of his words hit me in the chest as I stood frozen in his office.

No, God, not her. Anyone but her!

Paralyzed, my eyes scanned the security screen just as Rhys appeared on it and confronted Sandra. It was another series of clicks that went off as all the pieces fit together.

CLICK.

Sandra and Rhys knew each other.

CLICK.

And from the way he was glaring at her, I could tell she was his ex, and the previous owner of the club.

CLICK.

The woman he said he loathed…and sweet Bryce's mother.

Keep it together, Vi.

Sandra, the same woman who destroyed my marriage, and the woman we both hated. I didn't know whether to make my way out to the bar or continue to watch Rhys on the screen as he waved his hands toward the door angrily in an attempt to get her to leave. My eyes drifted to Alex, who was sitting with the man they came with. They seemed uninterested in the argument taking place at the entrance. Alex leaned over, his posture intimate, and brushed a piece of hair off the man's forehead before leaning in for a—what the fuck—kiss.

"WHAT THE FUCK!" I stormed out of Rhys's office and down the hall, thankful I'd had sense enough to wear a jacket that secured tightly over my lingerie-clad body. I rounded the bar, regarded Sandra for mere seconds as she argued with Rhys, and stood behind my ex-husband.

"You are gay!?" I screamed at the top of my lungs. The club was busier than usual and everyone, and I mean everyone, turned to watch me come apart, including Sandra and Rhys.

"Violet, what the hell are you doing here?" Alex turned on his stool to face me fully, completely confused and distancing himself from his lover as if he were ashamed.

My face heated, my anger surfacing further as I watched the man sitting to his left turn in his seat to face me, looking as if my name coming from Alex's lips pained him. I knew his name. I'd heard the conversations they'd shared, and recalled the last one when he had whispered his I love you.

"Well, Alex, I am fucking the man who owns this bar. What are you doing here?" I snapped, glaring at Chris, who was strikingly handsome. I could see the appeal. My fury evident, I grabbed Alex's drink and chugged it, the burn soothing me slightly. Rhys approached me from behind and grabbed my arm. I glared at him and jerked it away before returning my attention to Alex.

I kept my eyes trained on the man who had completely ruined my trust, ruined my confidence, all because he was too much of a coward to come clean. "All this time, I thought I wasn't good enough. I thought I wasn't woman enough and you let me think I wasn't! You could have told me, you selfish son of a bitch! At least I would have understood in some way that I wasn't MAN enough for you!" I took the rest of his drink and threw it at him, covering his dress shirt in ice and amber liquid. Rhys grabbed my upper arm and pulled me back roughly.

"Violet, let it go," he snapped, forcing me to bring my eyes to his. I ripped my arm from out of his hands again, cursing and blinded with rage.

Every person had their breaking point, and this was mine.

"And you, Rhys. You loved this...this bitch." I pointed at Sandra. "This whore...This monster!"

"Hey now, maybe bitch is deserved," Sandra said, coyly walking up to us and covering me with her clear blue gaze. She was smirking and enjoying every minute of the confrontation. I held her eyes, thinking Bryce did slightly resemble her, and shook my head, not wanting to make the connection. It was too painful. My chest burned with anger and there wasn't a rational thought able to compete with it.

I was in her office building a month ago, believing I watched a mouse at play before the snake struck, when in reality I'd been staring straight at the serpent.

She was the reason for so much of my pain, of Rhys's pain. She was the reason Bryce would grow up without knowing or feeling the love of his real mother. Rage boiled within me as I thought of Bryce and what he deserved.

"I didn't love her, ever," Rhys said plainly. "Violet, look at me." My voice trembled with fear of his answer, but I had to get my next question out.

"Did you know?" I asked in a harsh whisper. When he didn't answer, I asked louder. "Did you know, Rhys!" I demanded. My voice rattled with my next question. "Am I another one of your games?" I looked between Sandra and Rhys as what composure I had completely

left me. Rhys looked at me incredulously as Sandra took a step closer, unable to hide her excitement about the situation.

"No, Violet. I had no idea," he said quietly. His eyes pleaded with me to believe him, but I couldn't. In that moment, I hated Rhys for having anything to do with Sandra. I was flipping at my revelation and I was sure anyone in my position would be too. It was too much. I had to get out of there and fast.

"Violet, I'm sorry," Alex said, stepping up to the most fucked up circle of people I'd ever known. "I thought you knew and that's why I wanted a quiet divorce. When you said Chris, I assumed—"

"K-r-i-s, not C-H-R-I-S you fucking moron. How in the hell would I have known this?" I glared at him as he cowered away back to his seat as Chris grabbed his hand. I almost laughed at the way Alex needed to be consoled.

What a little bitch.

Sandra spoke next. I expected her posture to be hands clasped at her fingertips, eyes filled with mischief, an evil pose that let us all know that all of this had gone exactly according to plan. Instead, she looked between the four of us with pure delight. "Oh, this is too good to be true...I didn't realize my playthings could bring out so much emotion." Sandra shook her whole body in an exaggerated shivering motion and snickered as she looked back at Alex and Chris, who regarded her with contempt. "Little did I know when I took your husband, Violet, he would fall in love with me and my sub. I have your husband and his lover under my thumb. Why do you think that is?" She stood inches away from me and continued her torment. "You aren't woman enough and you never will be, especially for Rhys. I promise you that."

I turned to face her head on as Rhys moved suddenly, stepping in front of me. She took note of his protectiveness and her jaw hardened.

"Look at Rhys all grown up with a real girlfriend," she taunted. "Tell me, do you two make supper and watch reruns before you fuck? How is life in vanilla, Rhys? Do you really think this woman is enough

for you?" She laughed, but no one around her joined in. Not even her two subs at the bar, one of them being my ex-husband.

This was not happening.

I trembled with every breath I took as Rhys remained completely composed as he addressed her.

"I'm happy and it kills you," he said smoothly, his voice unaffected. "I want her and you know it and it's fucking killing you."

"You always did think a little too much of my need for you, Rhys." She waved him off, though her statement was far from convincing, her want for him evident in the way she regarded him.

"Really, is that why you made a house call for my cock just a few short weeks ago?" He nodded toward Alex and Chris. "I'm sure they would be interested to know their mistress isn't satisfied." Chris stiffened, his face contorted in anger while Alex remained impassive and unimpressed. Rhys took a step toward Sandra and she cringed slightly as he addressed her with nothing short of hatred. "When I walk out the door with my future in my hand, I will never see you again. I'm done with this place, with you, for good. If you come anywhere near me, Violet, or my son, I will ruin you." He leaned in closer so only the threat was heard by the three of us. "I will hurt you and you know I know just how to do it."

Rhys took my arm in an attempt to pull me out of the club. I passed her, but I had to get my digs in. I gripped the back of her head, digging my nails in her scalp as I whispered in her ear. "Your inability to keep your hands off what didn't belong to you led me straight to the arms of the man you wanted most. Your son will call me mother while the man you want fucks me, loves me, and worships my body. Keep Alex. We both know it wasn't really a fair trade, was it, Sandra? Enjoy the short end of the stick." I pulled back, inches from her face to see her shocked expression. She didn't think I had it in me, and that made two of us.

I saw the humorous light in her eyes die as she glared at Rhys and me as he pulled me out of the bar.

As soon as the cold air hit us, I pulled away from Rhys, furious with the night's events. "I'm a CLICHÉ!" I threw my hands up in the air. "Jilted wife finds out that her husband is gay!"

"Ex-husband," Rhys added.

"Seriously, why the hell couldn't he have told me? And she doesn't even know that the joke is on her. He loves Chris. I mean, she has to have figured it out by now, he can't love her." I racked my brain for answers that weren't coming. I saw Rhys's face harden as he ran his hands through his hair. His next words cut me.

"Why the fuck do you care who he loves?" he said harshly, his sudden anger with me stopping me from retrieving my keys from my pocket.

I looked back at the bar and then to him, incredulous. "No...no! You don't get to pull this shit on me! Are you kidding me right now? I was with that man for years and had no clue," I snapped, lifting my finger in warning.

"What shit am I pulling, Violet!? You seem obsessed with the man and what he feels. Why don't you go ask him? He's right inside that door!" Rhys turned away from me and began walking toward his car.

"Rhys, wait," I said, my voice shaking in anger. "What about you, huh?" I was freezing and all the adrenaline shooting through me from the last ten minutes was taking its toll. "What about you and your fucking obsessions? How could you have picked her?" My anger boiled over again and I was helpless to stop it. I walked toward him, refusing to let him leave. When he didn't answer, I pushed his back in an attempt to get him to turn around as he reached his sedan. "You picked her and she ruined both our lives! How could you ever have been involved with a woman like that? What does that say about you?"

Rhys whirled on me then, his eyes filled with hurt. "Who the fuck are you to judge me?"

"I'm not judging you, Rhys. I just find it a little hard to believe that you would mix yourself up with a woman like that for any reason and—"

SEXUAL AWAKENINGS

"I'm not perfect and I won't pretend to be for you. That in there was a mistake. My mistake and has nothing to do with you," he shot back, wounding me.

"I never expected you to be perfect," I defended weakly. "And apparently we can't separate our past from our future so it has everything to do with me!" I said, my entire body shaking with every emotion imaginable: embarrassment, hurt, shock, and outrage taking the lead.

He leaned against his car, arms crossed, eyes fixed on mine. "What exactly is it that you want from me, Violet? I'm not Alex. I can't make what he did right for you. I've already given you the ability to hurt me. What more do you want?"

"I'm not trying to hurt you, Rhys."

"You're not, but what you are doing is acting like a jealous ex-wife. You're making a damn fool of yourself and me, something I swore I wouldn't let you do again. You're expecting me to apologize and make excuses for mistakes I have already paid for...And you're pissing me off."

I glared at him as I addressed him next. "You don't want the jealous ex-wife, fine, how about answering to your current girlfriend? When exactly where you planning on telling me Sandra came for a cock-filled house call!"

He shook his head as his arms fell to his sides, his guilt apparent.

"No secrets or lies between us. I believe that was your line of bullshit, Rhys," I continued, my voice a shriek at this point.

"I may have an answer to that when you can calm down and act rationally. This is their mess, Violet, not ours!" he said, exasperated. He looked at me with contempt. "I moved on from that. I found you, let it go."

"Let it go? Let it go!" I shook my head, incredulous. "Well, she hasn't moved on, Rhys! You lied to me...again! That whore is the mother of your son, she ruined my marriage, and you think we can just walk away from this!"

"Yes," he said quickly. "I know we can."

225

"Maybe you can." I watched him slowly shut down in front of me and couldn't help my next words. "Tell me, Rhys, what is it that you're so damn angry about right now? You can control my body but not my emotions, is that it?"

His breath left him as he shook his head. "Tell me why you're so upset, Violet, because I'm pretty sure it has more to do with him than me." I saw a steely resolve cover his features before he spoke again. "Maybe I was wrong to pull you so close. You never wanted this, us, or maybe I just wanted it more. You signed up for something totally different," he stated, pulling at his door handle. I slammed it closed, forcing him to face me.

"What, Rhys..." I gathered my strength, the amount of hurt I felt making me tremble. "What the hell did you just say to me?" I clenched my fists at my sides as he stared at the gravel between us. "You're the one who was IN remember? No, Rhys, we were designed to be together and your ex had an unknowing hand in it! I mean, what kind of fucked up coincidence is this?"

"I'm thankful," he said, slowly reaching for me. "And I always will be." He pulled my face to him and kissed me gently then let go to get in his car.

"Rhys, talk to me," I said, my heart sinking.

"It's Christmas Eve, Violet. I have to go get Bryce."

"Violet?" I turned around to see Alex walking toward me and held my hand up to stop him in his tracks.

"Not now, Alex." I saw Rhys stiffen as Alex approached. I turned to glare at him but he stood firm in his refusal to give Rhys and I space. "All I am asking for is a few minutes, Violet."

Rhys darted around me, his face twisted with fury. "I thought I told you to stay the fuck away from her."

I jumped in front of Rhys, a question in my eyes as he looked past me, murder in his depths for Alex.

"I think you know I only want to talk to her," Alex snapped back,

challenging him. I looked between them, completely confused. Then it dawned on me they'd had this conversation before. I turned to Rhys.

"When?"

"The night before you left for the Caymans," he answered without hesitation. "He was at your house."

"Our house, Violet," Alex snapped behind me.

"Not anymore," Rhys challenged, taking a step forward.

"What in the hell do I have to do to get the men in my life to be honest with me!" I felt sick as I backed away from them both. I shook my head back and forth, trying to wrap my mind around the level of betrayal I felt in that moment.

"You," I directed to Rhys, whose eyes shot to mine. "You were supposed to be different."

"I am different and you know it," he said firmly. "I'm the only real thing you've got," he said, his eyes turning cold as he watched me.

"I don't think your fucking qualified to tell me what's real, Rhys," I snapped, keeping my voice even though my heart was falling away piece by piece.

"No," he said icily. "I guess your fucking fantasy is just a little safer, right? Don't worry, Violet, tonight I'll play the bad guy." He charged Alex and punched him square across the jaw, sending him to the gravel as he cursed and then glared between us. "You two really should learn how to listen. And, Violet, when you figure out just what in the hell it is that you want, we should talk."

"Something you are completely fucking incapable of apparently," I shot back, "honesty."

The level of hurt I saw in his posture almost knocked me down with guilt. He got in his sedan and left. I turned to Alex, who was still on the ground holding his jaw, then back to Rhys's retreating car.

Walking to my car, I did not give a damn about Alex or his newly aching jaw. As I was reaching for the handle, he protested.

"Just let me talk to you." I turned to face him. He was standing

now, still cupping his face as a small amount of blood trickled from his lips. I closed my car door and charged him.

"Talk," I snapped, ready for the answers I had deserved for far too long.

"I've always been this way and I've always hidden it. When I met you, I fell for you, Violet, I did. I truly loved you, but no matter how hard I tried, it was still there. I still wanted...men. And then I met Chris and it just happened."

"How long?" I asked, hating myself for it.

"A little over a year," he said, shoving his hands in his pockets, his jaw turning purple.

"I knew that." I couldn't control my disgust.

"I was going to end it, Violet, I was. Get it out of my system, be a better husband, but I fell in love—"

"Skip it, I don't care. How did Sandra fall into this?"

"We were away on that weekend retreat to brainstorm for new ideas for the Lux campaign and she brought him. She introduced me to him. It started with him, Violet. I had no idea about—they introduced me to all of this," he said, pointing at the club. "Everything changed for me. I had no idea how to explain this to you. I was completely selfish. I wanted him."

"So you and Sandra?" I asked, suddenly feeling guilty for even having the discussion.

"I hate her, but she has Chris, so I stay. She threatens me with outing me all the time to keep me in line. You know my parents. I would lose everything."

"So you aren't into—"

"I'm gay," he admitted.

"And all the phone calls?" I asked.

"At her insistence. And now that I think about it, I'm sure she wanted you to know. She's sick—"

I held my hand up. "No, it's you. Blaming her is easy. You did this to yourself and to me. You let it all happen. Jesus, Alex, how could you be so cruel?"

"Violet, just know that I'm sorry. What I did was unforgivable and I'll always regret hurting you, always."

"I can see you're sincere and I sincerely don't give a shit. I can also see that you're drowning in misery." I took a step toward him, my curiosity getting the best of me. "Tell me, Alex, why, if he's the one you want, can't you get him away from her?"

"He loves her," he said with a humorless laugh.

"Hurts, doesn't it?" I said, unable to keep the bite from my words. "God..." I exhaled. "What happened to when things were just simple," I said, not really wanting an answer. I turned from Alex, needing to distance myself from him, and from the entire situation.

"It looks simple with him, Violet...with Rhys. He seems to really care about you. I know I have no right to ask, but how did you end up here? Involved with him?"

I whirled on him. "You're right. You have no right to ask. And don't you dare give me permission, Alex. I don't need it from you." He nodded quickly, but was watching me closely.

"The vasectomy?" I asked, knowing the answer. It had nothing to do with Sandra or Chris. He hadn't met them when he took the possibility of a family with me away. It was simply the first nail in our coffin.

"I think I knew all along we wouldn't last, Violet. I didn't want to take that chance," he said, pushing gravel with his shoe, unable to look at me when he spoke.

"I'm sure your new Dom found it so very convenient," I said, disgusted. Disgusted with him, with his excuses, with the whole situation, I could no longer stomach any more truth.

I would never believe he ever loved me. I'd been nothing more than a cover for his sexuality, a way of him to save face and keep his secret from his parents. It was never a real marriage.

Alex took a step closer to me as I took one back. "You didn't do

*anything wrong, Violet. You were a good wife, the perfect wife, and I
never deserved you. Please know that," he said in a plea then turned
and made his way back toward the club. He looked back at me briefly
before entering the club, remorse in his posture, and something I'd
never seen written all over his features...defeat.*

I stood staring at the door as it closed.

*The very door I had opened months ago that led to my new ad-
venture, the door that led me to Rhys, was now the door that had answered so many questions; questions I had agonized over for almost
a year. I got into my car and stared out my windshield, all of the answers swirling around in my head.*

*The familiar heaviness in my chest returned. It had nothing to
do with Alex or the unraveled truth. It had everything to do with the
man who had just walked away from me...again.*

RHYS

I watched Bryce sleeping in the guest bed at my parents', unsure
of my next move. It was times like this that I was certain I was in
over my head. Physically, I craved her more than ever, but even
deeper I could feel the tear of her absence. It was debilitating and
had started to take its toll.

I'd watched her confront Alex in the parking lot. I knew then
I had nothing to worry about. He was never a threat to me. Then
again, as long as Sandra was around I couldn't be sure.

The revelation that Sandra's level of toxicity had spilled into
both of our lives should be more surprising to me, but it only af-
firmed what I already knew.

She was pure poison, and now, somehow, she'd managed to seep
into everything good in my life and taint it indefinitely.

When I saw Alex take a step closer to her, I cringed. I had no regrets when I right handed the son of a bitch. No problem at all with the crack of his jaw against my knuckles. Thinking that she still cared for him in any capacity had sent me over the edge. With her, I was selfish. I wanted all of her. I didn't want to acknowledge any part of her that still harbored anything for him, in any form. I watched their exchange closely, white knuckling my steering wheel, unable to tear my eyes away. Fucking vulnerability was not my strong suit and I had no cards left to play. I had to leave it all up to her. I had overreacted, but then again, so had she.

There wasn't a damn thing I could do to help her. My jealousy got in the way of that and might have pushed her away from me. That and the fact that I hadn't told her about Sandra's unannounced visit, or my short meeting with her ex-husband. Things that seemed so unimportant then might now be the reason I lose her.

She'd deserved the answers, and the apology attached to it; one I had no right to deny her.

The sinking feeling in my chest told me that I might never get a chance to explain.

⚬⚬⚬

VIOLET

I walked down River Street with my mother, still reeling from revelation.

"He was in love with a man, Mom. A MAN! I never in a million years thought that would be the reason. It all makes sense now." I spared her several of the details, knowing my mother couldn't handle it. I couldn't even handle most of it. I had been dying to tell her about the events of Christmas Eve, but up until now my father had been present.

"Violet, have you talked to Rhys today?" My mother gave me a sharp look.

"No, he's upset with me for my reaction. But, Mom, he had to know what a shock this is, and Alex—"

"Let's go in here and get a praline." My mother guided me into The Savannah Candy Kitchen and spent the next ten minutes shoving chocolate covered peanuts and pralines into my mouth—all of which she grabbed from various bags she was carrying. I was trying to get the words out as she shoved the candy in. I needed her perspective. I opened my mouth again and she shoved in a chocolate covered pretzel.

"Mom, stop it," I said, chewing quickly. "It's very good. Are you listening to me?"

"I am but are you taking my hint, kid? I don't want to hear about Alex and his lover. I'm happy you got your closure but you are dwelling on this a little too much, don't you think? Do you still love Alex?" she whispered as the cashier rang up her purchases.

"Of course not. I love Rhys," I said, honestly. "I just can't believe—"

"Believe it, accept it, and move on. It's a lot to process, baby, I know. And I know it's all a shock, but where your heart belongs is where it *is*. Forget Alex. Forget Sandra and Chris. Think about you and what makes you happy, not what happened." She stepped onto the cobblestone street and I followed her, watching as the trolley passed us by. She grabbed my hand and wrapped it around her elbow as we walked.

"Have you talked to Rhys?"

"Mom, you just asked me that. I told you no. I'm upset with him. I texted him earlier and he never replied." I was irritated. She wouldn't let me vent. I couldn't stop thinking about the insanity of it all.

Rhys spent Christmas on Tybee Island with his family and was staying until after the new year, as he'd planned. Although I was unsure of turning down his invitation to join him prior to our fight, I was happy with my decision now that he'd never bothered to answer my text. I had become accustomed to his silence when he was angry. Well, I was angry too and had every right to be. I wasn't sure even a phone call was a good move at this point.

My mother read my mind as she said, "He probably didn't reply because I'm assuming he's a little hurt and could use some reassurance right now."

"What do you mean?" I asked.

"Listen, you have an amazing thing with that man and you are blowing it by obsessing over what could have been." She turned to me quickly. "Get your head out of your ass, Violet. Stop worrying about the man who left you and start paying attention to the man who loves you."

"Mom, it's not that simple. He said some things—"

"Things that he didn't mean," she scolded.

"He lied to me again."

"He protected you, again," she said as she let go of my arm. "You have got to learn to choose your battles, baby. He's not in this to hurt you and right about now he's thinking you're not in this at all."

I paused in the street, thinking of how Rhys must have felt when I reacted to the situation. Of course I had hurt him. I was so worried about me, how I felt, too selfish to think of how it affected him. My reaction to Alex and his shit was ruining my newfound happiness...for the second time.

Did the details really matter? Why did I care so much about the way things happened? What is it in me that couldn't just let it go and be thankful like Rhys was?

No, when it came down to it, the details didn't mean anything.

Rhys was all that mattered, and his silence was deafening.

☙

I left my mother on River Street to finally head home and get on with living. As soon as I stepped through the door, my phone vibrated.

"Hey, Molly," I answered, less than enthusiastic.

"So do you have plans tonight with that hot as hell new boyfriend or did I just get lucky enough to catch you without any?"

"Tonight?"

"Yes, Violet. It's New Year's Eve."

I had spent an entire week at my parents!? No wonder my mother was ready to kick me out. I had been nothing but a moping pain in the ass.

"No, he's at his parents' house until tomorrow. But I will never go out on a holiday again. I'm cursed."

"Come on, Violet, just a few drinks before the road becomes dangerous. Then we can bring in the new year at your house."

"What happened to Roger?" I asked about her current fling.

"He's on a last minute business trip." I could tell from her tone she was lying. From the sound of things, she needed me. I looked down at my clothes and caught my reflection in my freezer door. I had once again turned into a slob of a woman, a pitiful mess agonizing over a man.

Old habits die hard.

"Fine, where?"

"Girl, you won't regret it. We will have a relaxed night, I promise."

God, how I wanted to believe her.

VIOLET

Molly and I sat at the bar, laughing hysterically at the events of Christmas Eve. Though the situation was anything but funny, she had a way of making the disaster seem so as she tried to put it all in perspective.

"You are an insensitive ass, Molly, really," I said, catching a tear from my last bout of laughter.

"Seriously, Violet, you can't make shit like this up. I mean, dear God, what a fucking story."

"It's not funny," I said firmly as the corners of my lips lifted. She stared at me for a full minute before we both burst out laughing.

"Okay," she said, lifting the cocktail straw to her mouth, "if you honestly want to know what I think, I say take him with all his flaws and his baggage, Violet, because he has to take you the same way. It's really very simple. In this fucked up situation, even with all the drama, you two make each other happy. Your coincidences make you miserable, but they are no longer in the picture. *She* is no longer in the picture. He's going to fuck up and so are you. That's a given. I don't blame you for holding your ground on the 'omission' thing, but don't drag it out until you two are strangers. You are so ready to stand up for yourself in this relationship because you didn't do a damn thing in the previous one to defend yourself, but you are punishing the wrong guy."

"I will not be treated like that, ever again," I whispered to her, and to myself.

"And I'm glad you've seen the light. Just don't let it blind you from seeing the guy who deserves you," she said, nodding to the bartender to refill her glass.

Maybe I was being an ass by dragging it out, or maybe the Old Fashioned I was drinking was doing a good job of making my situation a little less serious, less devastating. Either way, I was less angry, and for the first time in a week, I felt like I could recover.

And I missed him.

"Ladies, these drinks are on the gentlemen at the table behind you." We looked over our shoulders and lifted our glasses in thank you.

"*Thank you,*" Molly said flirtatiously in a singsong tone.

"Happy New Year's," I said cheerfully.

235

Minutes later, the four of us were making small talk. I had pro-tested Molly leaving the seat next to me, and was stuck in the po-sition of entertaining Luke, a dark-haired, dark-eyed friend of the gentlemen that Molly had quickly become smitten with. I made polite conversation, but gave no indication whatsoever that I was interested. In truth, I felt guilty and was on edge with the way he was looking at me. I had dressed in a sexy, form fitting, backless dress and worn a curtain of pearls that draped down the center of my back to cover some of my exposed skin. After a week of info-mercials and Ben and Jerry's, I wanted to feel like a woman again, a decision I was regretting as the man to my left fucked me with his stare.

Nothing about the situation felt innocent and suddenly I needed to talk to Rhys. I pulled my phone from my clutch and saw I had just gotten a text.

RHYS: He couldn't make you come with a detailed map of your clit and an instructional video.

Oh, shit!

I looked over my shoulder and scanned the bar, coming up empty.

I sat stunned as Luke spoke in circles. Pausing when it was my turn to reply, I completely drew a blank.

"I'm sorry. What were you saying?"

I could feel his eyes on me, though I couldn't see him. My mother must have told him where to find me. She and I would have to have a long talk about boundaries. She had never interfered be-fore, but I couldn't help but smile about the fact that I knew whose side she was on tonight—or in the last week, for that matter; it wasn't mine. Luke trailed his hand down my shoulder and I flinched at the contact. I looked over my shoulder and found Rhys standing close, fury in his stare. He closed his eyes briefly, as if in pain, and walked out of the bar.

"I'm sorry, Luke, but I'm in a committed relationship." I took a twenty out of my purse and signaled to Molly that I was leaving. She gave me a 'please don't go look' as I stood, waiting for her to join me, but she refused.

"I expect a call or text in a few hours," I said to Molly, shrugging into my coat. As I made my way toward the door, I quickly texted him.

VIOLET: Where are you?

I walked outside the bar and saw his taillights as he drove out of the parking lot.

What in the hell?

I got into a cab and was at his door within minutes. I turned the knob and was rewarded. He stood at the foot of his stairs, looking gorgeous in a tailored suit as he gripped the top of a freshly filled tumbler that rested on his thigh, his phone in hand. The house was completely dark except for a small amount of light gracing the stairway from above. I could feel his frustration and see it in his eyes.

We stared for a full minute before I took a step toward him.

"Don't come any closer," he cautioned, eyeing me. "I'm angry."

"Why did you leave?" I asked, ignoring his warning. "Why are you so angry, Rhys?"

"Why?" His laugh did not indicate in any way that anything was funny.

I unbuttoned my jacket and let it fall to the floor as I took another step forward.

"Don't, Violet," he warned, gripping his drink and tapping it lightly against his thigh, making his ice cubes clink. I stared at his glass, mesmerized by the memory of what those small cubes could do to me. As if he read my mind, he threw his glass against the front door, shattering it along with my confidence.

"You never do listen do you, Violet?" This time he took a step forward. "You took yourself away from me for another week. I give

237

you space and I find you at a bar, dressed like *that,* sitting next to a man that's not me. I'm angry, Violet, and right now I want to hurt you with my cock. I want to fuck you until it really hurts, and if you take another step forward, I'm going to do just that."

I damn near moaned at his words as I pulled my arms out of the sleeves of my dress, baring my breasts to him, letting the remainder of my dress rest on my hips. He refused to look at my peaked flesh as he glared at me. I swallowed hard, pushing the material over my hips slowly and letting it fall to the floor. I pulled the curtain of pearls from my back to the front of me, covering my front half with the silky strands as I took a step forward. He pulled his belt off and held it as his side. I took another step forward as he held up his hand, trying to pin me where I stood.

"I need you, Rhys. Please don't make me beg."

"What do you need? Me or *my cock,* Violet?" I took another step toward him as he perused my body, lust clear in his eyes.

"Both," I admitted, taking yet another step forward. "I don't want to fight. I just want —"

"You don't know that, either," he said, gripping the belt tighter.

"Rhys, I wasn't with him. I was—"

"This is me..." he said, pulling me to him by my long necklace and twisting the pearls so they constricted around my neck, "jealous."

I placed my hands on his chest, staring into his cold gray depths, mouth parted and pussy aching to be filled. He turned me to face the front door as he gripped my arms behind my back, securing them just above my elbows with his belt. It was painfully tight and the buckle dug into my skin. He pulled back on the pearls so that I was looking up at the ceiling, arms bound and completely at his mercy. I gasped at the strength in which he was handling me. I braced myself for the slap of his hand or more harsh words, but he stood there, his breathing heavy, his erection brushing against my back.

"Fuck, please, Rhys...please." I felt the warmth spread between my legs as my heart pounded. I didn't care how desperate I sounded. I needed his touch, his cock, his lips, and fingers covering and consuming me.

He turned me around to face him again as I leaned in, bracing myself for his touch. He ripped the triangle covering my center away easily as he covered me in his steely gaze. One swipe of his finger or flick of his tongue would ignite me, set me off. He was so insanely beautiful. No man had ever looked this appealing to me. His shadowed, chiseled features, angry eyes, and full lips had me licking mine in anticipation. His anger aroused me, though I hadn't done a thing to provoke him. He was being possessive and jealous, and I loved every minute of it. It meant he wanted me, that nothing had changed for us physically. Emotionally, we would deal with the rest later. It was raw need driving us together now and I couldn't wait to be filled by him, fucked by him, to be made his. His jaw twitched as he watched me arch my back as he took me in.

"I need you inside me, Rhys."

He gripped my necklace again, twisting the beads so I felt the pinch on my skin. "I don't want to hurt you," he gritted out. He was on the verge of snapping. I did the only thing I could to provoke him further.

"Would you rather I'd entertained him? Asked for his cock? Let him continue to touch me?" Thousands of pearls scattered down my body and onto the floor as he ripped them away. He turned me then pushed me onto the stairs, my head pressed painfully to the side of one of the hard wooden steps as my knees pressed against one another, my bare pussy exposed and ass out. He struck me hard with his hand right on my sensitive clit and I screamed out, tears coming to the surface. Another hard slap to my clit left me pulsating as I braced myself for another, my shoulders against the harsh surface of the stairs. He thrust his fingers inside me suddenly and I heard my arousal as he fucked me with them roughly. The unzipping of his pants had his cock at my entrance in seconds and I moaned in anticipation.

"You want me? This is what you want, Violet? Are you sure? You didn't seem so certain last week. Tell me what you want!"

"I want—" The words barely passed my lips before he buried his thickness inside me. We both moaned as the sensation overwhelmed us.

"You want me?" he taunted as he circled his hips, pushing hard as I urged him on with my moans. His fucking was tortuously hard, almost painful, and I pushed my ass back, begging for more.

"Fucking take it, Violet," he snapped, his hand coming down over and over again as he blistered my ass and thighs, my arms painfully bound as he gripped them with his and slammed his cock inside me. My knees screamed as the wood scraped away my skin and the weight of him bruised them as he punished me. I came almost instantly as he ripped away at my pussy, his strokes never slowing, never stopping. I heard his harsh exhale as he channeled all his anger into his fucking. He stopped abruptly, pulling me up by my bound arms, sitting down on a step and pulling me onto his length, facing me away from him.

I was rewarded with a deep moan that fueled me. "Remember this, Violet," he snapped, his hands molding to my hips as he began to move, pulling me down roughly with each thrust. I arched my back, resting my head on his shoulder as he continued to punish me. He was referring to the first night he had taken me, the first time he'd had me, the night my body became his.

"I love you," I confessed as he punished away, pretending to not hear my words as he continued his assault.

I came again seconds later and completely slumped against him as his strokes slowed and then stopped.

I looked back at him, our bodies still connected, both of us gasping, and his release still inside of him.

"Rhys?"

"I have to leave." He breathed heavily as he released my arms from the belt and stood me up. He retrieved my dress from the floor and tugged it up slowly around my body then pulled my arms through the sleeves.

"Rhys, please don't do this. Don't pull away from me." I stood there as he dressed me, like I was a helpless child, and without the right words to say.

"I have somewhere to be," he snapped as I reached for my coat, carefully stepping around the debris on the floor. I went to the kitchen and grabbed a broom to clean up the pearls and glass, but it was snatched from my hands.

"I have to leave," he said, grabbing my hand and leading me toward the door.

"Stop! Damn you, Rhys Volz, just stop!" I said, pulling away from him.

"Goddamnit, you stop it!" he said, his emotion coming through his voice. He took a step toward me. "I can't keep wondering if the woman I'm with is *with* me! I can't keep dreaming of a future with a woman who can't let go of her past. And I can't continue to let you be a part of my son's life or mine if you aren't certain about what you want or me! Regardless of what I've told you, this"—he gripped his chest with his fist—"is all new to me. I've never felt this way. I've never wanted a woman as much as I do you and I've never...been jealous, Violet, ever." He covered me with his gaze as I stood stunned at his admission, unable to comment or even wrap my head around it as he continued.

"I have traded subs without flinching. I've let go of lovers I've had for a year without giving it a second thought. So when I look at *you* and my chest hurts, my body aches, and you say those fucking words to me, I need you to mean them. Bryce needs you to mean them. This isn't just about me anymore. This is about us both. And we are *both* falling in love with you," he admitted with a resigned look.

241

His phone rang as tears slid down my face and I took a step toward him. He looked at the screen and answered. His eyes turned to me, his gaze unwavering as he spoke.

"Hi, Mom. I know. I spoke to her fifteen minutes ago. I'm on my way," he said, giving me a look of regret. He hung up and pulled me toward him so our foreheads touched. "I'm sorry. If I hurt you, I'll never forgive myself. I should never have taken you when I was this angry. Not like that."

"You didn't hurt me, Rhys. I'm fine," I assured him as he wiped my tears away with his thumbs.

"Heidi's in labor. I need to go."

"I'll go with you," I offered, hopeful.

"No." He pulled away from me, making me instantly cold. My heart sank as he pulled his jacket on and regarded me carefully. "I need you to decide to trust me, decide to love me enough to stick around when things are good or bad. And decide that no matter what happens you won't let it shake us. No more back and forth between us. I can't take it, Violet. With you, I'll always be selfish. I want all of you, not just what you're willing to risk. *All* of you."

I nodded as the tears kept coming.

He looked at me regretfully before he spoke. "I'm sorry. I have to go. I promised I'd be there."

"Go," I said, wiping my tears away and reaching for the door. "Goodnight." He reached for me and pulled me close as his mouth sealed over mine in a beautiful and gentle kiss. He stroked my tongue with his and I melted into him, wrapping my arms around him as he deepened it. He pulled away as we both stood completely wrapped up in the feeling, in each other. I leaned in again for more when he brushed his lips gently against mine before whispering, "I can't change anything about my past, Violet, and I don't want to." He pushed my hair away from my face and added, "You have to let go or we can't move on. Text me and let me know you got home safe?"" I nodded and he kissed me again before walking out the door.

I watched him drive away as I dialed a cab. I got home just in time to watch the ball drop on New Year's Rockin' Eve.

∝⊗๖

RHYS

I can't work.

Fuck this mouse. No, fuck this job.

I should just get the hell out of here for the day. I hadn't done anything at all but stare at my screen for the last three hours as I thought of her. I felt terrible for leaving her at my house the other night. Other than her text letting me know she'd made it home, we hadn't spoken. I felt like our time was running out.

One thought raced through my head constantly. The thought that kept me on edge, kept me from picking up the phone every hour.

I had kept my promise to her. I was all in. I had fallen hard, fast, and for a woman who had the ability to break me. So now the question remained...Was *she* all in? For years and years I'd had relationships with women, never giving them the kind of power Violet held over me. I grabbed my coat with every intention to head to my parents' house. Bryce loved the beach. Even though it was winter, the weather was mild outside. I could bundle him up today. With a plan in mind, I headed for the elevator, but just stood there.

You're fucking miserable. Just call her and see what she has to say. Anyone would have had that reaction. You can't punish her for it.

I really hated the reasonable guy I was becoming. I used to be able to just be angry without justification, take it out on a sub and call it a day. Now I had to think my feelings through without unleashing them. I hated myself for the way I'd taken Violet. I had lost control, and for the first time it was due to my emotions, not my sexual appetite. I had come a long way since I started. I had taken the steps I needed to rid myself of my destructive urges. I had no desire to even attempt the things I used to.

I wouldn't trade these days for those, anyway. I wouldn't trade my life for anyone else's. That thought alone had me jonesing for the sight of her. I could no longer imagine being with anyone else but Violet.

I'd come a long, long way.

If she still had lingering feelings for her husband, I supposed that would be understandable given the circumstances. But at the same time, I couldn't help but wonder why she would considering what we'd shared. She had moved me, weakened me, and was now breaking me.

You're acting like a pussy. Work this shit out. You can't turn your back on her because of your jealousy.

I didn't get the chance to call her. I'd just gotten a text with an address, from her mother.

<hr>

VIOLET

"All rise." Everyone stood as directed by the bailiff. I hadn't braved a glance to my left at the man who had attacked me. The minute I set foot in the courtroom, I felt nothing but terror knowing that the bastard who tried to kill me was mere feet away. I shook violently as I poured a glass of water, splashing a majority of it onto the table. My lawyer gave me a reassuring nod as I sat back in my chair and looked behind me. My mother sat close to me, giving me a similar nod, and I turned back to the action in the courtroom, completely oblivious to what was being said. I was, for the first time since my birthday, reliving the night I had almost died. I hadn't realized just how much I had masked my fear until today.

"Violet," my lawyer, Jake, whispered to me when my name was

called. I stood quickly, my knees knocking as I approached the stand and was asked to hold up my hand.

"Do you swear to tell the truth, the whole truth, and nothing but the truth, so help you God?"

"I do," I whispered, unable to find my voice.

"Please speak up, Ms. Hale," the judge urged.

"I do," I said firmly, taking a seat on the stand and refusing to look to my right. I saw his profile as he sat next to his lawyer in his filthy fucking brown suit, but couldn't bring myself to look at his face. I closed my eyes tightly as Jake went through the events of the night, detail by detail. I blocked them out, thinking of the man who saved me. I stumbled through my lawyer's questions and drew a blank as I watched the table to my right out of my peripheral vision, completely disabled by fear. By the time his lawyer started his line of questioning, I was terrified. The stench of him filled my nose as the memory gripped me. I fingered my scar absently as I felt the pinch of the knife all over again. I closed my eyes as I recalled the splash my fingers made in my own blood.

"Ms. Hale?"

"Yes? I'm sorry, could you repeat the question?"

"Is it true that you couldn't see the faces of your attackers?" the defense asked.

"Yes," I said weakly, looking at my hands as I twisted them in my lap. I bit the inside of my cheek hard as I tried to keep from crying. I answered as I replayed my own account of that night, refusing to look in his direction. If I did, I would know his face for the rest of my life, regardless if he were incarcerated for the rest of his. I didn't want that memory. Instead, I remembered Rhys.

"He knows you love him, honey. If he didn't before, he knows now. Don't you, Rhys?"

Remembering the medic's words, my eyes swelled and all I could do was sit silently and nod with an occasional "yes" loud enough for the record when I was forced to. I couldn't breathe.

Thoughts of Rhys raced through me as I let my tears fall at his memory, his sincerity. I needed him now. It felt foolish being apart from him. My fucking pride might have ruined my relationship with him, but right now, all I needed was the mere sight of him. It would have been enough. I said a prayer as I wiped at my face furiously, though it was useless.

The details didn't matter. Rhys had saved me in more ways than one. All he was asking of me was what I wanted from him. Our relationship was so simple, yet our lives had made it seem so damn impossible. The only thing standing in our way now was...us.

"Ms. Hale, do you need a minute?" the defense attorney asked as I hiccupped on a sob, trying desperately to regain some strength.

I longed for the gray eyes that had captured me and held me hostage. The tears fell heavy as I mourned for my love, no longer afraid of the bastard who had robbed me and left me for dead. Now, I was more afraid of the growing distance between myself and the love of my life. When I looked up into the faces of the courtroom, I saw the eyes I had longed for.

Rhys.

I almost cried out in relief as we kept each other's gaze, his eyes telling me everything he could not say. Saltwater slid down my cheeks, and I hoped he could see the *I love you, I love you, I love you* in my eyes. I had to keep my chuckle in when I noticed he was wearing his noncommittal sweater. As if he could read my mind, he gave me a reassuring nod and small smile. I gathered all my strength as he watched me and finally let my gaze wander to my right to face my fear. I glared in the direction of my attacker as he cowered in his chair, refusing to meet my eyes. He was older—maybe in his early fifties—and a true to life scumbag with greasy hair and bad skin, no doubt a junkie or alcoholic. There was nothing terrifying about him. I sat up straight and answered the questions Jake had drilled me on the previous day, more certain than ever that when I left the courtroom today, I could close this chapter of my life.

"Ms. Hale, do you need more time?"

I looked right at my attacker. "No, I'm fine," I replied, my voice growing in strength with each word spoken. The questions continued as I answered honestly through his cross-examination.

"I have no more questions, your honor."

The judge looked at me, eyes filled with sympathy. "Thank you, Ms. Hale. You may step down."

I was sure then the sentence would be fitting to the crime.

It was over.

My mother nodded at me, her tears mirroring mine, as I walked toward my seat. Rhys winked at me and I had to resist the urge to walk over to him and launch myself into his arms.

When court was adjourned, I stood immediately to go to Rhys, but was stopped short by my lawyer. Rhys left the courtroom and all the air left my body. I fought the small crowd and made it through the door, finding Rhys waiting next to the elevator, his gaze on me.

"Jake, Violet will call you," my mother interrupted as she watched my reaction to Rhys. Jake nodded, slightly confused as I approached Rhys and we slipped inside the elevator.

RHYS

"I've been trying to give you space, Violet, but I can't do it anymore," I whispered, trying my hardest to keep my distance. My chest was full as I sifted through my thoughts, carefully trying to convey to her in the best way I knew how that I needed her.

Fucking words.

"I'm not asking for it and I don't want it."

She looked so fucking beautiful wrapped in her black winter coat, her lips painted a perfect shade of pink and long blonde hair cascading down her shoulders. Her swollen eyes locked on mine.

I charged her when we were alone in the elevator and pinned her to the back of it.

Possessive is all I felt in that moment as I looked down at her face, so beautiful, so beyond perfect.

I felt a part of me rip as I asked her my next question, afraid she would see the hardest part of me no longer existed with her this close. I had come undone, and all for her.

"I guess my question is," I said, my chest heavy, "do you still *want* him to love you?"

Her tears fell as she looked up at me. "No, God, no," she answered, her voice shaking. She shook her head back and forth, her tears coming down fast. I wiped them away, searching her eyes, desperate to believe her. "I never want you to think I do, Rhys. I love *you*. I gave you everything when I got back from my trip. I was just so fucking shocked that night. I let it shake me."

I cupped her face in my hands as she looked up at me. "I'm sorry I didn't tell you, but I only did it to protect you, Violet. I don't want to lose you, but I can't and won't share you with anyone else, ever."

"You won't ever have to. Please believe me. I know I acted like a fool. What *we* have is all I want. I don't care about them. I want them out of our lives for good. I need to be with you and Bryce. I don't care anymore that I wasn't enough for him. I only want to be enough for you."

She grabbed my face and brought her lips to mine. I pressed hard then pulled away as I brought my hand up to grip her chin. "All of you. I want it all." She nodded in response as I grasped her waist, pulled her close, and leaned in, taking her mouth roughly, thrusting my tongue in and tasting her as she whimpered, meeting my kiss. I wrapped my arms around her, gripping her tighter before pulling my lips away to catch her eyes.

"Rhys, I want to know *everything*, no matter what. You get all of me, and I get all of you. It can't be any other way," she demanded as I smiled. I leaned in and kissed her jaw, stroking her throat with my thumb.

"I'm serious," she scorned as I slid my kiss down her neck.

"Oh, I know you are," I said, taking her lobe in between my teeth. "I think we both know you win this round, but if you need to prove your point further, can you wait until after I sink into you?"

I moved my kiss to her lips and took her mouth until she pulled away, gasping. "Rhys, I need you inside me. Now, right now. I'm so fucking wet, please." Her eyes were closed and her mouth was parted. I groaned, thinking of a way to get her alone, to get her what she needed, what I needed. The doors opened and I gripped her firmly by the hand and led her to the garage. We got in my car and she lifted her skirt then pulled down her panties as I turned on the ignition and began to circle the garage, looking for some privacy. She looked up at me, her eyes filled with need.

"Touch yourself...now," I commanded roughly. She pulled up her skirt, exposing her perfect pussy, and began making circles on her clit as she spread her legs. My greed taking over, I dipped a finger inside her and brought it to my mouth as she played with her center. She ground her heels into the dash while I glanced over to watch her. "You're so fucking beautiful," I told her as I found an abandoned parking space on the top floor and parked quickly.

"Rhys, God," she panted, her fingers drenched, her arousal showing all over her flushed body. I adjusted my seat, shifting and tilting it back then quickly unzipped my pants, pulling out my cock and stroking it as she started to come undone. She moaned as her legs began to shake. I leaned over and stroked her cheek. "Come for me," I whispered, pushing my fingers inside her as she stroked her clit.

"I'm coming." She threw her head back as her release took her and I pushed my fingers deeper, twisting them and rubbing her g-spot as her body shook. I took her wetness and coated my bottom lip then licked it clean before grabbing her quickly by the hips and pulling her to straddle me.

"Fuck me, baby," I growled as she braced herself above me and slowly sank down on me, making us both insane.

"I missed you," she said, leaning in as she started to move, keeping her eyes on mine.

She rode me hard as she ground her hips, milking my cock with her tight core. I thrust up hard and she bit my shoulder, bringing me close to losing my load.

I pulled her lips to mine as she exhausted herself, rising and falling so she took every inch.

"Fuck yes, Violet," I groaned at the feel of her. I felt the pull but waited for her as I felt her start to clench around me. I pushed her skirt up around her waist and shoved my fingers in her mouth as she moaned, close to the edge. She sucked and licked them before I pulled them out, reaching between us to massage her clit. I felt her let go and thrust hard as she bucked wildly, her orgasm coating me. When she was good and gone, I gripped her hair, pulling it hard as I buried my dick and came inside her, shaking with my release.

"I'm yours," she whispered, curling herself against my chest. "As long as you want me I'm yours, Rhys."

VALENTINE'S DAY

VIOLET

VIOLET: I am not leaving this house. I'm cursed.

RHYS: You are being a little dramatic, don't you think?

VIOLET: No, take the baby and run far far away from me.

RHYS: I want to see you tonight.

VIOLET: Not on a holiday. I want nothing to do with it. On Halloween, I was robbed, Thanksgiving just sucked, and do I need to remind you of the disaster at Christmas and New Year's?

He gave up, thankfully, and I resigned myself to a quiet night of watching a Hallmark marathon. I had no patience for Murphy's Law tonight. None. I had endured enough. I popped popcorn and snuggled up on my couch, unable to brave lighting a fire in my fireplace, though I longed for it. I had done everything imaginable to protect myself from this day. I had fancied the idea of wrapping myself in bubble wrap for the twenty-four hours it lasted. I couldn't wait for it to be over. I craved my men with me, but didn't want anything bad coming to pass today. I was overreacting and didn't care what a lunatic I might seem like. I needed peace. Just one holiday with some peace. My doorbell rang and I ignored it. I refused to open

251

it. Danger lurked in and out of these walls and I buried my head under the blanket to keep from hearing it ring again. But, it did.

Okay, Vi, it's probably your mother. Stop being a baby and open the door.

I threw my covers off, angry at the intrusion. Looking through the peephole, I noticed no one was there. Shortly after I turned back toward my living room, I heard the bell sound again and I went to look. Once again, I saw nothing. I cracked the door, looked through my screen, then my heart burst. Baby Bryce was standing in a tuxedo screaming "Vi tet!" as he waved a single red rose in his hand. I opened the door quickly and greeted him.

"Oh, baby, it's so cold! I'm so sorry!" He smiled and waved the rose in front of me, his father to the left of the door, egging him on. "Give it to her, buddy. Good boy." I scooped Bryce up, taking a huge cheek in my mouth with a kiss and rubbed his back to warm him up. Rhys came into view then in a matching tux and I nearly fell to my knees with Bryce in my arms.

"Get dressed. We are going out to eat," he said, smiling as he came toward me. I tried to keep my eyes on Rhys and nearly stumbled as I made my way to the kitchen to set Bryce on the counter, leaning on it to help hold me up.

"You look—Wow, you both look so...handsome," I said, cupping Bryce's cheek as he smiled up at me. Rhys pulled out the rest of the roses, that I hadn't realized he was holding, from behind his back. They were absolutely beautiful. I took them from him, leaning over Bryce, who sat in front of me on the counter, to give Rhys a kiss. He took my lips gently then swiped his tongue over them to let me know he was hungry. I met his tongue, quickly letting him know I felt the same. When he pulled back, he took a look at my clothes and began to laugh.

"Oh crap," I said, burying my head in Bryce's neck as he giggled at the tickle. I was wearing adult footed pajamas that I had purchased on a whim a few months ago.

"This is definitely not what you are wearing out tonight." Rhys laughed fully now as he took in my pajamas and I blushed, ignoring him, listening to Bryce. It had apparently been a big day.

"I am not going anywhere. I mean it, Rhys," I warned in a light tone, smiling at his son who looked like an absolute doll in his tux as he pointed to his feet telling me about his "shiny shoose."

"They are shiny shoes, buddy," I encouraged.

"Just dinner, and then we will come straight home," Rhys pleaded, coming behind me as I held Bryce on the counter. "I'll make it worth your while." His hips brushed my back and I could feel how hard he was. I lost my breath, trying my best to hold on to Bryce, pushing my ass back to bump him away from me. It backfired and we both groaned.

"Highly inappropriate, Rhys. Highly," I scolded as I kept my focus on his son, who was still telling me everything about everything. I felt Rhys's chest at my back as he leaned forward, moving my hair away from my ear to whisper, "Then maybe it would be going too far to tell you I can't wait to suck your pussy, to fill you with my tongue and torture you with my cock while I watch it go in and out of you."

I gasped and Bryce mimicked me, doing the same then giggling. I turned my head to the side and saw the fire in Rhys's eyes.

"Behave, please," I scolded, taking Bryce from the counter and bringing him the toys from my room that I bought him for Christmas.

"Our reservation is in an hour," Rhys reminded me and I shrugged.

"Violet, please." Rhys hardly ever used that word. He looked so damn handsome in his tux, it was impossible to say no. I reluctantly agreed and was in my bathroom sliding on my negligee minutes later when Rhys appeared behind me in the mirror. I smiled and so did he as we studied our reflection.

"I'm afraid I have one last thing I've been keeping from you, Violet." His tone was serious and I was instantly on edge.

No, no, no. God, no. What now?

"Damn holidays. I knew this was a bad idea," I said, shoulders slumped. He chuckled as he brought my chin up to meet his eyes in the mirror.

"I've never had a type," he whispered behind me as he slowly snaked his arm around my waist, pulling me back to him to hold me tightly. "I knew I appreciated certain features on a woman, and I knew what turned me on, but I never really had a type. A few years ago, I was standing in line for dinner and there was a couple standing in front of me." He slid his hand down my negligee as I leaned into him so my body was at his disposal. "The moment she spoke, she had my attention. Her voice instantly made me hard. And though I could only see the side of her face, I knew she was beautiful and I wanted her instantly. I was coveting another man's wife."

I frowned as he cupped my breast over the material. "Not a very good story —"

"It was you, Violet. I saw you and you were so fucking beautiful and so in love and that's what drew me to you. And when I saw the way you looked at him, I'd never wanted anything so bad. So when I saw you on the screen at my club, you seemed so familiar and the reason was because I had thought about you for weeks after that day. Dreamed about you even, your voice, your beautiful neck," he whispered, cascading hot kisses down my neck as his fingers slid to my center, circling slowly. He turned my head and kissed me deeply as I opened my legs and rotated my hips. He pulled away as he held my face and continued to whisper to me as his fingers filled me. "Maybe then I knew you belonged to me. Maybe then I knew that one day"—he pulled my orgasm out as I shuddered and moaned his name—"I would possess you this way."

He continued to stroke me through the satin as I asked about Bryce.

"Sleeping," he said as his tongue tickled my lobe. With skilled hands, he covered my chest over the material, making his touch feel surreal. I closed my eyes and moaned.

"Eyes on mine," he reminded gently as his hands continued to stroke me with his expert touch.

Our eyes connected, our faces washed in desire as he held me tightly, his mouth to my ear, making sure I heard his next words.

"I will be your everything. I'll be the man who fucks you, possesses you, and the man who loves and cares for you. You have to know I love you, Violet. I wanted you even when you belonged to someone else. I wanted you to *feel* it from me before I said the words." He cupped my mound again, sliding his digits in deliciously slow, moving my wetness all over me. With his chest behind me and hunger in his eyes, he captivated me with his gaze as he confessed to me. "Words can get lost, become meaningless and fall away. And promises have a way of getting broken. I want more for you. I want so much for you. But believe me, right here, right now, when I say that I can't imagine a day will ever come when I won't feel this way. And there will never be a day, good or bad, when you won't feel it from me." Two silent tears slid down my face as his features filled with emotion. As I stared at his reflection and saw his vulnerability, my chest squeezed.

"Rhys," I said, cupping his neck behind my head as he circled my sex, pulling me to the edge a second time. I felt his hardness at my back and rubbed myself against him as my chest rose and I began to pant heavily. His fingers plunged inside me and I let out a whimper as my knees buckled slightly.

"Fuck it. I can't wait." He lifted me off my feet, carrying me to my bed as he spread me before him. "Fuck, I love that you're mine," he growled as he lapped up my entire sex in one long, slow sweeping motion with his tongue. Still dressed immaculately in a tux, I was overwhelmed at the sight of him, the smell of him, his mouth devouring me. Awestruck by the skill of his tongue, I watched it dart out to lick my clit before he wrapped his lips around it and sucked. I burst in his mouth from the sight of him alone. He looked up at me, his gray eyes filled with satisfaction. I couldn't help but ask for more.

"Will you do that again? Just like that?" I begged as his eyes smiled, his grin was unmistakable. He said nothing as he brought me to the very same peak the very same way. He stood then, as I lay sated, watching his every move as he removed his jacket.

"You love me," I said, repeating his words to me in a daze as I watched him take off his bowtie and shirt.

When his pants and briefs were gone, he moved from the foot of the bed, crawling slowly over me, stopping at my sex for a quick tender kiss before he came up to my mouth, entering me slowly as our bodies aligned. Once I was filled with him, he looked down at me with nothing but gentleness in his eyes.

"I love you," he promised as he cupped my face while grinding his cock into me so I felt every throbbing inch. Soon his gentle thrusts turned into a vicious pounding, neither of us holding back as he completely stretched me, fucking me harder and harder until I unbuckled. I wrapped my hands around his neck and pulled him to me tightly as my orgasm subsided. He kissed my collarbone as we both lay panting and sweating, his eyes penetrating me.

"You sure do love me," I said, chuckling as he dipped down with a grin to take a nipple in his mouth. His hand clasped the side of my face as his thumb stroked my cheek. I rolled him over on his back, grasped his still hard length and watched his eyes fire up at my touch.

"Always working so hard for my benefit. I think it's time you let me reciprocate." Before he could say a word, I had him buried in the back of my throat. I heard his sharp inhale as he pulled my hair, instantly lost in his arousal. He pulled harder as I gripped the head softly between my teeth, gliding my hand down his shaft, pushing hard on that sensitive spot below his sack. His cock jumped at the sensation and I looked up to see his mouth parted as he stared down at me. I caught a good amount of pre-cum with my lips as it escaped him and he swallowed hard, unable to hide his need.

"So good, Violet." He thrust his hips up, but I stilled them, knowing I was more than capable of bringing it out on my own. I straddled his thighs, gripping his cock tight like a vice as I sucked the rest of it, soaking him up with my mouth. When I was sure he was about to burst, I swallowed him whole, never letting up, taking him deep into my throat, squeezing him so tight I knew he wouldn't last long. I heard his loud moan as I looked up and saw the shock and awe and undeniable lust pouring from him then pumped harder and faster with my hand and lips, taking him all the way in.

"FUCK! FUCK! Fucking take it," he hissed, shooting his orgasm into my mouth as I jerked it out of him fast and hard. When I was sure I had taken all he had to give, I sat up, watching him come down. He was in a daze as he looked at me. I smiled at him, rubbing my hands over his chest and planting small kisses on it.

He looked at my bedside clock and with a quick "oh shit" grabbed me. Minutes later, we were out of the shower, rushing to dress to make our dinner reservation. Rhys left me standing in the very spot I was in half an hour earlier at the bathroom mirror with a promise of a long night filled with more of what we'd just shared. He loved me, and in truth, I had known well before he said the words. I felt it every time he looked at me, in his smile, his touch, his embrace. I stood in a daze in the bathroom, praying and praising like I was accepting another Oscar.

Instead of the long night of lovemaking, we managed to get a quickie in at three a.m. Bryce had been a total adorable monster and stayed up well past his bedtime. We lay in our dress clothes, exhausted as we watched him run in circles until finally passing out.

SPRING

VIOLET

"**O**h my GOD!" I screamed, studying my face. I had run to the restroom half an hour ago, sensing an oncoming attack. And at the moment, I looked like the deformed Sloth from that movie *The Goonies*. I was a cauliflower ear short of being his double. My eyes were swollen shut and I couldn't stop sneezing.

This was not good.

Rhys knocked on the door and I stuck my foot in front of it to keep him from coming in, shut it quickly and locked it. I turned back to the mirror in the bathroom at his parents' house, watching my face explode from an allergic reaction.

"Rhys, get me a Benadryl!" I said, searching the cabinets desperately for an antihistamine.

"What the hell is going on? Everyone is waiting downstairs," he said impatiently.

"Nothing," I said, trying to muffle my voice. My swelling tongue would impair my speech for a while.

"You're full of shit, babe. Now open this door!" he demanded, his voice filled with worry.

"Can't a girl have some privacy?" I asked, every single word coming out strangled.

"Violet, please open the door."

I splashed cold water over my face, as if that would help, and stood to my full height. I warned him about my allergies, but it just so happened my first attack of the season occurred the very night his parents planned a dinner party so the family and I could get better acquainted. I couldn't stay in the bathroom. They were waiting. This was going to be bad.

I opened the door and saw the horror cross Rhys's face.

"Oh my GOD!" he exclaimed, mortified as he gripped my shoulders.

Yeah, it's just as bad as I thought it would be. I'd never seen him so horrified. I began crying immediately as he raced out of the room.

Man, that was fast. All it took was one look at my Shrek face. *Vain bastard.*

I sat on the edge of the bed sobbing as Rhys rushed back in the room with four Benadryl in his hand and shut the bedroom door, clearly not wanting anyone to see me.

"This is just allergies?" he asked, wiping my tears away.

"Yeah, for years the doctors said it was a food allergy and then they said it was something in the air. There's no way of stopping it. It happens at least three or four times a year. I'm sorry but I can't face your family. You can take me home."

He pulled me to him as he whispered in my ear, "I wouldn't leave you, even though you look like the elephant man on steroids." He chuckled as I elbowed him in the chest. "I'll be right back."

I sat at the edge of the bed, feeling terrible about ruining the dinner party I knew his mother had worked so hard on. She'd been planning this for weeks, and though I had been out with Heidi a few times and we quickly became close, I was excited to get to know the rest of his family.

The last few months with Rhys had been the exact opposite of our first months. I'd refused to peek around the corner, dreading the next disaster, and because of that they'd been the best months of my life. I was certain with my new love there would always be something there that threatened to shake us, but I was more certain I would refuse to let it get in the way. I heard Bryce calling for me from downstairs and my heart squeezed. I knew my appearance would only frighten him.

It's just an allergy attack, Vi.

Rhys walked in a few minutes later, carefully balancing two plates of food, two plastic glasses, and a hand full of movies as his arm cradled a bottle of wine.

"They are going to watch Bryce and you and I get another picnic in bed," he said, setting the plates on the nightstand next to me and sliding off his shoes. He walked over to me, stripped my dress off, and gasped at the rash on my back. "Oh, man, this is... bad." I nodded, embarrassed, then quickly got under the covers. He pulled me to him and kissed me gently.

"I'm sorry," he whispered. I nodded again, still a bit emotional from him seeing me this way. But he loved me and it showed now more than ever. I felt sick and took two of the Benadryl he offered. He quickly handed me the movies to choose from.

I sifted through them. "*How to Lose a Guy in Ten Days, Steel Magnolias, Cider House Rules*...Rhys, these are all chick movies."

His smile was devastating. "I know. I told them to hand me the cheesy love ones," he said, putting our plates on pillows and setting mine in front of me.

"This is awesome. Thank you so much," I said, my voice shaky.

"This is us. Good or bad. Butt ugly or not," he said as he deadpanned, "I may have to brown bag your head and get you from behind tonight."

"NOT FUNNY!" I said, offended, as he laughed. He cupped my face and pulled my swollen lips to his. I couldn't help but laugh with him.

He pulled back as he chuckled. "Told you I can be a prick."

❧

I walked through the market picking up various items to cook for Rhys tonight. We had the house to ourselves and I wanted to do something special for him. The last few months had been amazing, and though my skills were rusty, there was no time like the present to remedy that. I smiled when I found the aisle that carried his favorite bath salt. I reached for it when I heard a voice behind me.

"Predictable."

I didn't bother to turn and look at the source of the voice. No good would come of it.

"What do you want," I hissed.

"Nothing," she said passively. "I just thought I would come over and see how the happy couple is doing."

"Ask Rhys," I said, facing her head on and gasping at the sight of her. The whole left side of her face was purple and swollen. Her lips were busted and I saw a small amount of dried blood in the corner.

She completely ignored my reaction to her. I had no doubt her condition was a direct result of her sick fetish. "So tell me something," she said, trailing her pointer on the box of salt I was holding in my hand. "Do you think you satisfy him?" Her eyes were icy as she tried to regard me calmly, though there was nothing but contempt in the air between us.

I ignored her question and stepped past her. She gripped my arm painfully, forcing me to confront her.

"Sandra, I won't let you do this or anything for that matter. No matter how hard you try, you'll never come between us. Whatever you're thinking, give it up. We are too strong and you won't succeed," I said confidently.

"I'm well aware you're the woman he wants. What I can't figure out is why," she said, studying me.

261

"Maybe because I'm nothing like you," I said, ripping my arm away.

"Maybe, and maybe you are just better at playing the game."

"And just what the hell is that supposed to mean?" I asked, taking an intrusive step toward her.

She smiled at my irritation. "Oh, come on, Violet. We both know you came after me. You found out about Alex and me and went after Rhys. He may not have figured it out, but I have. I took your family away so you—"

"No, Sandra, you *gave* me my family. It was never a game for me. I'm not a sick bitch like you. I don't thrive on other's misery. I didn't have to play with his emotions to get him to love me. I didn't have to manipulate my way into anyone's life. I won your game without ever picking up the dice. Deal with it. I'm nothing like you." I watched her wheels turn at my admission. "By the way, I heard through Alex's parents that he moved to Atlanta with his best friend Chris. Sorry for your loss."

I smiled as she stood speechless. "I've got to get going now, Sandra. I have to go home to cook dinner for my Dom. You know how it is, supper and reruns before I let him tie me up and fuck me. And don't worry, Sandra, whatever he practiced on you, I can assure you he perfected on me." I smiled sweetly as I handed her the bath salts.

"Looks like you could use this more than us. Take care." I walked out of that store, certain we would cross paths again one day. But no matter what, I'd be ready for her.

I drove my route home, loving the way fall crept in on the heels of summer so subtly. I reveled in the crisp feeling of the season's air as I rolled down my window and welcomed it, a smile on my face. It's arrival brought the realization of how much had changed since I'd last taken notice.

A year ago, I was completely miserable, unable to please a husband who no longer loved me and left me unfulfilled. And close to becoming another divorcee who sat on a shrink's couch and whined about her husband's inadequacies.

I stepped out, hurt, afraid, insecure, and scared.

The bravest thing I ever did was take a chance and step out of my comfort zone to experience what I knew I was missing. The smartest thing I ever did was go with my instinct about Rhys and force him to give me another chance. The hardest thing I'd ever done was ride out the aftermath of my failed marriage, hoping for a silver lining.

I now lived in that silver lining.

I had been crazy to think I could replace my reality and live in a fantasy with something else. Rhys tried to keep his from me. He'd wanted to protect me, to keep as much of the fantasy as possible just as I'd needed to be disillusioned. Because, in the end, that's all there is...reality.

My knight in shining armor was a sex-crazed, ex-Dom that carried a diaper bag. But he was also a smart, sensitive, and sexy man who loved me. I wasn't the damsel in distress I had led myself to believe. I was worth more and capable of much more than I imagined. Rhys helped me embrace it, while Alex tried to rob me of it. In the end, I realized the people I surrounded myself with determined the quality of my life.

I loved my reality. I loved my silver lining. I smiled hearing the ping, knowing the source of my message.

RHYS: Pussy here, NOW!

My mind raced at the ever-changing possibilities that awaited me.

VIOLET: On my way. Don't I get a color?

RHYS: GOLD.

My chest squeezed as I turned into our drive and stared at the porch—*our* porch. In a few billion steps, I would be in his arms, where I belonged. I'd just sold my house and made his my permanent residence at his urging and I couldn't imagine it any other way. Rhys was home, as he promised he'd be. Bryce was my world.

It may have taken me a year to get here, to this place where I felt safe and happy and sated all at the same time without feeling guilty or afraid it would end. Deep down I knew I deserved it, that the bad realities that had come to pass would help me to appreciate the good. And that's exactly what I intended to do as long as I was living...be thankful.

For the first time in my life, I was truly in love...alive...and awake.

❦

RHYS

I had waited for her at the door after I'd just lit the house with every candle I could find. I was nervous, a feeling I hadn't felt in years because of a woman. *I* was the one who intimidated and slightly manipulated my way into their psyche. This whole year had been a new experience for me and I was fine with that. But on this night in particular, I really wanted that control back. I was used to it, taking calculated risks with partners when in reality I already knew what the outcome would be. In this case, I was screwed.

Doms don't often propose.

Celebrate the union of

Rhys Thomas Volz

and

Violet Marie Hale

together with their families

Saturday June 30, 2015

One o'clock in the afternoon

at

The Ritz–Carlton, Grand Cayman

EPILOGUE

3 ½ YEARS LATER

"**F**our bedrooms three and a half baths, hardwoods throughout, vaulted ceilings with crown molding, a state of the art kitchen, and as you can see, plenty of living space downstairs as well as a bonus room upstairs." I walked through the house, pointing out various selling points. I looked amongst the crowded room and found a few of the couples attending the open house had wandered on their own to tour the home. I quickly took inventory of the few whose attention I still had and froze when I saw a pair of familiar eyes. I couldn't help my smile as I continued on to the study with the remaining interested parties, minus one Dom who looked at me with expectancy.

"What year is this home?" a lady in what looked like her late sixties asked innocently as I stared at the man behind her who hadn't taken his eyes off me. My heartbeat spiked as I gazed back at him, growing hotter with each passing second. His stare was filled with hunger and his posture let me know he had every intention of getting his fill. The air thickened as I took in his perfect appearance. His thick black hair was combed back immaculately. His black suit fit him too well, and I wasn't alone in appraising him. A few of the wives spent an enormous amount of effort trying to conceal their obvious lust. His full lips turned up only slightly as I licked my own lips and my sex began to pulse. I took my bottom lip with my teeth as I smiled at him, curious about his intention. His answer was in

266

his eyes undressing me, fucking me as his blazing eyes stared at my lips then my throat, letting them glide down to my rising, rapidly moving chest then further down and back up, achingly slow.

"Umm, I'm sorry. It was built in '97," I said, trying my best to regain my ability to concentrate on the questions flying at me.

I felt my phone vibrate and checked the text quickly.

RHYS: You have 97 seconds to take off your panties.

"No," I said firmly and indirectly to the man behind the lady questioning me. "I'm sorry. It's '99 and the roof was replaced just last year." I averted my gaze to the younger couple staring through the family room window to the backyard. I felt him close behind me, my arousal growing with his proximity. I was wet, soaked, and had to squeeze my thighs together at the discomfort. I felt the burn start in my neck, the heat rising to my cheeks as I continued to try to keep it together.

"There's plenty of room for a pool and garden as well as an additional half acre—" My phone vibrated again, cutting into my train of thought.

RHYS: Sixty seconds.

"No!" I said quickly, confusing everyone around me. "I'm sorry. Where was I?"

I felt my pocket vibrate again and instead of looking at the screen, I excused myself to address Rhys briefly as he grinned at my frustration. I closed the short distance between us as he leaned in and whispered to me, his breath hot on my skin.

"Twenty seconds, Violet, or I take your pretty pink pussy in front of all of these fine, interested buyers."

"This is not funny. I'm at work," I whispered.

His eyes hardened as he leaned in close and whispered firmly, "And I'm not laughing. Ten seconds, Violet, or I'll do it myself."

I excused myself to the restroom in a near sprint to keep his threat at bay. Seconds later, I was out of the bathroom with my panties in hand and stuffed them in Rhys's suit jacket pocket on my way back out to the group. Less than a minute later, my pocket vibrated. I looked at him, shaking my head no firmly as he took a step toward me. I quickly looked at my phone.

RHYS: I'm going to need to fuck my pretty pussy within the next two minutes. Make it happen.

I groaned out loud in frustration as I read the text. Was he fucking serious? I had a house full of people; there was no way I could clear them out that quickly. I texted back as I showcased the kitchen.

VIOLET: Rhys, this is my JOB!

RHYS: I'm priority. One minute.

"And over here we have the dining room," I said, already hot at the thought his cock would be inside me in seconds. There was no denying him; he would make sure of it. I was soaked with thoughts of him filling me. I was also panicking and needed a plan.

"Okay, if everyone will step upstairs and have a look around, I will be up shortly." I saw Rhys smirk and grew furious with the position I was being put in.

"Can I ask a question about the flooring?" the oldest woman of the group asked as she thoroughly inspected the wood for scratches.

"Actually, if everyone could head upstairs, I will answer all your questions," I answered quickly, ushering the way to the second floor.

She hmphed and continued her questioning. "I just wanted to —"

"Upstairs! Everyone upstairs!" They all looked at me surprised at my insistence and quickly moved upstairs as Rhys approached me from behind, sliding my skirt up inch by inch as I watched the last of them ascend the steps.

"Rhys," I snapped as I whirled on him. He picked me up, quickly wrapping my legs around him, his engorged cock pulsing against my wet center and walked me toward the wall. As soon as my back hit the hard surface, he cupped my breast roughly and all my words fell away.

"Tell me you need it," he grunted, releasing his cock from his pants and sliding his thickness along my wet center, making it impossible for me to catch my breath. He pinned my arms above my head and commanded my attention, sliding himself back and forth against my soaked clit. I heard the shuffle of the people above us and quickly tried to free myself from his grip.

"Rhys, not right here," I pleaded as I glanced behind me at the empty stairwell.

"Right here, right now," he answered as he pushed inside me completely in one thrust and I moaned involuntarily. His face strained as he said, "Perfect."

"Oh God, Rhys, please." My protest diminished and turned into a plea at the feel of him.

"Tell"—thrust—"me"—thrust—"you"—thrust—"need"—thrust, thrust, thrust—"my"—thrust—"cock"—thrust—"Violet."

I gripped his hips with my thighs in answer and clinched my sex tightly, watching the heat in his eyes amplify at the feel of me. I leaned in and bit his bottom lip hard as he punished me, my blouse catching on the snags of the hard surface of the wall. Letting go of my arms, he pumped into me hard and fast, my back resting on the wall as he pulled our bodies away slightly so we were joined at an angle and I could feel every hard inch of him.

"If you won't tell me, Violet, your body will. It always does. Do you feel how well we fit?" He lifted my shirt, sliding his thumb over my nipple then pinching hard as he drove into me, gripping my hip with his other hand and squeezing hard. "Do you feel how much I want you? Answer me," he demanded.

"Yes, Rhys. Oh, God, I—" I lost the ability to breathe as he thrust in harder, slamming my back against the wall.

"Don't ever try to deny me; it's pointless," he bit out as I tilted my head back. I bit my bottom lip in an attempt to stifle my moan.

"Eyes on mine as I fuck my pretty pussy," he ordered, his hands on my hips digging in deeper, grinding his thickness into me. Our connection grew more intense as we watched our reaction to each other, mouths parted, our need undeniable. His eyes told me what his body reiterated with each movement, and what I knew without a doubt: I belonged to him.

"Fuck me," I urged as I reveled in the feel of him moving my hips hard and fast in perfect rhythm.

"Mrs. Volz?" I heard the call from above. It was that same damned woman. "Mrs. Volz?"

Rhys sped up and gripped my throat hard as I clinched around him. I burst, taking quick breaths as he fed on my reaction. "I'm coming!" I gasped out in reply to her as he worked me, his hunger washing over me. He licked my nipple then trailed lower to bite the swell of my breast as he continued to rip into me relentlessly. When I felt him thickening in anticipation of his release, he let my legs down and pushed me to my knees. I looked up at him just as his thick, coated tip brushed my lips. "Rhys, I need your cock." I took his orgasm as he stroked my face tenderly. When I had taken all of it, he pulled me from my knees and swatted me playfully on the butt. "Way to be the good little wife," he teased.

I raised a brow at his smug smile. "I'll let you get away with that once," I said, turning toward the stairs. "And, Rhys, please go pick up our sons. Apparently, I have to work later than expected."

I turned back to smile at him as he watched me climb up the stairs. His grin was unmistakable as he whispered, "I love you," our thoughts the same.

This was happy.

ABOUT THE AUTHOR

USA Today bestselling author and Texas native, Kate Stewart, lives in North Carolina with her husband, Nick. Nestled within the Blue Ridge Mountains, Kate pens messy, sexy, angst-filled contemporary romance, as well as romantic comedy and erotic suspense.

Kate's title, *Drive*, was named one of the best romances of 2017 by The New York Daily News and Huffington Post. *Drive* was also a finalist in the Goodreads Choice awards for best contemporary romance of 2017. The Ravenhood Trilogy, consisting of *Flock, Exodus*, and *The Finish Line*, has become an international bestseller and reader favorite. Her holiday release, *The Plight Before Christmas*, ranked #6 on Amazon's Top 100. Kate's works have been featured in *USA TODAY, BuzzFeed, The New York Daily News, Huffington Post* and translated into a dozen languages.

Kate is a lover of all things '80s and '90s, especially John Hughes films and rap. She dabbles a little in photography, can knit a simple stitch scarf for necessity, and on occasion, does very well at whiskey.

Other titles available now by Kate

Romantic Suspense

The Ravenhood Series
Flock
Exodus
The Finish Line

Lust & Lies Series
Sexual Awakenings
Excess
Predator and Prey
The Lust & Lies Box set: Sexual Awakenings, Excess, Predator and Prey

Contemporary Romance

In Reading Order

Room 212
Never Me (Companion to Room 212 and The Reluctant Romantic Series)
The Reluctant Romantics Series
The Fall
The Mind
The Heart
The Reluctant Romantics Box Set: The Fall, The Heart, The Mind
Loving the White Liar

The Bittersweet Symphony
Drive
Reverse

The Real
Someone Else's Ocean
Heartbreak Warfare
Method

Romantic Dramedy

Balls in Play Series
Anything but Minor
Major Love
Sweeping the Series Novella
Balls in play Box Set: Anything but Minor, Major Love, Sweeping the Series, The Golden Sombrero

The Underdogs Series
The Guy on the Right
The Guy on the Left
The Guy in the Middle
The Underdogs Box Set: The Guy on The Right, The Guy on the Left, The Guy in the Middle

The Plight Before Christmas

Let's stay in touch!

Facebook
www.facebook.com/authorkatestewart

Newsletter
www.katestewartwrites.com/contact-me.html

Twitter
twitter.com/authorklstewart

Instagram
www.instagram.com/authorkatestewart/?hl=en

Book Group
www.facebook.com/groups/793483714004942

Spotify
open.spotify.com/user/authorkatestewart

Sign up for the newsletter now and get a free eBook
from Kate's Library!

Newsletter signup
www.katestewartwrites.com/contact-me.html